HISTORY OF
THE UNIVERSE

HISTORY OF THE UNIVERSE
A Novel

Jennifer Bartlett

MOYER BELL LIMITED/NIMBUS BOOKS
NEW YORK

Jacket and book design: Kiyoshi Kanai

A co-publication of Nimbus Books, Inc., Brooklyn, New York
and Moyer Bell Limited, Mount Kisco, New York.
Printed in the United States of America

Library of Congress Cataloging-in-Publication Data

Bartlett, Jennifer, 1941–
  History of the universe.

  I. Title.
PS3552.A7654H5 1985   813'.54   85-15332
ISBN 0-918825-12-1
ISBN 0-918825-26-1 (LTD)

Hypochondriacal, or windy melancholy . . .

In Body   Wind, rumbling in the guts, belly-ache,
             heat in the bowels, convulsions, crudities,
             short wind, sour and sharp belchings,
             coldsweat, pain in the left side, suffocation,
             palpitation, heaviness of the heart, singing
             in the ears, much spittle, and moist, &

Or In Mind   Fearful, Sad, Suspicious, Discontent,
             Anxiety &. Lascivious by reason of much
             wind, troublesome dreams, affected by
             fits &.
                      Anatomy of Melancholy—Robert Burton

She was more interested in birds than flowers although she
wasn't really interested in birds.
                              Ida—Gertrude Stein

HISTORY OF
THE UNIVERSE

Family

Born at night. Fewer houses than now. The ocean and bay covered and flooded the land in a storm at night. Fish were all over the land. Apartment not house. The land began receding. I was accidental. My mother made more money than my father. She got toxemia at Harriman Jones Clinic when I was born and she might have died. She had Rob, Jon, and Jenny. She got arthritis at Harriman Jones Clinic, Seal Beach, California, when Jenny was born. A lady named Hortense, called Horsey, burst into the front room where my father was reading *Frankenstein* and scared him to death.

My first memory is of lying on the bassinet. I opened my eyes a little. My mother changed me in her coat, having just come in. She was surrounded by two other people, who said "How cute," and my father.

I lay on the kitchen floor forcing my eyes open to look awake. I asked my mother where Arizona was, about the news on the radio, and other questions. Sitting on a stool, she answered at length. She spoke eloquently that night as she stirred the orange dye into white grease to make margarine. She told me about food stamps and my father through the thick yellow light and my dizzy eyes.

We walked to the Glider Inn—it has a real airplane crashed on the roof. My mother pushed Rob in a stroller, while talking to a friend. The air was gray in Seal Beach evenings. The Glider Inn was lit yellow inside with high wooden booths, finnan haddie, and boiled potatoes with parsley. When we moved inland to Falcon Avenue, my mother moved less easily than she did in Seal Beach, by the ocean, walking loose-jointed, talking to her friend.

Ellen Bates Tauber is the sixty-year-old mother of four children, and wife of a construction engineer and contractor, Henry Tauber. A handsome, healthy-looking woman, she takes care of her clothes and body. Ellen is a perfectionist and becomes agitated when things are out of order. She lives by the ocean in Long Beach, California, despite the severe arthritis which developed during her fourth pregnancy and now cripples her legs and twists and enlarges her knees and hands. Arthritis (from the Greek—*arthon*: joint; and *itis*: a suffix used medically to mean inflammation) refers to any disease or disability in which there is an inflammation of a joint. The ravages of the illness have been felt for 100,000,000 years. Unmistakeable evidence of arthritis has been found not only in the skeleton of a Neanderthal man dating from 40,000 B.C., but also in dinosaurs of the Mesozoic period. "There's no cure, it's too late for acupuncture," they said at the University of California, Los Angeles, Medical Department. "One operation possible, if it doesn't work the legs must be amputated." Ellen said, "No way, no way will I take that chance." She swims three times a week in an Olympic-size pool and continues to live in the wet clinging ocean air rather than in a dry climate more suited to her condition. She loves the home which she and Henry built in 1963. A six-foot-wide boardwalk separates the house from the sand. The downstairs has a two-car garage, washer, dryer, laundry chute, storage cabinets, hall, Japanese garden, pebbles, bamboo, ferns, thick-leafed plants growing up two-story windows, kitchen, bathroom, dining room, patio with slate floor, wrought-iron furniture, aqua cushions, living room, cork floors, fireplace, white naugahyde curved couch, coffee table, end tables, chair, lamp. Upstairs are four bedrooms, *shoji* screens separating master bedroom from small living room, white shag carpeting, central vacuum, fireplace, balcony of a white pebbly material. At five P.M. she mixes a bourbon and water, puts on some classical music and watches the ocean moving, the sun going down. "It saved my life after my stroke. If it hadn't been for that view I'd be dead." She thought she was dead, a slab of meat, couldn't talk, walk: she watched the ocean and slowly recovered. Stroke is the term used to describe the combination of signs and symptoms produced by damage to a portion of the brain. The onset may be massive in its effects, producing wide-spread paralysis, inability to speak, coma or death within a short time, usually several hours or days. However, the outlook has been improved by modern treatment. Ellen was born in Washington, D.C. Her mother Renata was a teacher, her father James ran a hotel across from Union Station. He died of a heart attack when she was eighteen. James left little insurance. Ellen went to work to help support her mother. Ellen attended Fullerton Junior College with Pat Nixon, who responded civilly to a letter from Ellen suggesting the White House purchase works by younger American artists instead of decorators' selections. Ellen's oldest child is an artist living in New York, her youngest is an art student at Long Beach State College. Mrs. Nixon assured her this was being done and signed the letter personally. "She probably doesn't remember me," Ellen remarked, "but it was still nice just the same, don't you think, even if I don't agree with her husband's politics, particularly Vietnam." Renata developed arteriosclerosis at the age of seventy, and almost starved to death in her Los Angeles apartment because she insisted she had no money to buy food. Ellen put her in a nursing home in Long Beach. Renata ran away, convinced that the doctors and nurses were poisoning her and the other residents, stealing what few possessions she had left. Diseases of the arteries cause more disability and death than any other group of troubles in the Western world. Ellen's husband, Henry, has undergone a series of operations for arteriosclerosis. He has had his veins scraped, his arteries replaced by dacron tubes, and three valves in his heart reconstructed during open heart surgery. The succession of operations, the expense, his absence from work, caused his business to collapse. He started over. Ellen worries continually about his smoking, drinking, and the long drive to work in San Diego. Ellen has met a President of the United States in his office and has rolled eggs down the White House lawn on Easter Sunday. Her aunt was a photographer and took a picture of her wearing a white dress, with dark eyes and dark bobbed hair. Her beautiful doll Janie had dark brown real hair, a china face with rosy cheeks, brown glass eyes, and tiny teeth. She gave it to her eldest daughter, Jane, who broke it. Summers, Ellen played under her aunt's broad-leafed grape arbor. She went to Alaska, drew, wrote poetry. After graduating from Chouinard Art School she became a fashion illustrator, and made more money than Henry during the Depression and the first years of their marriage. After having Jane—a birth complicated by toxemia—she quit work, and had James Robert eighteen months later. Six years later she gave birth to George Jonathan and, finally, Jenny Ellen, four years Jon's junior. Jenny's name was Laurie but was changed because it sounded like a dog's name. During Jenny's birth Ellen was annoyed that the nurse made her go to the delivery room: she was at an interesting place in a detective novel. Henry complained of pain in his arms, went to the doctor and was told he had leukemia. He entered the hospital immediately. Ellen went to the hospital every day, twice a day, concerned about traffic and parking. She distressed Henry with her worry, her health, her talking and tidying up. "Take care of your mother, don't upset her," he said. They called late at night. "He's in critical condition." Only Jenny was home. Her boyfriend took Ellen and Jenny to the hospital. Henry was dead. The rest of her children came to Long Beach. "You look so nice, Jane, that's such a pretty skirt. Rob and Jon have been wonderful." People brought food. Ellen made arrangements for the funeral: simple, short, no coffin, no graveside ceremony, "That's what he'd want, that's what I want." Her eyes were swollen from crying, her knees hurt, she sat on the beach, ate her lunch, wrote thank-you notes for the donations of blood and gifts of flowers. She was remote. The funeral was short. They went to friends for dinner, talked about Henry, drank and listened to original records from the 'thirties. "Oh, remember this?" Ellen would cry, "Hank would love it." Henry's lawyer informed Ellen she had $25,000 clear and the new white shag wall-to-wall carpeting. Everything else would be sold to pay bank debts. Henry had mortgaged the house and borrowed on the insurance. She moved to a small apartment in Naples across the bay. The house went for $300,000. "I have a view of the water from my bedroom," she said, "you don't know how important that is to me. See, you can see the water. I can't afford it, it's going up to $325 a month, I can't get health insurance, I'm not old enough for Medicare, four insurance companies have turned me down. I can't impose on friends like that, anyway he's not in health insurance. There's no way I can work. Who would hire me? What can I do? I'm sixty-two years old, no one will hire me. Don't talk to me when I'm driving. That was how my accident happened; an empty street and she smashed right into me. Luckily no one was hurt. I've never had a traffic ticket. I only have two dollars. Can you cash a check for me? I don't want you to do that. I'll just have a taco. Well, thanks, here's two dollars. No, I can cash a check tomorrow. Did you send that check? The only reason I'm asking is Rob said you had, and I didn't want it lost in the mail. Oh. Well, I'm not asking, I thought it was so generous, you don't have to, I'll just put it in my savings account and keep it for you. I don't want to be a burden on my children. My mother was. You know daddy had intended I get $150,000 but the bank got it. I couldn't stand going to one of those homes. Well, you're all wonderful. Don't look at me, I'm a mess, it's small surgery, preventative for skin cancer. They got it in time but I can't go in the sun any more, not at all, unless I'm all bundled up. I don't want people to know, that's why I can't ask, they'll just turn up their noses at Daddy. Well, maybe you're right. I'm so busy taking care of your grandmother's affairs, she gets so mad, she's so ungrateful. You know your aunt hasn't done a thing, she sent your grandmother flowers for Mother's Day and never anything about Daddy. I don't understand it, her own brother. She's very lucky to have two women there, but you know, her money's going fast. We've gotten her to stop smoking so much in bed, but you know, she just won't. Her lawyer says I'm doing exactly the right thing, I shouldn't cash in her stocks, it's her security. She'll outlive us all. I went to a party, the woman who bought the house was there, I wouldn't have gone but my friends have been so wonderful to me, she came over and said, 'Mrs. Tauber, won't you please come to see what we've done to the house, we just love it.' 'Well,' I said, 'no thank you, it's just too soon and I'm not able yet.' She's put a big self-portrait of herself right on the downstairs fireplace. Can you imagine? Over that beautiful stone, a big self-portrait. The view of the water means everything to me, they're building right in front—a Mafia organization. Yes, in Long Beach. You don't know? They own half of Naples, but I can still get a glimpse of water from the other window. It's so convenient: there's a market down the street and a washing machine on the first floor. Be careful, don't put any kleenex down the toilet, it clogs up, I just had it fixed. I put a towel out for you. Did you see this memorial plaque of Daddy's from the Associated General Contractors? I just received it because I had moved. They must think I'm mad as a hatter, writing a thank-you note this late. Don't touch the television, its leg is broken and it's just propped up but it works beautifully. I could go any time with my blood pressure. I can't swim now. No way. I'm too busy with Nana's affairs. When I die I want my ashes scattered over the ocean, no funeral, just cremated and my ashes scattered over the ocean. I had a man to dinner, he was like an adolescent, he chased me round and round the apartment, it was awful. I am proud of you, send me all the clippings. I just know Daddy knows somehow. I'm taking them to a Book Club, they always ask me but I've just never gone. Look at these, aren't they beautiful? These fruits we got in China, that was a wonderful trip, and that darling little captain, I just love them, they're all semiprecious stones. Daddy and I just loved that trip, even the typhoon. He got beautiful pictures of all of us on the stepping stones in the pool at Hakone. Of course I look so clumsy, but it was so beautiful there and Daddy enjoyed it so much. He had a new camera. We ate shabu-shabu."

I packed my bag to leave home, a flight bag from Arizona where the Navajos lived in hogans, a gift from my father who was there for the Johns Manville Company. I took all food. My mother helped me pack.

Galloping over the grass in Sara McComb's back yard after school, Dale Evans said to Dale Evans, "Where's Roy? He must be in trouble."

At nap time in the schoolroom at Longfellow Grammar in kindergarten I ran out as the teacher distributed the white nap mats. I had been accused of talking in the hall to Joanne with braids and no bangs. I walked around the school over and over until my mother came and walked me back. We played "Step on a crack, you'll break your mother's back." I didn't step on one, but cried sitting in the teacher's lap while my mother watched.

Tony the policeman smoked big cigars. "I smoke a cigar every day before breakfast," I told him. "Little girls don't smoke cigars," he said. I smoked a cigar, I turned around, walked out the door, across the street, in the door, to the bathroom, and threw up crying. I loved Tony. He rode me on the handlebars of his bicycle. I fell off. My leg caught in the spokes turning around.

Sara watched me arrange my chicken farm in the alley. I bought fuzzy chickens with feathers for wings in red, blue, yellow, green, and pink, in two sizes. The small ones were two for five cents, the large ones five cents apiece. All the small chickens were divided into pens according to color, each group had a large chicken of the same color guarding them. The leftover chickens went into a mixed pen with no guard.

Al and I ate hard candy and listened to *The Shadow* on Sundays. He had lived all over and had a girlfriend. His mother had blonde hair and was divorced. She had a boyfriend. Later, they moved to Texas.

I built a room from cardboard in the garage. It was a beauty shop. I made preparations from toothpaste, powder, the insides of pills, shampoo. I gave Sara and Al permanents and treatments. I came out to play, clean from the bath, my hair braided. Sara and Al threw hundreds of gutter worms at me. I screamed. They hung from my hair and body. I began to dream the invasion of the world by worms. The worms would start crawling out of the gutter, getting bigger and bigger as they crossed the lawn. I climbed to the peak of my roof and sat there as the worms made their way up the four sides of the house.

In a recurring dream: I am walking home at night in the fog. There is a lady walking a fast yellow dog a block behind in the empty street. The moment I reach the dark open garage of my house, the lady and the dog turn into a man in a yellow shirt chasing me. I am rooted to the spot.

It is an extremely black night. A girl is lying in her bed scared by small sounds. Huge, gray, and soft, the worms come in through a window someone left open. They don't make any noise as they bump into furniture. They are soft and moist. If they break, they lie limp over the edges of tables. They don't bleed, they leak. They are inexorable. They are dumb. They clog up the house. Some die, others crawl, slowly sliding over the dead ones. They come out of the sinks, thin at first, then swell up outside the drains. No one can get to the telephone to call the police. The phone is covered with worms. The police phone is too.

I told Douglas Wade, "I drive my father to work every day." "No you don't," he said. "Yes I do, do you want me to prove it?" We got in the car parked on the sloping driveway, a Buick. I carefully and accurately released the emergency brake, placed my hands on the wheel in a ten-to-three-o'clock position. The car moved backwards and down the hill, gaining speed. It stopped abruptly in the side of a car parked opposite and perpendicular. Douglas Wade wasn't allowed to play with me after that.

Before I went to sleep I would think this: I am walking along a wide street inland, with nice houses and green lawns in front. There is no one on the street except me. A man and woman come running, grab me and drag me inside a house. They take off all my clothes, even my underpants, and put diapers on me. They force me to take naps and burp me. They won't let me talk, just make noises. I have to wet my pants so they can change me. There are other cribs in the big room. This man and woman kidnap children and force them to act like babies.

My brother Rob and I weren't allowed to eat dinner. We had to be at the hospital at six A.M. for the operation. The nurse gave me a white gown and a shot. I felt dizzy. "Don't be scared," she said, wheeling me on a cart into the brightly lit center of a

10

dark room. Everyone wore masks. The doctor, in a green coat like the tiles on the wall, put a black rubber cup over my face. "Don't be scared. Breathe in deeply and count from ten to one." I counted and began dreaming I was running through a long black corridor. Metal gates clanged open and shut in front and in back of me. I woke up in a bed and was allowed to eat vanilla ice cream and vomit blood into an oval enamel pan.

We went to Dr. Berkaw's for a checkup. "You didn't tell me I had to have a shot," I yelled. Dr. Berkaw blocked the door, his arms folded over his stethoscope, a mirror on his head. I ran around the table, the nurse chased me. I couldn't get out of the room. My mother squeezed one arm hard while the nurse gave me a shot in the other.

I spent time behind the sofa. I kept my blocks there. It was the only place I sucked my thumb. Rob tried to crawl in. To keep him out I bit his hand so hard he had to have it cauterized. Out in the tangled alley behind the house playing, a cat jumped and bit me on my hand, we went straight to the doctors and had it cauterized.

I went to ballet lessons. The teacher wore a tutu and her hair pulled straight back. She was born in a foreign country. I wore shorts. She taught us to lean over, curve our arms in front of us, extend one leg behind and point our toe. The doorbell rang, she said "Hold that position." She came back, I fell down. Everyone who was standing got a gold star.

James Robert "Rob" Tauber is thirty-three. He received a bachelor's degree from the University of California at Berkeley and lost his father the same year. His major was pre-law. He hates for people to congratulate him, "You know all they're thinking about is how long . . . that I'm stupid . . . how long it took me to get through, they're just looking down on me, feeling superior about their own children." After serving three years in the United States Army he entered college as an English major. Moved deeply by the works of authors such as Joseph Conrad, Rob would read a novel line by line, word by word, searching for the true meaning hidden in each book. He wrote a long paper, turned it in, got a B, became infuriated by the instructor's criticisms and wrote another paper disputing them. This, coupled with the attention he felt each book demanded, caused him to fall far behind in his work. He smoked dope, switched colleges, quit, returned to Southern California to work for his father. He contracted hepatitis, lived in a monastic modern apartment in the dry flat town of Poway, California, ate Shakey's pizza, hamburgers, ice cream sundaes, watched TV, worked, and listened to records. Jane was having a hard time in New York City, recently separated from her husband and hard up for money. Rob sent money for a trip to Puerto Rico and asked her to buy him a good print of his favorite painting, Paul Klee's *The Twittering Machine.* "What do you think it really means?" he asked. "It must mean something." She never answered the question or sent the print; he bought it himself and had it framed. Rob had no friends. His isolation and paranoia increased. He felt other members of the company were lazy, inept, and morally careless. He despised the offers of friendship made to him by his father's secretary and was proud that he refused all dinner invitations. He worked fifteen hours a day, gained weight from his sedentary, obsessed life. "When I ask Rob something it's all detail," his father said, "he has no grasp of the general picture. I know he works hard, though." Rob took almost no salary when things were bad. The strain of working in a business where his long hours went unappreciated began to tell on him. He was haunted by the idea that Henry had hired detectives to follow him on the San Diego Freeway. He had three apartments, two of them listed under assumed names. He quit and returned home. His psychiatrist's son committed suicide. Rob recovered and reentered school. At the age of four he developed periostitis in his leg. The disease softens the bones of the joints, and there is no cure except to immobilize the affected limb until the disease has run its course. He was put in a hip-to-ankle cast for three years, and dragged himself from room to room trying to play with his friends. Jane hated to wheel him around the block in his wheelchair. The cast was replaced by a harness and crutches. A black-and-white photograph shows four boys dressed in identical Hopalong Cassidy outfits, one with a harness and crutches. Rob would slip off his harness, drop the crutches, and try to run. Ellen punished him, "You'll be crippled, permanently crippled." He recovered in sixth grade and began to participate in sports. The years of inactivity made his progress difficult despite his unusual height and size. He quit and started playing poker every day and night with friends his parents disapproved of. He kept a chart of his winnings and losses for five years. Rob's dream was to be a dealer in Las Vegas. He enlisted in the Army after high school graduation, a course approved by his father. "The discipline and responsibility will mature him," Henry said, "then he'll be ready for college." The night before he left for Germany with a security clearance, he got in a violent fight with Henry and left the house in a rage. Jon, Jane, and Jenny followed him to get him to come back, explaining, "They really love you but don't know how to express it." He had tried to hit Henry with a fireplace poker. He did well in the Army, traveled through Europe, accepted responsibility, and returned with banderillas, a sword, plaques and brass cups from Spain, music boxes from Austria, cuckoo clocks from Germany, posters from Czechoslovakia, a glass boot, and other presents for the family. Rob believes the Taubers, who have low foreheads and hairlines, occupy a lower place on the evolutionary scale than other human beings. "Well, look, look at apes: brain capacity is indicated by the size and the shape of the forehead." No arguments could move him from this position. Rob finds himself preoccupied by two childhood memories. One, he was responsible at age four for the death of the family dog, Button, a Kerry Blue Terrier, one of whose puppies had a successful movie career. Rob's mother stood on the street talking to a neighbor. Rob saw the gate to the back yard was open. "I pulled at Mom's skirt to tell her the gate was open, she got mad: 'Rob, don't interrupt when I'm talking to someone.'" With an abundance of good spirits Button raced through the gate, down the street into an oncoming car. She died whimpering, with her eyes open. The second memory proves to Rob his possession of sadistic tendencies and involves feeding goldfish the wrong food or even trying to torture them in some way. He is the second of four children.

I read all the Oz books. I read over and over the part about Tip, a boy who knew the Strawman dispersed and whole, the Tin Woodman, magpie nests full of jewels and money, and sawhorse speed. In a day he was changed by a witch's incantation, behind floating curtains, into Ozma of Oz.

My grandparents lived on Granada Street, in a stucco house which looked Spanish. Flowers grew in the back yard as well as the front. The back door always had a black key in it. A trellis of wild roses grew around the garage window. In the garage were boxes full of Enrico Caruso records from Idaho Falls. My grandmother didn't have a record player. She would fix me peanut-butter-and-Karo-syrup sandwiches. I didn't like Karo syrup but I ate them anyway. Another time she and Big Rob took me to the mountains for a picnic. I got carsick on the way in their cream-colored Buick. I saw a deep scoop in the ground, ringed by pines and filled with granite boulders, where the rattlers came to shed their skins in spring. They lay on the hot flats of gray stones, thousands, rattling while blue jays squawked from tree to tree.

Alice Hartwell Tauber is an eighty-seven-year-old bedridden grandmother who retains her will and her reason. She was born in 1889, in Idaho Falls, Idaho, into an upper-middle-class family. Her father was first a telegrapher, then in the lumber business. Her mother was a converted Catholic who bore five children: Mabel, dead; Alice; Margaret, dead; Vincent, dead; and Agatha, the baby. Alice attended a convent school that had smallpox and typhoid epidemics. Summers were spent deep in the mountains, beside a river. The men hunted, the women tried to keep them from drinking the moonshine liquor hidden in cold river water. The nights were dark and still, often bright with stars. The children's gloves and beaded purses were made by local Indians. Alice was four feet eight inches tall, with bright red hair, and was punished frequently by the Sisters for sneaking from the convent to keep assignations by the schoolyard fence. Vincent caught typhoid at school and died at home. Her father, a heavy man who didn't usually attend services, cranked his car violently and took the family and a visiting priest to church. From the violence of his cranking he developed a fatal strangulated hernia. Dr. Kern came. Alice heard her father shout, "My God, Kern, you're killing me." Dr. Kern had attempted to push the hernia back into place, thus worsening Alice's father's condition. Before his death he said something to each of the children. To Alice: "Take care of your mother, don't be a burden." After his death at forty-six, Alice's mother became even stricter. The family wore deep mourning, Alice was forced to dye a new favorite maroon dress black. The Tauber brothers, Glen and Rob, came to town. On the night of Alice and Rob's wedding, his mother died. They visited Utah and Colorado, then returned to Idaho Falls where their first child, Henry Hartwell Tauber, was born. He was big and heavy, the birth was uncomfortable, and Alice was not happy to find herself pregnant again with Barbara. "Lord, Henry was in and out of Mama's house all day. Even though she was strict she had a real soft spot for Henry." Rob and Alice moved to California. He worked in the shipyard, Alice at home. They had little money. Henry insists he slept in a drawer. Letters came regularly from Idaho Falls. Firecrackers exploded in Henry's pocket, severely burning one thigh. Doctors were consulted, skin grafts implanted, "I walked him every day along the ocean in the deep sand to exercise the leg. My God, that proud, proud, red flesh, it was a real bad burn. Oh, he had a lot of friends—Phil, Scrub, Box, they were over here all the time, coming up outside honking their horns. He didn't do real well in school, they were out a lot, doing a lot of I don't know what. Well, Barbara now, Barbara was real different, they seemed to get along but Barbara was real quiet and studied real hard. Henry was more social, she was smart and, Lord, in high school, I don't understand it—a woman like that—I found a poem, or a book rather, a book of poems, from her high school English teacher, by Sappho, and the inscription was a love letter. Lord, I didn't know what to do and after that Barbara went her own way. Now she's come back with different women. I never could understand it. We asked the doctor. Then she just went ahead and moved back to the East Coast. She was always real smart and became a computer expert. Henry worked for a bank, then married Ellen and worked for the Johns Manville Construction Company. Barbara has always been thoughtful, sending presents to the family, but I don't know, she and Ellen never got on, and then she just stopped visiting. Well, then, Jane was the first grandchild so she was sort of the favorite and then James Robert, sort of a mama's boy, so naturally we saw more of Jane. The kids would dump her off here for the weekend. Then Jon and then Jenny." Alice knitted outfits for Jane and James Robert. Her husband Rob died unexpectedly at night, in his bed, of a heart attack, leaving half a peeled apple in a saucer. He would wake up with a sweet tooth at night so he kept a large box of See's candy by the bed. He had inherited money, invested in stocks, quit the shipyard and become addicted to drink, spending every afternoon at a local bar. Alice didn't drive their cream-colored Buick and his death decreased her mobility. Their relationship did not include many friends, but they went on long drives to the country for picnics with their grandchildren. Alice walked to Second Street to shop, bank, and have her hair done. She bought a color television, continued to knit, entertain her grandchildren, drink sherry and smoke Camels. Barbara would write. She answered. Every six months a friend would call. She visited her younger sister Agatha and husband Lloyd in Hawaii where he was president of a bank. He was killed by his electric lawn mower. Agatha got double indemnity and moved to San Francisco where her son Farrell and his wife Mona lived. Agatha remarried at seventy-two, a man thirty years old. Farrell was furious. Alice said, "You know, Agatha always liked pretty things and had a lot of spirit." The man was homosexual, Farrell got the marriage annulled on the basis of non-consummation. The man's family wanted a settlement. Agatha married again, the owner of a combination beauty salon and dress shop. He was thirty-five. They moved to the Midwest, which stopped the visits between the sisters. Farrell's son Mark became a hippy. Mark's best friend, the son of Bishop Pike, committed suicide with a revolver in a New York hotel room. Bishop Pike died in the desert. Mark became addicted to heroin, was found in New York, cured, then went to work for Uncle Henry's construction company. The daughters finished school and married. Farrell's wife Mona went on a crash diet, contracted pernicious anemia and died slowly. Farrell fell in love, remarried and died of a heart attack at his desk the day following the ceremony. Every year Alice would fix either Thanksgiving or Christmas dinner, often becoming drunk on sherry before the meal was served. The silver, china, lace tablecloth, linen napkins from Idaho Falls, and a seasonal centerpiece, graced the table. Everyone dressed up, bolted their meals, groaned in the living room about the amount they'd eaten, and came over the next morning for turkey sandwiches. On Christmas morning Henry would pick up Alice for the opening of gifts. They went to a restaurant on Easter. Alice inherited money and loaned some to Henry for his business. She fell late at night breaking her hip, was unable to get to the phone. Neighbors broke in and rescued her. She was hospitalized. The doctor visited five minutes a day, charging $25 for each visit. Her hearing and sight failed, she was no longer able to redecorate her home, tend her garden, consult with John the gardener, walk to Second Street, prepare Thanksgiving or Christmas dinner, go out with the family for dinner, make herself up, sleep in her pink satin bedroom upstairs, buy clothes, bathe herself, read, knit, watch television and get drunk. She insisted on staying alone at night and making her breakfast alone. She worried about her appearance. "Lord, look at me, I'm nothing but a bag of bones, an old dried up woman." She became angry and sentimental after three glasses of sherry in the afternoon, often crying and yelling. Jane, Rob, and Jon had left Long Beach. Jenny continued to visit. Henry's business had taken him to San

Diego. Ellen called but they had never gotten on. Mrs. Starr, a trim widow with a married daughter, came to take care of her. They became fast friends. Henry and Ellen gave her a lightweight red transistor radio which she could hear turned up full blast. There was an all-night news program. Henry died of leukemia. Barely able to move, she was agitated by grief, his picture sat in her room a gray blur, over and over she'd ask, "Why not me, I'm just good for nothing?" She wanted to die. She began giving things away: crystal and silver to Mrs. Starr; figured china to Ellen; mink stole and lace tablecloth to Jane. She couldn't stand the idea of strangers coming into the house and taking her possessions, many of which had travelled from Idaho Falls. She wouldn't eat or take her medicine. Barbara didn't write. Sometimes Alice saw the family as conspirators after her money. She put in her false teeth whenever anyone visited. They were kept in her bedside table wrapped in kleenex, the kleenex sometimes got caught between the juncture of teeth and gums. Jane read letters from Idaho Falls. Alice couldn't sleep. "I'm just ready for the dump heap, there's no reason for me to live, no, now I'm just good for nothing to myself or anyone else. Now listen, I'm having Mrs. Starr take me to Dilday's and I'm picking out my dress and casket." Both were pink. "I don't want anyone coming to the funeral."

Mrs. Starr writes:

> I do not know what to tell you 'cept here at your
> Nana's is about the same. She is getting weaker and
> hardly gets out of bed except to clean up. Today was
> her shampoo and bath day. I made a chicken salad and
> will stuff a tomato for her to eat when she gets hungry.
> The appetite "ain't what it used to be," she still enjoys
> her hi-ball at 3 each afternoon—what a remarkable
> woman, and how attached I have become—sometimes I
> think each of us leans on the other somewhat.

We moved back to the peninsula in September. The first day I went to the bay to swim. I climbed the low concrete wall and saw the gray water, the tide in all the way almost covering a concrete mound on the invisible beach. I swam around by myself, frightened there might be an octopus. I walked along the bay to the Seaside Inn and bought some red and black licorice. The red tasted like strawberry. Another gray day I charged a TV dinner at the market. I had never seen anything like it. I cooked it when my mother wasn't home and took it out on the back porch to eat.

I went to swimming lessons at the bay. The lifeguard wore red trunks, the water was blue, the sky was blue. I learned to kick hard; deadman's float; back float with my eyes open looking at the sky, blue sky; dog paddle, blue water; elementary backstroke, blue sky; elementary breast stroke, blue water; side stroke, blue sky blue water; scissors kick; crawl; swim under water; butterfly; dolphin; artificial respiration; cross-chest carry; how to jump into the water keeping my head up; how to make people drowning unconscious so I could rescue them. I won a medal in a freestyle race. My brother Jon is an All-American swimmer.

Across the street along the ocean beach ran a boardwalk of splintering planks, six feet wide. It extended from the edges of houses or vacant lots to the retaining wall three and a half feet high. There were supposed to be rats under the boardwalk. The water came up to the wall, the waves splashed over. I would get wet walking by. In places, the wall dropped down as far as ten feet to the sand and piles of big rocks. It was noisier, wetter, brighter and bluer than it is now that the beach has been widened two hundred yards. In the rocks were Pismo clams, six inches at the widest point. Some people wearing blue denim pedal pushers, probably from inland, would hunt the clams and eat them raw sitting on the rocks.

I went down to swim in September when the beach was empty. The sky was blue. I looked up from the center of the waves breaking and saw a man in red lifeguard trunks. I got out of the water and walked past him. He was playing with his penis. I started running, he started running. I thought he was chasing me. My mother said he was probably just running away, that he was more frightened than I. He wasn't a lifeguard. My mother and the neighbors agreed that beach and resort areas attract a lot of strange people and perverts.

I imagined dancing in a huge auditorium for a ballet recital. I'm doing my solo, wearing a white tutu with silver on it, executing an incredible series of turns on the points of my toe shoes. The audience is totally still and surprised. I stop the turns and do a huge leap, just like a bird. The ballet is *Swan Lake*, I'm the good princess. Everyone claps, the ladies-in-waiting come out. Jane Johnson is a lady-in-waiting. I do a dance in the middle of them. I look to the back of the auditorium, and there is Roy Rogers on Trigger. I keep on dancing. It is the best dance the audience has seen by someone my age, so they don't notice Roy Rogers. Roy Rogers takes out his lasso, lassos me around the waist, pulls me off the stage, puts me on Trigger, and rides off. Margot Fonteyn is in the audience. Her sister lives in Long Beach, that's why she came to the recital. She says, "Who is that girl? She's the best dancer I've seen for ten years old. I'm going to take her back with me to Sadler's Wells. She will be a genius by the time she's eighteen."

"I have to take my script with me if I go to Frank and Janet's at all." Their yard was warm and sunny and smelled of barbecue. The adults were drinking and talking, the kids played volleyball on the beach. Frank said, "What are you reading, Jane?" "I'm memorizing my script." "Are you in a play?" "Yes, *The Princess and the Frog*. I'm the princess but we have to be familiar with everyone's parts, not just our own." Frank is the commander of a ship in the Navy and was in World War II.

Pepper Brown and I are practicing baseball on the beach. Two men walk along the boardwalk talking. I am batter. Pepper pitches, I hit the ball, a perfect hit. The men on the boardwalk sort of laugh, they think it's an accident. One man is a scout for the New York Yankees, he is visiting his brother in Long Beach. Pepper pitches another, I hit it again, even farther. The Yankee says, "Wait a minute, let's watch this." His brother wants to go.

Pepper pitches. This time I hit it as far as her house, three blocks away. Pepper just picks up the ball and walks into her house, because it's time for her dinner. The Yankee says, "Who is that girl, I've never seen anyone play that well so young." His brother answers, "It's Jane Tauber, she goes to Lowell." The next day I'm playing baseball, all the bases are loaded, two boys have struck out, the hardest pitcher is pitching, I go up to bat, I tap my bat on the plate. Everyone's really worried, a girl up and it's the last inning. The pitch comes, I hit it so hard it goes into the Rogers Junior High playground. I start running, the first baseman trips me. I skin my knee so hard blood is gushing down my leg. Everyone's in. Some guys from Rogers throw the ball back, I make it anyway. Stan Musial says, "Who is that girl? She could bat .350 easy. When she wasn't batting she could be the catcher."

We used to take white pillowcases to the ocean on windy days. The ocean was dark blue and choppy in the afternoon. I soaked the pillowcase in water, filling with water the holes between the threads. I would hold it open, spin around filling it with air, pull it together at the neck and float. The air was squeezed out by my weight and I would fill it up again with wind.

Grammy Bates wasn't home. The gray interior of her garage smelled of soap and old cardboard. The sun coming in through the square window lit the corrugated metal surface of the clothes scrubber. I took off my clothes and ran naked, my heart beating, into the backyard. The air hit my body. I ran back into the garage and put my clothes on.

Jane Johnson's mother gave her a notebook with a ballet dancer on the cover; a pencil box with eight pencils, each a different color; two pencil sharpeners; a compass; a ruler; colored rubber bands; and two erasers, one shaped like a cat.

My father brought home twenty-six three-by-six-inch pads of white note paper for telephone messages. Each pad had fifty-eight pages. Nana gave me the jumbo box of crayons, one hundred and five colors, including gold, silver, and copper, with an attached pencil sharpener. Again and again, lying on the floor in the sun by the radio, I drew Cinderella. Sea green, yellow green, olive green, peach, salmon, melon, pine green, magenta dresses, ribbons and trim. Cornflower, periwinkle, violet blue, green-blue eyes. Mahogany, tan, yellow, black, brown, maize hair. Sometimes birds hold her ribbons, sometimes rabbits. Grammy gave me colored pencils. I didn't use them, there were only twelve.

Renata Bates is dead. She is survived by a daughter Ellen and a son Jim who was in the United States Air Force during the Second World War. Jim married, divorced, then married Jeanne, a French nurse whom he brought to the United States. Both Ellen and Jim are strong-looking, attractive people. Renata had six grandchildren. They called her Grammy. She was married to James who died unexpectedly of heart trouble in Washington, D.C. He was manager of the old Congressional Hotel, no longer in existence. The family lived next door to the Speaker of the House. Ellen and Jim rolled Easter eggs down the White House lawn. They visited President Wilson in his office. After James' death, Renata and the children moved to Southern California. Ellen went to Fullerton Junior College with Pat Nixon, then to Chouinard Art School, after which she got a job illustrating fashion for a department store. Renata was unable to teach in California and lived off the inadequate estate left by James. Ellen helped support her. Her family came from Vermont. Renata didn't like Henry, Ellen's husband. She had steely white waved hair, an aquiline nose, a strong jaw, and an imposing Edwardian figure. She was a black Republican and hated Roosevelt. Her mind began to go— senility, caused by a lack of blood and oxygen to the brain, a constriction of veins and arteries. She locked herself up in her Los Angeles apartment, she believed she had no money for food. Ellen found her unconscious from self-imposed starvation. Ellen put Renata in an old people's home in Long Beach. She ran away: she thought the other inmates, the nurses, the doctors, were trying to poison her. She died. Ellen went to the home to pick up her things. All that was left was a cardboard box of old shoes, everything else had been stolen.

On Parent's Night Bob had two drawings up: buildings and fighter planes, car crash. Tom had one: airplanes. Nancy, two: horses, side and front views. Sarah, two: girls in front of houses. Al had one picture of his family in a blue and tan car. I had four: one, Irish people on stage acting in sad play; two, Spanish mission with Indians working in fields of vegetables, priests and nuns walking and watching, Indians working, bell tower, fire with smoke, rain clouds, sun, cliff, ocean, boats, large land mass in background; three, underwater scene, people swimming different strokes, shells, crabs, fish, sun, waves, sailboat, sailboat sinking, octopus, eel, seahorse, starfish, shrimp, whale, killer shark, sand shark, hammerhead, bullhead, floating garbage and lifeguard; four, self-portrait in red jumper. Aunt Jeanne says French schoolchildren have more education in, and command of, drawing than American children. Their drawings, though not as large, look real.

Jeanne Bates is French-Italian in her late fifties, in good health with crinkled but trim face and body. She is a nurse, and was a member of the Resistance with her brothers in the Second World War. One had his leg blown off; another, Germano, opened a restaurant in Tarzana, California. Jeanne is married to an American named Jim Bates, who began to get arthritis. The doctors could do nothing. Jeanne started reading all the medical literature on arthritis and developed a treatment for Jim, who was cured and now plays a good competitive game of tennis. She has two sons, Jimmy and Philip. Both speak French. During menopause she treated herself with hormones and got through that period of her life in relative comfort and control. Germano has a large house on Lake Como between Italy and Switzerland. Jeanne becomes friends with her sons' girlfriends, and continues the relationships when they break up. She is organized, thinks Moroccan cooking is the best in the world, has a strong accent and is fluent in English. While working for the Resistance she got on the wrong train. It was filled with German soldiers going to Germany. She got off somehow. Jeanne misses the sound of car horns in Paris streets since the new regulations, and thinks General de Gaulle a great man. She drives most of the time when she and Jim go out, in case he is too tired or tight. She wears a watch, sweaters, skirts and tailored dresses, her hair is short and wiry. Her son Jimmy graduated from college and was operated on for cancer. The operation was a success, but he must be checked regularly to see if it has grown back. He lost his job—a record of cancer made him ineligible for the company group insurance plan. Jeanne and her husband don't speak often. The relationship is on and off. He lives in a small room off the garage.

Swimming, I pulled down my bathing suit. Debbie sucked my nipples underwater, underwater I sucked Debbie's nipples. I lay on my back, on the floor of the service station restroom, bathing suit pulled down. Debbie felt me up and brushed a matchstick over my clitoris. She lay down on the floor, I brushed her clitoris with a matchstick.

I made the butterfly wings with crayons, wire, brown paper, and wrapped them around my body. Jane Johnson read my story of Hedy Larva wrapped in a gray cocoon, hanging off a branch, mocked by birds and butterflies. In spring she felt the cocoon split, her back twitch, and giant colored wings spread open. She opened her mouth and began singing opera in Hollywood.

I got off the school bus at 62nd Place. I couldn't decide between Hostess Angel Food Cake or Oreo cookies. I charged a double package of cookies and a pound of cherries. I ate them on the dock in the late afternoon sun before going home for dinner.

The lawn is bright green and sparse beside the yellow school bus. "She isn't that fat. See, I can get my arms around her waist," Jane Johnson said, putting her arms around my waist, me crying. Sullen in the cafeteria, I said, "I'm quitting this school, I'm transferring, everyone hates me here." My friends said, "No, they don't really hate you." I walked out of school to Nana's, smoked, and went back to school the next day.

My mother took me to the doctor, he sent me to the dietitian in another part of the hospital. The dietitian said, "There's nothing wrong, she just eats too much." I ripped up the diet she gave me and threw it on her desk.

Everyone went to bed. I stayed up and wrote a story about the captain of a ship caught in a furious night storm at sea. Waves forty feet high crashed on the deck as the captain relived the events in his life. At dawn he felt a strange tranquility. Mrs. Taylor gave me a B. There were grammar and spelling errors. I ripped the paper in pieces and threw them on her desk.

Phil and his friend invited me into the office of the Christmas tree fort. I was flattered. They made me lie down and tied me up, my face in the dirt. They rubbed my shoulder bones. "Shall we turn her over and feel her up?" I wouldn't stop yelling so they untied me and let me go.

"I have something to tell you," I told Jane Johnson, and walked with her across the wide gray beach to the wet sand where no one could hear. "My mother's pregnant, she doesn't know what they're going to do, she told my father." We both agreed we would do intercourse but we would never take off all our clothes in front of men.

Jane Thomas Johnson Kempner is a thirty-four-year-old mother who graduated from Stanford University, studied art history in graduate school at Berkeley, made her debut with the Junior League in Long Beach, California, and married Dave, a banker from Northern California. Dave didn't want her to wear miniskirts when they were fashionable, or to get her ears pierced; he thought both were cheap-looking. Her mother and stepfather were buying the entire family diamond earrings. Jane has three boys. She grew up in Long Beach on the oceanfront, her room had green wall-to-wall carpeting and a toy stove that worked. The family Christmas tree was always decorated with white and gold clouds of spun glass, gold balls, white roses and ribbons. Her mother is a gourmet cook, nearly six feet tall, slim and blonde; she is a docent at the Los Angeles County Museum, interested in theatre, music, literature, art. She hangs the work of young artists, on loan. She is an accomplished skin diver, swimmer, sailor, world traveler, and a member of the Junior League. She divorced Mr. Johnson, Jane's father, who is committed to religion, and married a man with business interests and a sloop, who participates in the Trans-Pacific races to Hawaii. Jane has an older sister who taught Spanish on both coasts, had several medical problems, became painfully thin, and has been married two or three times. She has a younger half-sister who is tall, slim, and looks like her mother. Jane received excellent grades in high school, was a member of the best sorority and the best welfare clubs. Her mother shops at I. Magnin in Los Angeles. Jane gained weight and wore muumuus, wouldn't leave the house except for drive-in movies. A friend came to borrow some boots for the snow. Jane wasn't there; her stepfather went to her closet and picked up the boots. Dozens of candy wrappers fell out: Campfire Girl candies Jane had been selling for her troop. She loves her children, thinks about the excitement of others' lives and of going back to school when the children are older. She visited New York and has traveled in Europe and Hawaii. Her china is Limoges, her crystal Baccarat.

We were standing in the skeleton of a new house. Jackie Fish said, "You have to climb to the second-floor rafters to be a member, everyone's already done it, it's the rules, just do it then you'll be in." I was scared, my stomach hurt, everything was confused up here, I was almost crying. Somehow I got down. Jackie said, "O.K., now all you have to do is smoke two cigarettes in a row. That's all, I promise."

Jack had red hair, he came one summer to take care of Rob and see that he kept the brace on his leg. I wanted to be with Jack all the time. I pulled out the blue drawer in front of the bathroom door which served as a lock. No one could get in but they could peek through a small crack. I was in the bathtub, salty from the water, sunburnt and fat. I could hear them whispering and giggling. I yelled at them, they ran away.

Dezell Kelly was our maid. She was brown, thin, and quick. She knew what we were up to. She made angel pie and homemade rolls. Some Sundays she took me to a church where she testified and was called "Sister." She had a gold tooth with a white heart showing through. From Dezell I learned to testify. I learned that people who fast end up fat, that a person could go into real estate or be an Avon representative instead of a mother.

A man pulled up in a car, yellow and tan. He said something. I was walking my bike on the sidewalk. I stopped and looked in the dark car at the man looking out, playing with and showing me his penis. I was surprised and might have yelled but he started to drive away. I looked fast and got his license number. My mother called the police. I went to Kelly's dime store and asked Mr. and Mrs. Kelly if they had seen anyone suspicious hanging around in a yellow shirt with this license number. I also asked Pete the butcher and other people in the market. The police caught the man and came to my house. "No one ever testifies in these cases so we just have to let the man go." My mother didn't want me to testify. I said, "I will testify." I got dressed up to go to court, I was cross-examined in the box. The defense attorney said, "Couldn't he have been applying calomine lotion, not paying attention to you because of his infection?" I didn't think so but didn't know and was confused. The man was convicted, received a suspended sentence and was not allowed his Navy pension. That night I baby-sat for my sister and heard a noise at my bedroom window facing the alley. I saw a man making faces at me, he probably wanted to kill me for getting him in trouble. I ran out of the house. My parents didn't think it was the same man.

I heard my parents say that Jane Johnson had been assaulted or touched wrongly by two men who rowed her out to sea on a starry night in her sabot. One man sat in the bow, the other in the stern. They assaulted her, then rowed her back to shore prostrate. Jane was the first person I met who had my name. It would seem, considering the structure of a sabot—a small, blunt dinghy that sails—that had there been a man in front and a man in back, light from the stars and jetty, then Jane must have been in the middle, the oarsman's seat, rowing herself out to certain misadventure.

In my father's drawer I found some playing cards with pictures of naked women on them, some rubbers, handkerchiefs, and socks.

Our house on 58th Place was a desert pink stucco rectangle with three rectangular bedrooms, bathroom, glassed-in porch, living room, hall, kitchen, and washing machine porch. The dining room had a round table and chocolate brown wallpaper with a green and salmon Dutch colonial design. It was the nicest room; we ate green salad there every night. The television was on the front porch. I could turn it around and watch it through one of the living room windows from the couch when my parents were out. At night we would watch *Your Hit Parade*, sponsored by Lucky Strike, with Dorothy Collins and Snooky Lanson. Photographs of both Jenny and Jon as babies were taken on the front porch the same day mine was taken in a plaid shirt, stocky with an older, lunatic grin. My mother was young.

George Jonathan "Jon" Tauber is twenty-six years old and attends graduate school at the University of Southern California in Civil Engineering and Ecological Construction Management. He maintained an A average last semester; this semester looks more difficult. Jon is the third in a family of four children and is close to his father Henry, who has taken a great deal of interest in him. He was slow in school. During a test he looked out the window and the teacher asked, "Why aren't you writing?" Jon answered, "My pencil is broken." Sometimes he would stand sharpening his pencil, turning the crank handle over and over, staring out the window. He loves music and built his own stereo. His teachers at Progress, a school for students with trouble in school, called him dreamy; his brother called him stupid and goony; his older sister said he had a goony smile. He played with his younger sister Jenny. As a baby he ate sow bugs by the water faucet and threw them up with his lunch. He grew up by the ocean. His older brother was crippled between the ages of four and ten and bad at athletics. Henry gave Jon swimming instructions. He was gifted and swam every morning before school and every evening after school, breaking his own times. Jon got a stopwatch and a fancy bicycle for Christmas. Henry felt a boy needs an interest to structure his time, to build a sense of responsibility and self-worth. Jon began winning medals, shaved his legs and became an All-American, butterfly stroke. He was offered scholarships, went to UCLA, joined a fraternity (he needed the security, he told his sister Jane), made the finals in the Olympic tryouts, went steady, had a beer. He went to a psychiatrist for two reasons: one, both his older brother and sister had been; and two, it was hard for him to make up his mind, he never knew exactly the right thing to do. Jon, a friend, and their dates were almost beaten up by some thugs in Los Angeles who called them fraternity boys. He became engaged. His family disapproved, then changed their minds. Jane asked, "Why don't you live with Shawn instead of getting married? Travel more, farther east than Ohio?" He said it was what he wanted, what he needed, the security of marriage. Jon was hired as a management trainee at J.C. Penney, developed a pre-ulcer condition, quit his job and went back to school. His wife Shawn is working at J.C. Penney and earning her degree in Physical Education at Long Beach State College. Her parents take them on camping trips. Jon met Shawn at the Pacific Coast Club pool. She was the lifeguard. There was something different about her. Jon is generous with everything, has a drawer full of medals, a good, kind nature, rows of trophies, his junior high school diary, a notebook of his swimming times, and all the copies of *Rolling Stone* magazine for a two-year period, a gift subscription from his sister Jane. He didn't like the magazine. He is six-three, attractive with brown hair, brown eyes, narrow waist, large shoulders, and powerful arms. He doesn't take drugs, smoke or drink. Jon's mother gave him a book on sex when he was ten. Jane stood on a stool looking for something in his overhead closet, found the book put away in the back. "Why?" she asked. Jon said he didn't think he was ready for it yet. He made short movies about burglars with a friend, taped his lectures in college, and took his art history teacher several of his sister Jane's early paintings. Jon received his master's degree and went to work for his father. Jon and Shawn heard at eleven P.M. WDT on September 14, 1975, that Henry was in critical condition at Community Hospital in Long Beach. He called Jane in New York, packed and drove from San Diego to Long Beach. Shawn said Jon was in a daze. Henry died before they arrived. Jon went to the airport with Jenny to pick up Jane. He returned to San Diego as president of the Oceanside Construction Company. The business was in a state of chaos. Bankers called demanding immediate payment of unsecured loans. The federal government had a warrant to arrest the four children if withholding taxes for employees, totaling $15,000, were not paid immediately. The phone rang, the lawyer had no idea of the extent of the loans, debts, accounts payable: "He didn't tell me anything, I don't know what he's done." Jon's Aunt Jeanne told him: "Your father said to me before he died, 'I just need two years, just two years, to put it all together.'" Jon met with lawyers, bankers, and company personnel. He distributed Henry's many suits and ties to field workers who had been with him for years. Rob got angry: "Dad would have wanted me to have the clothes, I need them for school." Rob is four inches taller than Henry and found the clothes too short even for alteration. Jon explained his plans. He was president of the company, the secretary became vice president, Shawn treasurer. "That's the way Dad wanted it, we talked before his death. We became very close when I started working for him. We ate together all that year. Henry was sad about Rob and cried about his failures as a father." Jon met with Jane and Jenny in the company's office. Jon sat in his father's chair behind the desk. Jane took notes.

Jon said, "I'll get you both a copy of this photograph." It was a formal portrait of Henry as president of the Associated General Contractors. He explained his plans. Jane, Jenny, and Rob would have no controlling stock. He would buy them out as soon as the company paid its debts and became solvent. Jane asked, "What if we don't want to sell our stocks, what if we want to remain in the business?" Jon countered, "If Shawn and I are assuming responsibility for the company, we should at some point have the freedom to develop it with no interference from the family. Mom will be salaried by the company and own the house." The conversation went on, covering detail and strategy reaching years into the future. Jane was angry and aggressive. She thought Jon was taking everything over. "You're nothing," she snapped, "you're nothing, just like the Snopeses, white trash on the way up." Jon was sad and still. "Who are the Snopeses?" Jenny was torn between the two, confused by Jon's desire to separate himself from the family, and by Jane's anger. The desk was shiny. Boxes packed with papers were stacked on the floor. "Dad wrote me fifty pages on yellow lined paper about his life and business plans for the next two years. A nurse threw them away cleaning up his room for the next patient." They returned to Jon and Shawn's home in the brown California hills near Poway. The atmosphere was strained. Jon withdrew, not speaking. Jane felt guilty. Jenny teased Shawn. Ellen repeated herself over and over, complimenting Shawn. Services were held. Jon greeted all the field men who had come up from San Diego and Tia Juana. Jane apologized to Jon. By October the company had failed. The house and property were put up for sale. Jon went to work for a competitor. A small company. The lack of honesty and energy depressed him as much as being a J.C. Penney executive trainee. Their baby was born, John Henry, after the Christian names of the grand-fathers. Jon planned to ask an old architect from Santa Barbara, who designed houses which made you feel you live outside, to work with him on a house. Jon makes tables and bookcases of polished inlaid wood, carefully cut and fitted together. He quit his job in the construction company, sold his house in Poway, bought one in Long Beach near Shawn's parents and the house he was born in. He set up as an electrician, a business from which Shawn's father earns a good income. Jon is an eager, sympathetic listener who displays anxiety and great curiosity about the mechanics of others' lives.

Jenny Tauber is twenty-one years old and two credits short of being a senior majoring in graphic design at Long Beach State College. She was a general art major who wanted focus but didn't think she was good enough in painting and drawing to become a fine arts major. She lives with her mother, Ellen, in Long Beach by the ocean. Her father Henry works in San Diego on pipeline construction and spends weekends at home. People say Jenny looks like Ali MacGraw. She is the youngest of four children. Jenny had two female blue-point Siamese cats, Ping and Pong. Ping was killed when Joan Corwin left the back door open. Jenny bought a male seal point after her father recovered from open heart surgery. Her mother named it Ping Two. It was killed by a car. Jenny cried for days when Jon got married: Christmas wouldn't be any fun. Jon and Shawn decided to spend Christmas at Jenny's. She is an excellent tennis player and for a year and a half has dated the El Rancho Country Club tennis pro, Ivo, born in Czechoslovakia, whose family, avid anti-Communists, fled first to Argentina, then to New York, which they found dirty and cold. They live in California and own a dry-cleaning business. Jenny feels she will never be a really good tennis player. When faced with a competitive situation she feels compelled to lose. She works in the tennis shop at El Rancho, owns many tennis dresses, and skis in Colorado. An older secretary at the club tried to question Jenny about her family, giving her many personal compliments while remarking on the widely varied talents of the family, particularly of Jenny's father Henry. The secretary now lives in San Diego and works for Henry. Jenny doesn't like her. Though gregarious, Jenny experiences herself as shy. Her friends travel to different places: Spain, Peru, Europe, around the world. They say, "We can all check in with Jenny and find out what's happening in Long Beach." Kathy, one of Jenny's friends, is on the Olympic team as a javelin thrower. Her dates challenge her to throw the javelin although most have never held one before. They get angry when Kathy wins and refuse to speak to her again. Now she dates only other Olympic athletes. Jenny has had many embarrassing moments which are mentioned at length in her diary. She sews her own clothes, spends time doing things for others, has olive skin, large brown eyes, a regular nose, a wide mouth, large breasts, a small waist and long legs. She giggles frequently and has a quick temper. She doesn't want to marry and would like to move from home but feels a responsibility to her mother. Jenny has won many prizes for her ceramics. A movie of her at work has been made for distribution in the Long Beach Public School System. She hates shots and the sight of blood, doesn't read much, owns the *Cosmopolitan* book on sex and joy which she keeps under her bedside table. She has countless possessions, many of sentimental value only. Her room is a mess. She doesn't like people to disapprove of her or push her into things. Jenny began dating Pete, an attractive, withdrawn, twenty-six-year-old designer with a dry sense of humor. He was working on the sets for a space movie by the director of the popular *American Graffiti*. Jenny maintains strong ties with all branches of the family, sends presents, handmade cards, stuffed animals, and letters with small drawings or stickers of timid bunnies affixed to them. Her handwriting is a round, elaborate print. Pete took Jenny and her mother Ellen to the hospital the night her father was declared in critical condition and died. Henry had leukemia and, like a friend of Jenny's who died from the same disease, found some consolation in religion. Jenny saw Henry the night he died. "He knew me," she said, "he lifted his hand and waved." She had visited the hospital every day during the forty days of his illness and watched him physically deteriorate and grow emotionally remote. Jenny was the only child left at home. Her mother Ellen and her grandmother Nana were devastated by Henry's death. Jenny hated the funeral. She had to work at the tennis club the day Rob and Jane went to visit

Henry's grave. Jane, Rob and Jon left Long Beach. Jenny stayed with Ellen and tried to visit Nana every day. The house was sold to a high school friend she used to pitty for being poor. The friend's mother had married a rich man. Jenny moved to a small apartment, painted, made curtains, furniture, decorations, and was evicted because of a previous tenant with prior claims. Jenny moved in with Nana. She says, "Nana hates me now." Ellen took her cat Pong. Jenny says, "Pong is driving Mom nuts." Ellen says, "There's no way I can take care of Pong, Jenny. I can't drive at night, cats get sick at night." Jenny's relationship with Pete continues. They are often apart. Pete's job is time-consuming. Jenny works days, full-time, at an art store. They live in different towns. Pete hopes they can open a design firm together. Jenny can't seem to concentrate or finish school. She plans to visit New York for two months.

I was embarrassed to ask my mother for a bra. Everyone had one. I went to Newberry's dime store. At the bra counter I told the lady who asked if she could help, that a friend had left her bra at my house after swimming that it had gotten lost and I had to buy her a new one. The lady asked, "What size?" "Oh, about my size," I said.

Rob went out to play early one morning in June. He found a wallet covered with blood in the bushes underneath the bathroom window. Mom called the police who came and took the wallet and asked questions. Rob was young and on crutches. The wallet belonged to a man who had dropped it under our window at six A.M. after killing his wife and child with a hatchet. He had walked from Belmont shore to the peninsula, thrown away his wallet, walked back to his house and tried unsuccessfully to kill himself. He was a veteran of the war in Korea. Rob testified in court about the wallet.

Watching a movie on television about white slavery, I kissed my sister on the lips. She was three. I was baby-sitting.

Kids, I'm writing in 7th period, what a drag. Are you going to Hodies after class? Don't be mad but did JK say anything about me in the bathroom at lunch. She's been acting real funny. Larry's been ignoring me all day, sob! He really hates me. Did you see what Stephie was wearing today, God! I'm really going to flunk this, she's looking right at me. What's happening Friday night, are you going to the gym? What's Larry doing, what are you wearing? Got to go. See ya. Rabbi Tauber.

I'm so ugly. UGLY UGLY UGLY. I have pimples on my chin. I cover them with Liquimat when I go on dates with boys. My mother says, "What is that stuff covering your pimples?" I have also been fat. I am rude to my mother's friends. I am rude to my friends, my mother says. I pick on them and talk behind their backs. I am evil and very bad. I am powerful and can hurt other people. I have a sharp tongue. I am superior. I am conceited. I have bad posture. I sweat under my arms. It smells. I can stop the smell but not the wetness. I keep my arms tight to my sides so no one will know I sweat, even when making out. My teeth are yellow. I have a lot of cavities. They are filled by the dentist every Wednesday. Afterwards, I always eat French fries even if I've had so much novocaine I can't taste them. I smoke Camels at my grandmother's and in gas station bathrooms. I run away from school. I bleed every month. I have the curse. It smells bad and hurts. My father had intercourse with our best friend. My mother got pregnant. I have hair above my lip, which is unnatural. Other people pretend to feel differently about me even though I pick funny clothes and make them mad.

I urinated on the floor standing in front of the open telephone booths at Buffums department store. I was arguing with my mother. The telephones were by the credit department. It was impossible not to, uncontrollable, a relief, an embarrassment. I stood behind a pillar watching the woman clean it up with a rag.

The space around my grandparents' house wasn't large, but was divided so precisely that it seemed immense. The back yard had a high wooden fence, roses, homey flowers in beds. Around a corner was an alcove with camellia bushes, meticulous blossoms, a murky fish pond, fast goldfish, and shiny green leaves. Magnolias climbed to the second story, blooming on the balcony. The front lawn was smooth and short, standing rose bushes, straight flowers, round stones leading to a thick oak door with a stiff brass knocker. Around the side, a six-foot-wide, geranium-lined space ran unbroken the length of the house, connecting the front lawn and the back yard.

The dining room: dark polished surfaces, cut crystal from Idaho, elaborate dull red and gold plates, sets of silver, bone-handled knives for luncheons, turquoise-studded indigo plates, turquoise blue enamel vases with scarlet snakes as handles. Downstairs bedroom: storage for unused Christmas presents, stacks of gloves, shiny pocketbooks wrapped in tissue, drawer of photographs, important family papers, records of transactions in brown paper files. Upstairs bedroom: tall dressers, marble-topped dresser filled with tiny buckled shoes, down comforter, beaded chiffon dress (pale green), velvet bodices, flowered skirts, jewels, and old watches. Master bedroom: twin pink satin beds, pistol in dresser drawer, rows of shoes in shoe boxes, matching jewelry sets, peacock pin, long rack of silk print dresses reaching back to a small yellow window looking out. The smell of powder. Tomatoes, sweet corn, pork chops consumed in my grandparents' formica kitchen. Grape Nuts with heavy cream, the newspaper, with my own section, Nana's big cup, Big Rob's bigger cup, the sound of wood-cased radio news, morning sun through thin white curtains. Nana, tiny, white hair mathematically waved, dressed in puffy mules and negligee or going out powdered in Shalimar. Big Rob, home at three, sloppy, often drunk, from the stock market and the Pago Pago Bar, big spaces, kitchen, long roads, cream-colored Buick, picnics, bluejays, dust, pine needles, small humiliations when he'd stumble in a store.

Pete the butcher held his hands out to catch the ground round as it squeezed from the meat grinder. He turned his head. "I heard your grandfather died today. He was a fine man." I looked at him, "He did not." I tried not to cry. Pete finished wrapping the meat in freezer paper and marked the price. I took it to the counter to be charged. I ran home crying. My mother was crying. He died in his bed in the night beside my grandmother. She woke up in the morning and tried to wake him.

Billie and Russell were our best friends. I ate corned beef hash at Billie's, tan sugar from Cuba, and English muffins. I stayed overnight at her house when Russell was out of town. I tried on her clothes. She had a full-length mirror. My father would come to take her trash out. She and Russell took me to Catalina Island fishing for tuna on a bright morning. I threw up Welch's grape juice in the sea. Russell said I was feeding the fish.

Billie Marsh in the late 1950s was an attractive woman in her late thirties with sexy clothes, lace underwear and short platinum blonde hair. She was compact, lived in a small house with early American decor on the peninsula between the ocean and the bay in Long Beach, California. Billie was a live wire and fun at parties. Her husband Russell was a mild-mannered, kind man who traveled a great deal on business. They had one child, then in his early twenties, and a house on Catalina Island perched high on a hill looking over Avalon Bay. She served raw sugar, neatly poached eggs on corned beef hash, toast with sweet butter, salt in a cellar and pepper in a grinder for breakfast. When she was away teenagers would smoke, barbecue, and masturbate in her garage. One close friendship was broken off when it was discovered that she was sleeping with her best friend's husband, meeting him in San Diego, sleeping with him in motels. She was encouraging and supportive. She moved away from Long Beach, perhaps to Texas, with her husband Russell.

I don't know what I'm going to do, the worst thing happened. I got arrested in Buffums just when I was walking out. I'd been to Dr. Longley's. I've lost twenty pounds. I went to the store. Mom said we had enough Christmas balls but we didn't. I took two boxes, some ropes, a choker, and one of those tiny little cameras for presents. Anyway, I paid for one box, the people at the cash register acted funny but I didn't really get it then. I went across the street to Buffums. All I did was ask them for a bag because I had too many things, the stuff I took plus the clothes I'd borrowed from Stephie, her orange lanamere sweater, etc. I just looked around and went out, a man and a woman came up grabbed my arms hard and pulled me into a little office. I was really scared, they went through everything and tried to say I'd stolen everything even Stephie's sweater which is really old. They were sarcastic. I was crying. They took me to Juvenile Center, they took my fingerprints on both hands, took everything away from me even my shoelaces and pencils and asked me why I had done it. I said Mom and Daddy liked Rob better and proved it by saying how much allowance we got even though I do a lot more since he's crippled and that I get the lowest of all my friends. I begged them not to call Mom. I wouldn't tell our phone number but they had it from my wallet. They put me in this dirty yellow room with a screen they look at you through. There were all these names all over the walls I think a lot of kids from Poly and Millikan High. I don't know how they wrote because they took all my pencils. Mom came down, God I hate her guts, she brought Dan Corwin because Daddy was in San Diego. She cried. I don't care. She said she was going to tell Daddy about me borrowing Stephie's sweater, God. What I'm really scared about is I can never get a job except at Daddy's office, or go to college because they always check to see if you have a record. I'm going to flunk typing anyway and probably algebra. If anyone finds out I'll just die, they will, she tells everything. Oh God, what's even worse, Tom Russell's father is president of Buffums. I don't even know if I should run away last time I got restricted for two weeks.

We had barbecues in Billie's garage when she was out of town. Once we tried to roast corn but it didn't get done. I wonder if at that time or any other of the many times we sneaked in there to smoke, if these were the times she drove down to meet my father at a motel in San Diego. To get food for eating in the garage I used to charge things at the market. Ruffle potato chips had just come out, corrugated rather than smooth, strong enough to eat with cream cheese.

Full circle white felt skirt with boatneck pink jersey, I sat laughing in the little lights, Main Street, Disneyland. Dick's friend said, "She's going to cause a lot of people a lot of trouble in a few years." Dick smiled. Returning, we made out in the back seat. I rubbed my hands up and down the back of his creaking black leather jacket as Marge had directed. Dick's friend said through the rearview mirror and refracted headlights, "That's some workout that jacket's getting."

Jane,
They said they liked both of you and were fighting about who was going to get who. They want to take you guys out, if possible this weekend. Do you think you would want to go out with them?
Answer, Margie

Margie,
Did they really say that? Later, who wants to take who out? I'm pretty sure I'm going out with Dick this weekend but I'm not positive.

Jane,
Harold wants to take you out and Mike wants to take Stephie out. But it doesn't make much difference which to them.

Margie is a skag. Judy let Phil feel her up. Mary is wearing a turtleneck to cover a hickey. Kris will make out with anyone. Mary G. has hot pants. Dixie is getting a really bad reputation. Linda smokes. Patty had to marry Mike. Leona went all the way with Randall. Susan didn't make Zygomas because she makes out in public.

Jane,
Jack was going with Jan Rycroft while she was broken up with Ray Snider. Jan was Soph. Pres. last semester and Ray was Jr. Pres. last semester. Jack came to

church with Jan quite a bit. I think he is real sweet. He is so funny. Anytime I was around him he kept me laughing all the time. I think he is real neat.

Margie,
He is, is Jan very neat? Is she in any sorority? I think he's really great but I don't want to go with anyone right now! Cause I still want to go out with Jack Duffy too! I'm going out with him Fri. nite too!

Jane,
Jan is real sweet (sometimes). She is real moody. No, she isn't in any sorority but she was asked to Anue but I don't know if she made it or not. She wanted to real bad. She is the type of person that will be real sweet to your face then turn around and say something bad about you behind your back. But I still like her. She is real cute and she knows it. I don't think she is as cute as she was a year ago.

Margie,
What does she look like? Who does she go around with? Is she neat? I'm just checking, cause Jack told me about her last night and he said she was kind of an oddball!

Jane,
He is right, I guess if you come right down to it, she gave Jack a dirty deal. I don't know who she goes around with at school, I don't even know what she is like at school. All I know is what kids have told me. Some of it I wouldn't repeat. She is a big flirt. She says she is going steady with Ray but she turns around and says she is going out with Jack Hall. She is all mixed up. Anything Jack says about her is probably right. He knows her better than I do.

At Woodrow Wilson High School Stephie was voted Sophomore Princess, B Song Girl, Sweetheart of Sigma Chi, Junior Princess, invited to Phi Gam sorority, elected Varsity Song Girl and Homecoming Queen. I developed an interest in poetry, painting, accumulated a number of appointed and elected student offices, accused people of cheating, went out with more boys than anyone on campus except Anne, prepared Crab Louis and cold artichokes in the girls' bathroom and ate it with Katie in the triangle at lunchtime while I read her my latest work.

The unbearable sadness of my life flattened me face down on the sand after school, alone, making up poems, my body in the shape of an X listening to waves break in the Pacific Ocean.

I wish the strength would break.
I wish the strength would break.
I wish the strength would break.
And I could slip into the dark unconscious
Until the making of the path is done.

Jim, drunk for the first time at a beach party at night in Corona del Mar, tackled me yelling, "I want to fuck you." Everyone was shocked. Jim was the star of the football team and a straight A student. I acted fragile and confused and was able to drive back with John French.

June 11, 1959

Dear Mr. Rickman:
I wish to apologize for my behavior today. I realize fully that it is not my place to dispute a teacher's decision and I am aware of what a grave error I made. I am sorry that you were the recipient of my temper outburst and I hope you will be able to forgive it. I was thoroughly shocked, though, when I learned that you felt there was an element of dishonesty in my behavior in Government Class. I wish to state that I have never attempted to "pull the wool" over anyone's eyes, and I am very hurt that you have interpreted my actions in this light. I have been in Government class three semesters and I have found them extremely profitable; it is disappointing to find that, apparently, my contributions have not equaled what I have gained.
I am sincerely sorry that today's incident occurred and I hope my apology will be accepted with the same sincerity in which it is given.
Sincerely,
Jane Tauber

41

6-12-59

Dear Jane:

Your good letter accepted without reservation. You are still my favorite Government student in spite of the fact of our tiff yesterday. It happens to all of us. Please hang on to your temper these last few days. There probably will be many more incidents before school is out but it is not my intention to blow clear up. Only part way.

I have removed the truancy from your record this morning on receipt of the very nice letter.

Good luck at Mills next fall.

Glenn Rickman

Marriage

There was no moon. I walked along the boardwalk past John Lane's house hoping he would see me and come out. He didn't. I walked on to the end of the boardwalk and back. I heard footsteps behind me. I began to get frightened. I walked faster the footsteps walked faster. I stopped and looked back at someone who looked back at me. For a moment my body dissolved I ran screaming. He ran after me. I cut across a vacant lot he did too. I ran to the nearest house banged on the door he ran past me. I was crying and sweating. My father picked me up. He didn't call the police. I took the plane back to Mills College.

A dream: I'm lying on a plank with tall wheels in a furnace room, a prisoner, drugged. The furnace man is an idiot in a white suit. He moves like a quiet, fast chicken. He wants to touch me.

I rested in Ted's bedroom, wishing he'd come in. He came in. "Jane?" I didn't answer or open my eyes. He felt my breasts. I didn't open my eyes. I decided to stay overnight at Ted's. We had to be quiet so his landlady wouldn't hear us. He wanted me to sleep with him. I wanted to but didn't know if it was the right thing to do, I hadn't with anyone, at least I thought I hadn't. Ted thought I slept with his best friend, Jim, by a stream in a marble quarry. Jim wrote, "Dear Ted, I have finally done the great deed . . ." I dreamed a fist-size crab dug into my calf. I shook my leg violently to get it off and woke us both.
"Come in me, don't finish outside."
"No, we can't."
"Why?"
"I don't have any rubbers."
"Why do you keep forgetting to get rubbers, don't you want to sleep with me?"
"That's not it, why don't you get something? Why don't you buy the rubbers?"
I was scared to get a diaphragm. I'd have to make an appointment with a doctor, say I was married, tell lies, show I wanted to, they would know.

Driving from Berkeley to Mills, Ted told me about his old

girlfriend. There were things she didn't like to do. I was pleased she didn't like sex. "What things, like touching your penis?" He laughed, "No, like kissing it."

A dream: I'm in my grandmother's living room watching a revolving circular unit, a lazy Susan. It's a refrigerator on one side, an oven on the other, some lamb chops are freezing and broiling. I'm petting a dog which stiffens into a plucked turkey. Jenny, Jon and I watch Frank Sinatra sing on television. His face comes forward and recedes, becomes my face then his. Someone knocks on the door. It's the boy next door. He wants me to drink a sticky pale green cocktail. Everyone says, "Don't drink that." I drink it because I am mad.

Carlos held up a reproduction of a Warhol painting, "When you see this what do you think of?" I looked at the painting of Campbell cans, cans I thought. "Hands," I said. "That's not the point," he said, "do you know what I mean, Rose?" Rose nodded, drank some more beer, and looked at the print.

My painting teacher served shrimp Creole at his house in San Francisco. All the graduate painting class was there. I was a senior. Rose fell in a bush drunk talking about Verdi and vomited. Leila left early with a Spanish instructor. Bibby got depressed and went home.

Leila Eckhart is a thirty-three-year-old victim of a recent rape attempt who teaches Spanish and English at an underprivileged junior high school in Oakland, California. Her father was the Eckhart sugar king. His father gambled with the last Hawaiian king. Leila's mother divorced her father and took no alimony. Leila went to Mills College for two years, flunked out, moved with her mother to Mexico, and entered Mexico City College where she fell in love with a boy named Jay who was interested in anthropology and American Indian tribes. She became pregnant, had an abortion. After the abortion Jay refused to sleep with her, and left to find an Indian reservation he could live on. From Mexico she moved to Southern California and worked at a Sears department store, at the ice cream counter, for three days. She was fired for putting too much ice cream in the cones, and took a job at Huntington Harbor, a luxury housing development with canals, as a receptionist, then as a secretary. She has a large jewelry collection—primarily gold, silver, emeralds, green and yellow topaz, coral, jade, opals, amethysts and pearls—purchased in Peruvian and Mexican markets for small sums. At five A.M. a man entered her bedroom. It was dark, he'd cut the electricity off from outside. He put his hand over her mouth. Leila said, "What do you want? Take anything you want and get out of here." He said he wanted to rape her and held a curved knife to her throat. "Don't scream," he said. Leila said, "May I light a cigarette." "Yes, if you don't light it to light up my face." She asked what he did, how he'd gotten involved in this business, what if she had syphilis or something and other questions. He seemed eager to get started. She asked, "May I go to the bathroom? I have a tampax in." He followed her in and out, then began to take off her clothes. She struggled but saw that it excited him, so she took them off herself. He began to touch her. She struggled but saw that it excited him, and lay across the bed on her back, ankles crossed, eyes closed, arms against her sides. Dawn broke, a few minutes passed. He said, "Well, you'll be glad I have to go now." Leila thought he couldn't get an erection. She said, "O.K. Would you lock the door on your way out?" He said "Yes," and left. He turned the electricity back on. Leila leaves her windows open. The cost of fixing them after continual robberies has become too great. She's thinking of moving to Montana to join some friends, one of whom is on a mucus-free celibate diet. He feels better than he ever has in his life. Before going to Sierra Leone, Leila married James Prentiss, a Yale graduate from the East Coast who played the violin and was interested in civil rights. His great-uncle discovered the ancient city of Macchu Picchu in Peru and his uncle is a senator from New York who was helpful in releasing James from a jail in the south where he had been registering voters. In Africa, they lived in a chiefdom of the Mendi tribe. The chief assured them he was monogamous and didn't believe in witchcraft or sorcery. James attempted to change some of the local customs by appealing to the logic of the tribe and was discouraged in his efforts. The tribesmen had to walk twenty miles to the main road. James helped them build a bridge. Some used it, most didn't. Leila felt they were taking jobs that could be done by the tribespeople. When an animal was killed the baby animals were brought to Leila. They had a civet cat and a monkey. Neither would come near James, who attempted to imitate them. The tribespeople put curses on each other which were generally effective. The swear tree was outside Leila's and James' house. An injured party was putting a swear on a young woman. He stood chanting with the agent who beat a stick on a turtle shell. The news of the swear spread fast and reached the young woman working in the fields. She ran to the village, clasped her belly, fell over in a coma, and died the same night. Leila and James were unable to help her. No one was allowed into the Bunda where women came of age. It was built much closer to the village than in previous years and was held for a shorter length of time, about two months. Leila could hear them drunk on palm wine, chanting all night. On a certain day a woman with a devil's mask came into the village. All men had to hide and couldn't look at the woman or they would become blind, paralyzed or killed by the sight of clitorises in a jar held and shook by the devil woman. The women's clitorises were cut out so they would have little pleasure in sexual intercourse and be faithful to their husbands. The tribespeople find stone carvings of small squat figures in their fields when plowing. No one knows who carved them, they come from the remote past. Finding one is good luck. Leila has two. When a twin died, a figure would be carved to keep the surviving twin company. Traders offered a considerable amount of money for these figures. The families would sell them, first hammering a hole in each eye to blind the figure so it couldn't see that it was leaving and where it was going. Leila doesn't know what effect this has on the surviving twin. James received his degree in law, Leila in education. He disappeared after allegedly handing a gun to Black Panther William X in his prison cell. They were divorced.

James wasn't heard from for years. A skull thought to be his was found but he appeared in Canada and gave an interview to the *New York Times*. Leila's house is filled with many objects. She doesn't want to leave it though she is very discouraged with the way things are now in society and doesn't enjoy meeting people. She writes:

> I have come to some drastic conclusions of late and have finally acted for once. All of a sudden everything seemed to click and fall in line. I finally decided I never really liked teaching from the beginning, mainly 'cause I just don't or haven't the knack. I've had the opportunity in the past year to spend a good deal of time on friends' farmland camping out and mellowing out a bit. I think my perspective has done a real flip. My father left a few bucks & so now I'm on a twenty-acre almond farm & am loving it. No postal delivery. No garbage pick-up. No supermarkets. Very little traffic. My world view is very dim & I figure with spaceships zapping human beings up into their glowing machines what the hell difference does any of it make. And why not sit back and enjoy the spectacle. I don't mean literally sit back because I do want to produce. But I just want to do it at my own pace & pleasure. Am into making baskets now & will hope to make time to get good at it. Lots of natural fibers growing beside the river—willows & cottonwood & cattails.

Ted and I were both accepted at Yale. I bought a 'fifties green station wagon. Ted learned self-hypnosis. We drove to St. Louis to meet his parents. The tennis courts were grass. We ate artichokes and pâté in linen suits and dresses. There was a bell attached to the table for the maid. We discussed the Comptons Shopping Plaza and hippies. I went to New York to stay in the Third Avenue apartment of a Peruvian Communist. The airshaft was filled with eight stories of hungry cats. No one else wore a French twist at the Yale art school.

I drifted in and out of sleep. Ted told me about a big polar bear rug and an aquarium. We were getting married in two days. In the street my mother said, "I'm going to faint, Jane, I can't talk about this on the street. The wife is always the last to know, you know that cliché. I still can't talk about it. She was a terrible woman, she actually followed your father down to San Diego." We made plans to meet in Princeton at 4 o'clock for the bridal dinner.

Laura Elliot wore an informal blue silk dress. John Elliot wore a lightweight dark suit. Ellen Tauber wore a fancy white silk suit and hat. Henry Tauber wore a dark lightweight suit. Laura Elliot wore a big aquamarine ring which turned out to be Bibby Cartwright's birthstone. Leila had on a topaz dinner ring the night before with a silk dress which Laura Elliot liked. Jenny and I had our pictures taken on the steps of the church in white, looking alike though twelve years apart, mouths open, eyes blank. Uncle Jim emerged later in photographs taken by Saul Brauner, confused son of the physicist. The bouquets and head dresses had to be taken apart because they were ugly. There was a dinner with champagne. I invited everyone to come to the Americana Hotel, not wanting to leave, which upset Ted. It turned out neither of us had brought contraceptives. The minister may have written *Bridge on the River Kwai*. My finger was too swollen to get the ring on. I did my own hair for the wedding. There were no ashtrays at the bridal dinner although I smoked heavily. I was angry at the wedding. My mother wanted me to pose for photographs, I didn't want to. I didn't see Ted, he was talking to his friends. The Elliots talked to my friends. I was grouchy. I watched us get married and laughed about the ring getting stuck on the first joint of my finger. Bibby gave me diamond earrings, my mother gave me a sapphire and diamond pin of my great-grandmother's, Ted gave me a leather pig, I gave Ted a Siamese kitten not yet born.

Honeymoon. They served a five-course breakfast at the Snow Inn, silver dishes with homemade bread and sweet rolls, overlooking the water. We took a picnic lunch, rented a motorboat and went to the sand dunes across the wide bay. We drank wine, we made love in the sand. Thinking how happy I was my stomach cramped, my bowels heaved. A dense fog separated us from land. I was terrified, sick and dizzy. We found someone. They took us back in a dune buggy. "She's sick." I had cystitis and took pills that turned my urine orange, kept me out of the sun, made me complain and feel guilty. I couldn't eat much.

Ted Elliot is a thirty-four-year-old psychiatrist living at the edge of a wildlife preserve in Bethany, Connecticut. He has mown the side of a hill smoothly, there are tufts of long grass between the cracks of boulders, around the circumference of boulders, where the mower is blocked. Recently he has become skilled at Tai Chi Chuan, a traditional Chinese martial art. This discipline, along with Chinese herbal tea prescribed by a Chinese doctor in New York and eight years of psychoanalysis, has corrected a severe back problem which caused him pain for years. A doctor in Berkeley, California, who owned an organ and all of the Bach organ works, many performed by E. Power Biggs, told Ted to pay attention to the Mayo Clinic's diagnosis of arthritis spondylitis, to realize that he could never stand up long enough to become a doctor, to move immediately from damp and foggy Berkeley to Arizona. Ted attended Brookhaven Country Day School in St. Louis where he was a gifted athlete: tennis, football, track and basketball, president of the student body and recipient of the Marsh Elliot Award for Leadership, an award established by his cousin Maxwell Marsh Elliot, a movie producer in Hollywood. Among Marsh's credits are: *Apache*, a Cannes prize–winning documentary film; *A World Affair*, with Bob Hope, about the United Nations, romance, and orphans; a war picture in which a dying Southerner has to accept a blood transfusion from a Northern black; a picture with John Wayne and Barbara Stanwyck, which was dedicated to the Elliot family, about an insane asylum and the need for more understanding between human beings. Ted went to Princeton University, joined an eating club and made the varsity basketball team. In one game he scored many points but after that had conflicts with the coach, couldn't sleep the nights before games, and was afflicted by frozen wrists the days of the games. He ran for a student office and lost, dropped out of school for a year and stayed at home in St. Louis. Among his majors were architecture, Chinese, and psychology. He went to summer school at Harvard for Russian, went to Nationalist China for a summer as a medical research aide, and learned about snakes and tapeworms. Ted decided to be a doctor and enrolled for pre-medical postgraduate work at Berkeley. His father John is in the grain business and originally from California where he was friends with the son of William Randolph Hearst, with whom he visited the legendary Xanadu overlooking the Pacific Ocean. John wanted to be a journalist but instead joined his elder brother Mead Sr. in the real estate business. Eventually they went into grain. Ted's mother Laura is from Cairo, Illinois, where her family was prominent. Her sister starved herself to death locked in a room, perhaps from a disappointed love affair. Ted's parents are members of the Friends of Art Society for the Robert Gardner Merritt Museum of Art, a group organized to enable that museum to buy the work of living artists. John is patron of the Willa Marsh Library of Science and has commissioned busts of, among others, Fermi and Einstein. John once met Buckminster Fuller and spent a lively evening talking; he found Fuller eccentric. He feels, using Albert Einstein's tennis shoes with no socks and unruly hair as an example, that a man can afford eccentricities once he has achieved success and world renown. Ted clapped his hand to his forehead and groaned. Ted began dating Jane, his best friend's girlfriend, an art major at Mills College. They began living together and both were accepted in the graduate school of Yale University, Jane in art, Ted in medicine. They were married with the grudging consent of Ted's parents and to the delight of Jane's. They were divorced after several breakups, reconciliations, and ten years. Ted now lives with his girlfriend Carol, a clinical psychologist who goes to a women's consciousness-raising group. Ted has entered the Psychoanalytic Institute for training, about which he still has some reservations. His parents were concerned that his elder brother

Foster's name sounded Jewish. The Elliots were to receive some money from St. Louis' wealthiest family, the Marshes, if Ted was a girl. They named him Edward Marsh Elliot, which they changed to Edward Atwater when the Marshes took no interest in him. Ted believed his mother was in love with him and imagined that she didn't wear underpants when he visited home on vacations. Ted plays compositions of his own on the recorder, and hymns on the piano. He and Carol have two goats, four geese, two cats, a dog, and one or two drinks before dinner. They have traveled in Nova Scotia. Six feet in height, Ted is very attractive with bright blue eyes, a wide aquiline nose, sensual mouth, mobile features, small shoulders and bad posture which has been greatly improved by his practice of Tai Chi. People have noticed his resemblance to Jean-Paul Belmondo. When Ted's uncle, Mead Sr., was ill, they rushed him to the French Hospital in New York. Mead Jr., Ted's cousin, allegedly got Mead Sr. to sign codicils to his will under false pretenses, much to the disadvantage of the rest of the family. Ted's father wrote many letters advising Ted to change his linen frequently, to watch the north side of the road for ice when driving in mountainous regions, and never to sully the family escutcheon. He offered to set up Ted's fiancee as his mistress because women are after men of family, education, and certain fortune. Ted's income is augmented by the interest from a rather large trust fund. He lives simply and has little interest in fashion. He used to squeeze tennis balls on the way to class to strengthen his wrists. Ted and Carol have married. Ted has decided to retire but worries about money. His metaphysical interests continue to be the focus of his life. He was deeply moved by a week spent in a monastery in New Mexico. Ted and Carol have divorced.

"You won't be able to have intercourse for two weeks."
"O.K."
Across the surface of the desk the doctor said, "My patients have two reactions to that: 'Oh no!' and 'Thank God.'"
I said, "It hurts when I have intercourse now."
"Where?"

"In the small of my back at the end of my vagina."

"That's impossible, there's nothing wrong with you."

"Can't his penis be hitting something that's sore?"

"No, put a pillow under your back."

"I've tried, it doesn't help."

"Have you ever had homosexual fantasies?"

"Not really."

"Then you have a depressed libido. Are you free with your husband about sex? My wife always encourages me to take pictures of girls in bikinis on island vacations, as many as I want. A man needs to feel his wife isn't jealous and encourages his sexuality. This in turn encourages his loyalty to her. He needs to feel free."

"Thank you. Two weeks?" I said.

A man in a cook's suit walks into the house at night. He has an axe raised over his head ready to hack the people in bed to pieces. I am awake Ted is asleep. I think about the man and the possibility of throwing myself backwards out the window. I think about waking Ted, both of us rolling the mattress over and pushing it into the axeman so he will fall on his own axe. If this doesn't work he will hack through the mattress.

The owner called the house on Martha's Vineyard a shack. It wasn't. It was wood-paneled, looking across Great Tisbury pond to dunes and ocean. The pillows matched the rugs, the rugs the bedspreads. The lamps were maps, the pots and pans complete. I painted in the garage. We had to get Party Boy castrated. Ted got 99.3 on his medical boards, we made love in the ocean and talked about having a child. We swam out to catch some waves and almost drowned. We panicked, swam, floated, and talked each other back to shore.

Jim lay on the road in his bathrobe, a surprise visit. Jim and Ted decided to take a trip. I almost married Jim. I said, "Fine, maybe I'll visit Phillip in Boston." I fixed bacon and scrambled eggs the morning they were to leave. I began vomiting. We drove to the hospital, I lay on the back seat holding a stainless steel pan. "Go ahead, I'll be alright, I'll stay with Meredith and Robin when I get out." They left for Maine. Meredith and

Robin went shopping twenty minutes down a twisted dirt road. "I'll be fine, I'd like to be alone." I felt exhilarated. I listened to my heart beat. The room was sunny. My heart beat louder and faster. I panicked, felt dizzy, and blacked out. Ted once told me about a doctor, allergic to bee stings, who had saved himself from dying by jumping into a tub of cold water. I got under the shower dressed. I called the operator for help and crawled to the porch to wait. The police came. Fading in and out of consciousness I cried, "Someone help me." I had tests, X-rays, thoughts of Rocky Mountain Fever. No one knew what was wrong. "Take this red sleeping pill," a resident whispered. "I shouldn't say this but I think your problem may be psychological."

Rose and her husband came to visit. Ted returned with Jim. I went to a psychiatrist who said, "Couldn't you be angry at your husband for leaving you?" "He didn't leave me, we have an agreement. People should be able to do what they want." Then I thought, I hate Ted and Jim, they aren't fair. The doctor gave me Stelazine and recommended therapy.

We cleaned the house and left.

Dr. Hammerstein said I sat with my legs wide apart so he could look up my skirt. He added that another psychiatrist had said the same thing and that he felt it was in the nature of a challenge. I believed Dr. Hammerstein but not the other one who didn't like me and made me angry.

Arthur was an incredible dancer. He had a girlfriend in Boston. Ted had left the party early to study. "Your body is really smooth," Arthur said. "Don't you have any rubbers?" I asked. "Don't you have anything?" he said. "No, I quit the pill for a month."

"It furthers one to cross the wide waters." I interrupted Ted's *I Ching*. He got a stomach ache and had to lie on the bed. I kept talking. "You should go if you want to get away." He went to Chicago. He brought me the new Beatles album, *Revolver*, as a present. He wouldn't touch me. "I met Helen in Chicago." "I had an affair with Arthur!" I yelled. I smashed the window open with my fist. I left and went to see Dr. Korn, recommended by Dr. Hammerstein for emergencies. Leaving his house I drove the car into a sand dune. He and Ted got it out the next morning. I crushed, bent, and stamped on *Revolver*. Ted said, "How can you do that?"

February 4, Ted was depressed. I said, "Do you want to have Buzz and Sue over for dinner?" I was jealous of Sue. Ted said, "No, I want to leave, things are no good." Ten days later he came by with two Halloween masks he bought on impulse. The masks were a monster woman and a very old man. It was Valentine's Day.

Ted showed me through the retarded hospital. There were people who couldn't move, who had never opened their eyes, fifty-year-old babies, twenty-year-old six-year-olds. A girl came up nervously, "Can you give me some pills?" Ted took her down the hall. I said, "Is that one of the patients?" He said, "No." I straightened up his room, looked through his mail, found hairpins in his bed and towels with dry vomit on the floor. Over coffee I asked, "Did you sleep with that girl?" He said something. His hands were shaking. He was as frightened as I was.

In June Ted bought a new car, a Mini Cooper S. It was our sixth anniversary. We decided to go to the country together. Fifteen minutes later we crashed into the back of a very large blue station wagon. Luckily it was right near Nelke Motors, where Ted had bought the car. We ate hamburgers and decided to go in a different car.

I visited Rose and her husband in New York, and went looking for a loft that Ted and I could live in part-time. Rose and I got off the subway. Her face was red, she was furious. "I hate that."
"What?"
"That man playing with himself, looking at us and leering."
"Really? I didn't see him."
We watched television. Bobby Kennedy won. Ted called at six

A.M. and said Bobby Kennedy's been shot. I went home on the train. I hated everyone.

Rose Ohearne is a thirty-six-year-old artist, born in Chicago, of Irish-Catholic extraction. Her father was a lawyer and an alcoholic. He wrote poems to Rose's mother on her birthday and Easter. As a child she beat up other children, lied, drew realistic pictures of her father's hands. She has an older sister, Dinah, whom she has been jealous of, and a younger brother, Johnny, who disappeared after he had been discharged from the hospital during the Vietnam War. He reappeared married, with children. Rose's father and aunt were in vaudeville, a tap dancing team. She attended the Chicago Art Institute and believes the Chicago Imagist painters are working out of early drawings she left around the school. The lake was cold and windy, she walked around alone in the dark. Her father and mother ran out of money when she was young. They lived in hotels and would sneak past the clerk when the rent was due. Rose never ironed her clothes or used deodorant like her sister Dinah. Her mother would play games to divert them in the hotel room. They would eat Wonder Bread and ride the El all night. Rose attended the Mills graduate school in painting. Her first year she listened to Verdi's *Requiem* frequently, ate Grape Nuts at all meals, and fell into a rose bush drunk, talking about Verdi. Her second year she was married to Vincent, a Sicilian artist from Chicago, by a black minister in San Francisco. She is fond of Einstein and his friend Steinmetz. Drunk, she told a curator from the Whitney Museum, "I am the James Joyce of painting." She laughed, reading *Ulysses* and *War and Peace* on the floor, went out with Tim who spent all day watching children through windows. She dreams about nuns, has black frizzy hair with white in it, a long body of average height, capped teeth, crazed blue eyes, a son Hughie, a regular nose, and wears jeans and tight sweaters. She is often depressed and worried about her work. In a rage she smashed all her windows, adding up the cost of each pane. She won't talk much about herself and once pushed everything off the table when a friend of Vincent's was boring. She has an interest in small measurements. She wrote newspaper articles against rock and roll in high school, published a newspaper called *The Monthlies* in which there was an article titled "Lady Leaks," about a woman who saved a penny for each year of her life and stuffed them up her vagina. Feeling ill, the lady went to the doctor who told her to stop doing that. She couldn't, she had no other way of keeping track of herself. Rose attended a Rauschenberg exhibition, someone put his hands on her shoulders, she turned to face an older man she didn't know who said, "My god, you're a girl, you look just like an Irish tough." He returned to his wife's side and both of them watched her as they left the gallery. The same day, teenagers in a car followed her nine blocks, she ducked into Astor Wines and Liquors, she didn't want them to see where she lived. They yelled "Hey baby, hey baby," and finally, when she wouldn't respond, "Hey baby you're getting gray." She bought some wine, the clerk gave her the change and said, "Thank you, sir, I mean ma'am." She returned home depressed. As a child Rose tried to kill a large tomcat she hated. "He chased my little cat Queenie into the water and made her break her leg. She limped the rest of her life. I thought he was evil, the devil, an evil cat, I wanted to get rid of him, kill him." She would wait for the cat to appear and try to grab it. One day she succeeded. Just as she was about to hurl the squiriming cat into the incinerator her father appeared. She feels if she had been allowed to carry out her plans she would have felt absolutely no guilt. Rose and Vincent separated. He went to live in the woods of Vermont, she stayed in New York. Her ceiling collapsed, she moved to a larger loft, summered by the ocean, painted, bought the complete line of Erno Laszlo products for skin care, tried to change, to improve the quality of her friendships, made new friends, began exhibiting at the Ana Martin Gallery, experimented sexually, entered therapy with a Lithuanian woman, taught in California, painted, took care of her son, energetically started and stopped relationships, became depressed, returned, got in fights, suffered, resumed therapy, had her astrological chart done twice (Virgo sun, Scorpio moon), had her palm read, painted, began doing three hours of Yoga a day, took Shiatsu massage once a week, painted, stopped smoking, started, stopped, stopped eating meat, began meditating (sitting technique), had an interview with a high Tibetan Buddhist, bought a Ping-Pong table as a physical outlet for her anger, and exhibited her paintings. She writes:

I loved getting your letter
I've started one of the shaped canvases—9 feet it feels exciting!
The work came back from California & it still (or finally) looks really exciting to me. This made me feel better.
I've been really, really, really depressed in spite of what a wonderful artist I am and what a great future lies in store for me (sometimes after 50 years of pain & agony when I'm drooling at the mouth & trying to find the switch to turn on my motorized wheel chair) I'm going through a lot of things with people & finding out a lot—basically I'm finally feeling all the garbage in me—rising to the surface—big shit balls & tar balls. I just feel a lot of urgency that I've got to clean up my act fast and there's no time to waste anymore. I'm doing a lot of Yoga and reading a wonderful book called THE LAWS OF FORM by G. T. Spencer—if you get a chance pick it up before Japan to contemplate in the monastery. I think I need this time to get prepared for the onslaught of the fall.
Ana is depressed too—she's out on the Island now though. I haven't really talked to her. I miss you here. I'm glad it's going well—it sounds wonderful & beautiful and you deserve it. Sorry about the Laszlo but it's a small price for a good trip. I love Holiday Inns too—I think they are far out!!! I might go live in one when I get to my wonderful old age—Say Hi to Yukie for me. I'm glad he's being good.
Love
Rose

Some titles of her paintings are: Beerglass at Noon, Will, Mars Violet Cross, Red Arc Yellow Painting, Dark Heart, Pink Spiral

Leap, Middleground, Heartbeat, Flamingo, Benita, Harry, Southern California, Rise, Rolling Ball, Singing School, Back, Beginner, and, most recently: Desire, Searchin.

Robin Slade-Ryan visited New York with Felix during Christmas. Ted went skiing in Colorado. It was so cold the car doors froze shut. I wore a green velvet dress with a yellow collar. Robin, Felix, and I celebrated New Year's. I stayed the night and decided to go to London for semester break to visit Felix. Ted agreed we needed more time apart.

Felix and I walked to Daniel's on Prince of Wales Drive. London was gray, the air bitter. Felix ran a stick along the metal palings of the fence. "This is all new, the old fences were melted down for raw materials in the recent hostilities." Daniel made an omelet, talked about literature, and served a salad. Two Burmese cats lurked in the corner. Felix said we were lucky Daniel didn't leave us alone with them. They had held two adult males at bay for six hours.

Robin Slade-Ryan is a thirty-three-year-old artist of wide reputation in England. He was born in Ireland, brought up a Catholic, and can no longer recite the Mass in Latin. He has a British-Irish passport, a house in Hackney, a good teaching job, a ten-year-old daughter, Virginia, a Dalmatian, Emma, and, in New York, an estranged wife, Meredith. Robin's father attended the same Irish boarding school that James Joyce did and he too had to break the ice covering the wash basin on cold mornings. He is with the World Bank. They lived in Peru. Robin made a movie about Macchu Picchu, the Inca city in the Andes. He went to Fordham University, despised it, had sad blind dates, transferred to Yale in art, began having an affair with Meredith three years his senior, a graduate student in painting. He had slept with two men; she had slept with women and was from Boston. They became engaged, Meredith got pregnant, they were married and honeymooned in Europe. Robin and Meredith took a job at a remote progressive school in Vermont where Virginia was born, they returned to New

Haven, Robin entered Yale graduate school in painting. Their apartment became the center of a clique of art students. His work changed from hard edge painting, he broke through to sculpture. The more Robin worked the less Meredith painted. They talked about the Vietnam War with their friends. Robin planned with Robert a design for a new world. "What are the other students' plans?" he asked. "Oh, one decided everything would be blue—a painter." Everyone laughed. The program fell apart. Robin and Meredith summered in Martha's Vineyard, cooking and caring for a seventy-year-old rich man. They decided to move to England, got jobs, Robin as an instructor in art, Meredith as the warden of a dormitory. Everything was packed and shipped: the Design Research couch, the Design Research stack-up china, souvenirs. There were bon voyage parties. A letter arrived. They no longer had jobs. They went anyway and both fell in love with the same student, Bran, who later baby-sat for Virginia and lost his virginity to an American art critic on their sofa. The art critic didn't like Robin's work, most of which was being used as furniture. Meredith knitted sweaters for Bran, spent their money on yarn and the ingredients for elaborate French meals, converted to an evangelical faith, threw stones against Bran's window at one in the morning, and went for long solitary walks. Robin was deeply troubled. The pain of the situation struck him in the middle of London traffic; he drove the car into a traffic island and began to cry. He started to exhibit and sell his work. They had a £2,000 bank overdraft, Yves St. Laurent suits, and an enormous number of friends. Meredith had an affair with a boy, Robin slept with a boy, everything came out. Robin was artist-in-residence at King's College, Cambridge, worried about money, drank fine wine and walked across the same lawn E. M. Forster did. Robin, drunk, slugged Meredith after a party on Martha's Vineyard in 1963. In 1973 Meredith, drunk, tried to push Robin over a balcony in London. Their friends explained to them the nature of their relationship. Meredith went to New York City, sub-let a loft. Robin wrote a letter asking for a separation: "We are destroying each other." Robin looks Irish, bought glasses at Yale with plain glass because they made him look more serious. He has an extraordinary sense of humor and impending disaster.

Daniel Francoeurs is one of seven brothers, three of whom may never have had any kind of sex. He is thirty-five years old, of French-Canadian and Algonquin-Indian heritage, born in Providence, Rhode Island, now a novelist living in London, England and Cortona, Italy. "How much longer can it last?" he asks about his looks and the probability of his body holding together, "I think everything that's going to happen in my life has happened." During college Daniel woke up, looked out the window, and even if the day was fine thought of suicide. He went to a psychiatrist. His roommate Bill said impatiently, "Daniel, why are you always so nice?" Daniel left for Europe on a ship, lost his virginity to Gloria, a black nightclub singer, recently dead, who sang "My Funny Valentine" to him at three A.M. in a Spanish bar. "Why don't you sleep with Omar? There's so little room," she said. Daniel said "Yes" and was seduced near dawn enjoying the best sex of his life. He wonders now if Gloria knew what she was doing, if he is congenitally homosexual or just prejudiced against blacks. He danced, drank, stayed up late, traveled with Omar, lived in Rome with a brother and sister, had tangled relationships, lost his faith on the roof of a Gothic cathedral in Louvain, Belgium, returned to America, taught French. He decided to marry Bill's sister, Maria. He'd been in love with Bill. He left for Greece, stopped in London, met a Greek man, Andreas, who suggested they live together, Daniel wrote Maria a long letter saying he was sorry, stayed, and has been with Andreas since. He wrote his first novel, *The Spectre of Henry Adams*, about five brothers and sisters from Boston who needn't work for a living and are estranged from, enmeshed in, attracted to, and repelled by each other and themselves. They go to Europe, something inexplicable happens. *Snapshots*, his second novel, deals with five friends who have complicated expectations, anticipations, and fears of one another, and who go to Europe and are altered somehow. One is transformed, possibly three. Transubstantiation is the term adopted by the Roman Catholic Church to express its teaching on the subject of the conversion of the Bread and Wine into the Body and Blood of Christ in the Eucharist. The Council of Trent defined it with authority:

> If any one shall say that, in the Holy Sacrament of the Eucharist there remains, together with the Body and Blood of Our Lord Jesus Christ, the substance of the Bread and Wine, and shall deny that wonderful and singular conversion of the whole substance of the Bread into (His) Body and of the Wine into (His) Blood, the species only of the Bread and Wine remaining—which conversion the Catholic Church most fittingly calls Transubstantiation—let him be anathema.

The third novel, *Kin*, tells the story of a brother and sister sinking clothes belonging to the brother's absent wife in water on a bright day. The water weights the floating clothes, causing them to sink; the brother and sister pick up a stranger, Russell, with whom they fall curiously in love; a woman appears in a long yellow dress who may or may not be real. There are sexual overtones between the men, sex between the sister and the stranger, sexual tension between the brother and sister, and an excellent description of a railway car which brings almost the entire world into its construction. *Shadow of the Act* is about a depressed woman who wants to do and feel nothing and beats her fists against the bedboard making blood. A man becomes preoccupied with her, they change places, he becomes stonelike, she active, in the end they make love and if they were standing they would be dancing. A new novel, whose title will be something about water and light, is about two men and their families. The names are Welsh though they are not. Daniel wants his characters from nowhere, dislocated and stateless. He considers himself one hundred percent American. His great-grandmother smeared on bear grease for warmth. Americans terrify him, their discontented presence suggests chaos, darkness, and great risk. In London, Daniel was cured of an ulcer by acupuncture. During the course of the cure he went mad, beat his hands against the headboard of his bed, wept, screamed, shook, shouted. Since then he hasn't been seriously depressed. Andreas, who is a poet and works in a publishing house, took care of him. One brother is in the Army: at the age of forty he told his parents they were living in sin because they continued to share the same bed though the mother was past childbearing age. The priest said "That's crazy" to the mother, who'd consulted him. She told her son, who gave them twin beds for their anniversary in response. He owns a condominium in Hawaii and told his mother he wraps his hands in rugs, beats them on the floor, to avoid masturbation. Another brother, thirty-seven, has the mentality of a fifteen-year-old. His friends are fifteen-year-old boys with whom he discusses boats. He exposes himself occasionally, lives at home, works as a printer. His room is filled with pictures of the baby Jesus and Jesus as a young boy. His name is Ralph. Another brother, Rex, is married to a Vietnamese woman who makes plaster painted casts of Lincoln, her favorite American statesman. She varies the color but not the shape or size as they are made in a rubber mold. Daniel loves Italy and will settle there eventually, needs ten hours of sleep a night and bathes for an hour a day. His mother has been treated for severe depression with shock therapy, and recently was thought to be dying of cancer. Daniel came to the United States, looked up an old school friend, Bill, and his wife Mary. Bill's sleep was troubled he didn't know why. Mary said, "Go and see Daniel." He appeared at Daniel's door at two A.M. Daniel said, "Get in bed," and slept with Bill, then with Mary, then with both. They sent the twins to their grandparents' house, Daniel stayed in bed a week, Bill would go to teach, Mary and Daniel would sleep together. Mary would go to teach and Bill and Daniel would sleep together. Daniel went to New York and slept with other friends. He left for Washington, D.C., to visit a man with whom he had been in love ten years ago, he remembered the end of the affair, which drove him mad, with clarity. They were at a bus stop. Daniel said, "Why?" The man said, "Because you're crazy." Daniel says, in retrospect, that the man, who has become fat and boring, was right. He returned to England. He writes:

I realized I have, since last January, been living in two worlds, a bright orange one and a thin blue one which sometimes becomes thin gray or thin green. I've given myself till the end of February to finish the first of the ten novels I talked to you about. It's my best novel. I've done things in it, things I don't do, and perhaps can't do, in life, I think it's a religious book, and it is most certainly bright bright orange. I have three chapters more to write and my obsession grows rather than diminishes as I get to the end. I wrote all summer in Italy, where I stayed till September and have been doing nothing else but write (or at least it seems to me I've been doing nothing else but write) since. I thought, "Well, I've got to make an act of faith, a real act of faith, and that's this book." My thin blue, grey, green outside life I hardly think about, and don't want to, because I know if I did, now, I'd have too much to think about—it'll have to wait till I finish the book. I owe taxes, they're after me for never having paid my national insurance stamps, I have no clothes, the flat has dry rot, the furniture is falling apart, I hate teaching, dinner parties demoralize me, I don't like going out at all and whereas I used to feel beautifully free in London because indifferent to it, I find myself truly hating the city.

Daniel, Felix, Robin, Meredith and I went to dinner at the Gibsons'. Meredith hated the organized perfection of the house, Gabriel hated Felix, Jessica was confused, Robin wanted things to go smoothly. We discussed Ted, Felix knocked over a bottle of wine, Robin broke a glass trying to clean up. Gabriel showed a photo album of his and Jessica's marriage. Meredith and I got stoned and went to sleep. Daniel discussed Jean Rhys. He said, "I saw Jean Rhys last winter, when she was in London. She got very very drunk and collapsed on the toilet, from which I had to rescue her and put her to bed. She later said, 'Now Daniel, I have some advice for you, the next time you find yourself with a very drunken lady, don't panic but get her on the bed, leave a sleeping pill and a glass of water by the bed, straighten your jacket and tie, leave very quietly, say at reception that the lady is resting and when you tell the story later leave out the name and make it funny.' I had been with her for about six hours; I thought at the end she was dying; she would suddenly burst out weeping, then shout, 'What a goddamn shitty profession, writing,' then laugh."

Gabriel and Jessica Gibson are married and own a white four-story house at Ten, Priory Walk, London, England. Jessica is younger than Gabriel. The basement is an office workroom for Jessica, who manufactures clothes and employs three people full-time executing her designs. She does two collections a year. The winter is best: "I have more of a feeling for wool." Her clothes are simple, direct, and in the Henri Bendel area of cost and cachet, lower than St. Laurent ready-to-wear. She thinks of quitting, the expenditure of time and money is great and causes friction in her relationship with Gabriel, a child psychiatrist. The first floor contains a large kitchen–dining room with a raw pine table seating twenty-two in the center and a small sitting room leading to a garden. Jessica received her culinary training at Cordon Bleu and prepares Sunday lunches for twelve to twenty-two. A typical menu might include eggs mayonnaise or quiche to start; a roast of lamb, beef, or veal; potatoes; vegetable; salad; and, for dessert, tart or fruit salad. The meal is always delicious, there is plenty of the wine Gabriel and Jessica buy in France and bottle themselves, thereby reducing the cost of entertaining. Wine in England is notoriously expensive. The guests are varied; journalists, artists, businessmen, and fashion people. In the sitting room is a push-button phone with lines connecting all the floors and offices in the house. Gabriel calls down to see if their guests have arrived. The second floor is the main sitting room and toilet. The phonograph and photo albums are there. Gabriel is an enthusiastic amateur photographer and has a large photographic record of trips, friends, and social occasions, plus some pornographic films. The third floor is the master bedroom, bath, and television. The fourth floor is the children's room. The two boys are both blond like Jessica. Gabriel and Jessica each have a car—she has hers washed outside once a week and cleaned inside twice a week. There is someone to help care for the children. Commenting on the effects and speed of today's air travel, Gabriel noticed that whenever he made a transatlantic flight he would fire the children's nurse. He now waits a week after his return before making any important decisions. Gabriel is worth about 200,000 pounds. Some of it is difficult for him to get to as it is in South African gold. They have just bought a house in Dorset near a lumpy brush-covered hill said to be an ancient source of energy. The house is by a dairy and large shaggy cows come up to the property line. The house has two stories and is being renovated now. It will have a large kitchen with a pine table seating twelve to twenty-two; adjacent to the kitchen will be a sitting room with skylights and a view of green fields and hedges in which violets grow. They walk through the spring mud in Wellington boots. There will be a garden but no proper swimming pool. There is the children's room with a room for the next person who takes care of them. Gabriel hates the new house the cowman built next door which he believes has spoiled their view. The second floor will have two guest bedrooms, two or three bathrooms, the master bedroom, a bathroom, and an office for Gabriel. A friend asked, "When you finish your country house what will you do?" He replied, "Sell the London house and get an apartment." The friend asked, "After that apartment?" "That's a good question," said Gabriel. Jessica is never depressed, loves to work and cook, she can't help it. She says she plays dumb so that no one will ever take her by surprise. She learned early to get along. Her father would say, "Isn't your stepmother a bitch?" Jessica would agree. Her stepmother would say, "Your father is horrible." Jessica would agree. She says that when agreeing with each she felt each agreement passionately. She didn't do well in the privileged boarding school she attended. Her father would say about her bad grades, "Darling, do you love your daddy?" She'd say

"Yes," and he'd say, "Everything is alright then," and send her a treat. Gabriel is South African, his parents are dead. He knows why women like him. "It's because I seem understanding and have money." Jessica is angelic-looking with fine short blonde hair and large eyes in a round face. She likes to dance and flirt. Gabriel is of medium height with thin hair and large slightly protuberant blue eyes. Jessica says Gabriel believes in honesty and tells her about his affairs; she would rather not know and have no reaction. Gabriel constantly questions people about their behavior and motivation. He is devoted to his work but questions its worth. He thinks the main function of the child psychiatrist is to alter the child's environment rather than altering the child to fit the environment. He needs a career, dreams about his own death (which upsets him for days), answers questions directly. Jessica and Gabriel are generous although he believes he can be tight and she considers herself selfish. It is odd that Jessica and Gabriel are English, for two houses, two cars, two white West Highland terriers, two children, two careers, two dispositions—cheerful and melancholy—and many friends suggest the attainment of the American dream.

Ted picked me up at Kennedy. The pills he gave me for flying to London made me scared. I got sick in Paris. Felix's bedroom was cold without the electric fire. There's no central heating in England. Driving back to Connecticut, Ted said, "We don't love each other any more, I had a terrible time while you were gone, and it seems true." I looked out the window. "I still love you," I said. He said, "We can't go on like this, it's bad for both of us."

I finished the dishes. Ted would arrive in an hour. I looked at my hand my wedding ring was gone. I dumped the trash on the floor and couldn't find it, it had always been too large. Ted and I went to Lucy's party. I told everyone we were separating.

I closed my eyes to sleep. A witch with a melting face is screaming and laughing inside my face at my face.

rage vi l
rage/'rag/n(ME, fr. MF, fr. LL rabia, fr. L rabies rage,
madness, fr. rabere to be mad; akin to Skt rabhas violence) 1a: violent and uncontrolled anger : Fury b: a fit
of violent wrath c: archaic : INSANITY 2 : violent
action (as wind or sea) 3: an intense feeling : Passion 4:
Craze, Vogue (was all the) syn. see ANGER, FASHION.

I am controlling my rage. I looked up the definition of rage.
I am violent, my anger is uncontrolled. I am in a fury. I am
infuriated, possessed by fury. I am active violently. I am crazed
I am in vogue I am in fashion. My teeth are clenched. I hate
ambiguity I would like to kill you. I would like to smash your
face to pulp. I hate men I hate women I hate myself. I am
insane because I am mad. To be mad is to be enraged is to be
insane is to be uncontrolled is to commit violent action is to be
fashionable, as of wind or as of sea.

Three-part landscapes. Blue sky, yellow field, dirt. Blue sky,
palm tree, sidewalk. Sky, sand, ocean. Jungle, wet air, plants.
Yellow field, red house, green tree. Black road, white line, tire.
Brown tree trunk, green leaves, brown leaf. Gray sky, yellow
sand, gray water. White sky, white sand, glass. Stucco house,
blue house, red door. White house with green door, white
house with yellow door, white house with small door. Mailbox,
fencepost, road. Moon, dark blue sky, light gray sand. Tan
plain, yellow sky, giraffe. Green lawn, red flowers, dog. Cool
breeze, warm bench, cold drink.

I dream I am on a wide flat plain at night. It is the night of
my initiation. The women are in one group, the men in
another. Around the huge fire the head women are instructed
by the chief of the tribe. It is very hot. The tribe begins
chanting. I am taken by the women behind the dry bushes. I am
left alone to slit myself open from my anus to my urethra. I can
see the tribe around the fire singing. I can't do this to myself.
There is a dead cow, her stomach ripped open lying on the
ground. I smear the blood from her wound between my legs
down my thighs and walk back to the fire. I am hugged and

congratulated. I am terrified. I will be discovered as false the first time I have intercourse. In any tribe I will have to marry. All are suspicious of, will kill, any woman who wanders. I must convince the man I am with to be in love with me, that I am right, or that this is a special circumstance.

Thousands of penguins scatter over broken ice to feed in the sea. A leopard seal waits for them. He will kill and eat all he can catch. His head is reptilian, his jaws huge, his body slick brown and spotted. The penguins go to the top of any icy hill. They find their old nesting spots and mates from earlier seasons. Everything is gray and white except the penguins and the seal. They carry stones in their beaks to build nests. Some stones are frozen to the ground. One penguin guards the nest against stone raids from immature penguins. The penguins mate. Among the seven- and eight-year-olds there is eighty percent fidelity. The females lay eggs and sit on them for three weeks. They go to the sea to eat, the males take their places on the nests. The females return, the eggs hatch. The babies are fat and gray. Some will die from storms, snow freezing their feathers in clumps of ice. Some will peck others to death, thinking them rocks.

Vincent visited. I hadn't seen him in over a year. He said, "I saw Ted last night with two witnesses for the divorce." I said, "What? When is it?" "It's today, didn't you know?" "No. Who are the witnesses?" "Some psychiatrist friend of Ted's who met you here and a nurse who met you at a party in New Haven, brown hair, fairly attractive." "I know who he is. I couldn't stand him but I was polite, the creep. I don't remember her. How were they acting, what are they going to say? It's going to happen today or has already? Why didn't he tell me?" "Maybe he didn't want to upset you."

The divorce. The oriental rug. The green car, the Mexican chairs two to four dollars apiece, the white formica table, silver from Kansas, lion bowl antique, large modern bowl, small modern bowl, modern shell dish, big dish cover with snakes.

MARRIAGE

The records, the stereo, the books, the cats. The date: February 9, the weather damp.

Bibby Dannon Cartwright is a thirty-four-year-old mother and Mills College graduate married to Bruce, a draft dodger. They keep the Cape Scott Light Station in Victoria, British Columbia. The landscape is a moonscape made of caves, fissures, and blowholes erupting geysers. Once a month the boat comes with mail, medical supplies, best-sellers, magazines, Sears catalogue, fuel, frozen and canned goods. Once a week they make the terrifying walk over three suspension bridges, narrow catwalks, to the foghorn. The bridges sway, rock and careen in the winds that frequently reach one hundred miles an hour in velocity. Six miles away live their neighbors, the tides allow them time to walk to their house, have a cup of coffee and walk back. There isn't much work to do, just being there takes all their energy. The wind blows, waves smash against the rocks, the sun rises and sets, weather changes, rain pours down, fog fills the air, the sun shines. Bruce walks all day, alone, collecting fishing floats, old *sake* bottles, shells, rocks. They make $12,000 a year with a free house, no phone bill, and nowhere or no reason to spend money. It doesn't snow, the climate is moderate, their day starts at ten A.M. and ends at eight P.M. Bibby is from an upper-middle-class family in Edina, Minnesota. She is blonde with classic features and was lady-in-waiting to the prom queen at Edina High where she wore pale blue and green sweaters and matching skirts. Her grades were low at Mills in sociology. She told a friend the day before graduating that she had wanted to major in art but hadn't had the nerve to mention it. Bibby skied every weekend each winter with friends but never became better than mediocre, it was too cold on the slopes. Disappointed often in love, using her energy in depression, she looked for direction, went to Europe after graduation and stayed on ranches in Spain and yachts in the Mediterranean, found it beautiful but boring. She went back to school in psychology and specialized in the treatment of autistic children, with whom she identified. She met Bruce, their affair was chaotic and sad, left him, visited New York, moved to California, then Canada. Her friends married, went mad, divorced, became artists, newscasters, teachers, had miscarriages, and moved. She dove for abalone to make money, lived with no electricity, no people, no running water, learned about isolation. The task of feeding herself took up the whole day. She and Bruce were reconciled and continued living in Canada. She wrote:

> I have missed the last two mail ships. Now there is a helicopter sitting outside, maybe I can finish this before it leaves. Living in isolation is like sitting in the shrink's office. I have mulled over every friendship I ever had and felt tremendous guilt over most of them. The last time I saw you I had a visual hallucination. You and I were sitting on the couch talking and I saw blood running out of your mouth. I think I was seeing the pain you were suffering over your divorce but at the time it scared me so much that I didn't want to admit to myself that it happened and I sort of shut myself off from you. A strange thing, isn't it?
>
> I am watching this helicopter work. It is taking slingloads of equipment down to the foghorn which is about a quarter of a mile from here. The other woman here broke her finger and they sent a huge transport helicopter to take her to the doctor. Nila is a beautiful child. She's easy. She just sort of raises herself. Her birth was the classic childbirth that you read about in magazines. Bruce and I did the Lamaze thing and it all worked. Everyone cheered when she came out, six student nurses observing the birth, all in tears. The contractions were painful but after a while it wasn't too bad because I could take them one at a time, I had no memory of the last one and I was incapable of thinking of the next one, that's probably the most immediate I've ever been in my life. By the time Nila arrived I was incredibly high and it lasted for days, even weeks later I would look at Nila and burst into tears because it was all just so lovely. I guess it really was the big event in

my life. My marriage is very conventional and so are
my everyday activities but somehow they never bore
me, I guess because we always live in weird circumstances, usually in isolation where conventional things
take on a lot of importance. And also because I am a
lot simpler (I wonder if that's a word) than I ever
wanted to admit.

She sent some photographs:
A white cubical building shadowed blue on one side with a
peaked red roof pink where hit by light, slanted red roofs of
adjacent buildings, a golden furze bush on a rock in the
foreground, a blue and pink streaky sky, and bluest, the faint
irregular horizontal of a distant mountain range. Evinence
Island. Pines on a brown hill hit by water, kelp-covered rocks in
the foreground, pale blue cloudless sky, rocky horizon, yellow
streak from defective developing. Cape Scott. Three scraggly
tall pines in the foreground, black fuzzy horizon, purple and
orange sky drawn to an intense yellow white point above the
horizon. Cape Scott.

Career

I had just bought my ticket to Rochester for my museum opening. I was scared and sweating. The ticket man said, "You'll have a wonderful trip; you won't even realize you're flying." I had to go to the bathroom. Some men were talking business, acting just like they didn't know they were going to fly. The plane was available for boarding. They stood up. I made it. Thought about what it's like to be the worst in the show. Returned to the motel room, constructed reasons why I wasn't the worst in the show. Walked around gallery, pretended to make adjustment in hanging. Dan Polakoff's wife was cleaning an invisible spot on the wall with Fantastik. I couldn't see any spots on my wall. Got drunk at party. Had a good time and felt guilty the next morning.

Before dinner Jack Komar had asked John, "Have you seen Jane's work? It's really very interesting." John said, "I heard about her show and couldn't make it. You know I've known Jane for two years and she's always been with that lovely boy, what's his name? So I always thought of her more as a lover." Jack asked me, "Does that bother you?" "Yes." Leaving, Jack asked Rocky Ross if he had seen my work. Rocky said, "Yes." Jack said, "I like it very much." Rocky said, "Oh." Delfine and I shared a taxi downtown: "Now I know why I've always been so mad in that situation. It isn't just my imagination." That night I dreamed I was visiting John and Clay's apartment. Clay sat in a rocking chair silent in shadow, his legs crossed. John and I were boyfriend and girlfriend holding hands. Time passed. Neither of us could decide what we wanted to eat.

Delfine Ford Komar Polakoff Ford is a thirty-six-year-old artist who had trouble picking a last name. Her father is Jack Komar, a painter who exhibits regularly in New York, her husband is Dan Polakoff, a painter who exhibits regularly in New York. She decided to use her middle name, Ford, which she received from Ford Madox Ford, a writer who was married at the time his death to Jack's sister Freya, a painter now living in Paris with her second husband, a French painter, Claude. Delfine has a son, Seth, with red hair. Delfine feels she has a laughing problem. Socially she laughs continuously in order to overcome difficulties and problems associated with the existence of other people. She sometimes forgets which last name to use. During an interview for a job at the School of Visual Arts she introduced herself to three different people entering the room at different times as Delfine Polakoff, Delfine Komar and Delfine Ford. They asked, "What is your name?" She teaches in Ridgewood, New Jersey. Delfine didn't paint for years, began doing drawings of feathers in the middle of the page (they reminded her of penises), then pencil drawings of dunes in Provincetown which were exhibited in Wellfleet, Massachusetts, a show including Delfine Ford, Jack Komar and Dan Polakoff. She began painting different surfaces on panels, colored or not, stroked, marked, or painted flat. She was afraid that in a given painting one panel would look like her father's painting, one like her husband's. Seth pointed this out. It's no longer a problem. Delfine is very attractive with brown thin hair cut short, a dancer's neck, a glandular problem which has improved; her body is round; her face has large, soft, clear-cut features; she has an infectious laugh. She studied dance with Clay Llewellyn who said to someone, "Delfine's getting very good." She quit dancing to study painting. Delfine went to Antioch College and became discouraged with art: her instructors loved the abstract paintings she did effortlessly, she felt like a fake. Her family didn't have much money. She went to a fancy high school in New York. Franz Kline and Fielding Dawson visited her late at night and early in the morning, unshaven and drunk. Delfine gets on very well with her parents and friends, is becoming less tractable and very busy. She met a woman in the hall at Westbeth with whom she had a nodding acquaintance. The woman stopped Delfine and told the story of her marriage. Her husband was involved with how she looked and never was satisfied: he made her dye her hair, lose weight, gain weight, wear wigs, make-up, buy different sorts of clothes, he had affairs and brought students home to pose nude with her, with him, and many other things. The woman told Delfine she had finally kicked him out. Delfine listened to the story, called a friend. "It's really extraordinary what happens when you ask someone how they are." Delfine is astonished by the difficulty of existing today, rising prices, and problems of morality. In September Jane called at four A.M.: "My father died. Can you come over till my plane leaves?" Delfine took brandy, forgot to cork the bottle which spilled on the floor of the taxi. She helped pack and left at six-thirty A.M. to teach in Ridgewood. Jane called back in October: "Do you think your parents could lend me some money to pay for an abortion?" The abortion was performed. Delfine called early the next morning: "I don't want to upset you but Dick Bitts has been mugged and is in critical condition at Bellevue." Dick has recovered and is preparing for an exhibition. Her mother entered surgery for a possible thyroid tumor which proved to be benign and she has begun to write. Delfine and Dan moved. A friend, Tom, helped build their loft. His girlfriend left town for the weekend. Tom stayed for dinner. Someone called; his girlfriend had been axed to death by her depressed brother in Canada. Delfine believes the United States is becoming an oligarchy by consent of the people. Eighty percent of the registered New York Democrats didn't vote in the Presidential primaries. Delfine is preparing for an exhibition and like her mother is a good cook, reads many books, enjoys movies and eating out. She is a strong swimmer with a relaxed, easy stroke. As a teenager her favorite couple was Rocky and Steve; she was upset when they broke up. Delfine worries about money and has been given some very expensive clothes by a friend of the family. She is having them altered. She has a younger sister, Claire, an anthropologist, who is in divorce proceedings. Delfine tells a story: "When I was sixteen an older boy I was sexually terrified of took me out and we went to the ocean at night and after three hours of persuading and insisting and coercing he finally got me to agree that I could see beach fires burning on the coast of Spain."

Dec. 3—134 lbs.
one tbsp. peanut butter and jam, one tbsp. chocolate sauce, 2 cups coffee with sugar, soup, 10 glasses wine, 2½ quarts milk,

bacon and cheese sand., 10 Cadbury Fingers, 2 cups tea, apple pie

Dec. 4—137 lbs.
coffee with milk, tuna sandwich, tomato, toasted cheese, pickle

Dec. 5—134 lbs.
tuna sandwich, 2 cups coffee with sugar, 2 whiskey sours, 1 toasted cheese, 1 pickle

I was being hurt. This was what it was like. I was waiting for Sonny, who was late. The Christmas tree was on. I was drawing, listening to outside car noises and music. Ashes fell on the paper. I drank champagne out of a paper cup. I had three cups. I discovered I had dropped my cigarette on the table. It left a little burn. I had another cup of champagne and thought about why Sonny, who was to arrive at twelve, wasn't here at one and how necessary it was. I thought I heard Sonny arrive. He would yell my name. I would throw down the keys. I was right. I threw them down in a paper bag. He was coming up in the elevator. He would smile when he came in the door. I wouldn't, I won't.

Sonny Bache is from the South. He is thirty-one years old and has attended thirteen schools. His father is a meteorologist in the Navy. His mother has red hair and is separated from his father. She lives in an apartment in Virginia Beach, Virginia, and is currently employed as a beautician. The father lives in their home with Sonny's grandmother and his youngest sister. Sonny is an artist and makes five-sevenths-scale female figures from clay which are cast in wax then bronze. He experiences technical as well as aesthetic difficulties. At the foundry he saw some recent de Kooning bronzes and was overwhelmed that an area he thought was dead could produce such good art. His work is handled by Tom Buckley. They had a flood at the foundry in the 1973 spring rains. Sonny takes tiny balls of clay and places them on a slab, following the energy flow of the figure he is looking at. He works from live models; it takes him at least a year to build a piece. He never turned his back on his mother in the kitchen because he thought she would stab him in the back. He modeled a pair of scissors in Linnea's hand. She quit modeling due to her involvement with guru Sri Chinmoy and consequently more limited time. Sonny removed the scissors. He was frequently late picking her up to model on Sundays. They ate after work at a Chinese restaurant every Sunday for a year. Sonny has rebuilt a Reichian orgone box or accumulator which he obtained from his ex-girlfriend's ex-husband. It is the wrong size, with insufficient lining. Sitting in it one day after working he found it gave him a new energy or made him less nervous. Sonny wants a stable relationship, both partners working, then seeing each other exhilarated after work at eleven P.M. They would spend the night together and touch at parties but still flirt with other people. He had an affair recently, long term, one year. He contracted V.D. from a one night stand that weakened him. Sonny has a beautiful curved smile, clear fair complexion, blue eyes, blond hair. He can lift great weights, wanted to be a monk and was celibate until twenty-four, when a woman, Sara, sucked him off. He enjoyed the sex and did a sculpture of her lying on her back, legs spread, in black bronze. She left before the piece was done. Sonny likes the baby Sara had with her new boyfriend, also named Sonny. Sonny has complained about his back. He went to a doctor who said you have a disintegrating neck vertebra complicated by gout. The doctor gave him pills for the gout though he can't really cure it. Sonny will try acupuncture. He tries to get along with strong women, can't, wants to change them, make them happy, they won't, he won't. Buckley said, hearing about his gout, "You really are in the nineteenth century." Sonny likes to be touched. He teaches at Hofstra University. A student who does medical photography photographed his pieces in good light. Sonny has devised a lighting system which allows him to work at night. He goes to a Reichian therapist and shudders from the breathing discipline. His doctor thought he was catatonic. He smiles frequently and laughs when nervous, heartily. He has read recently Linda

Nochlin's book on Realism and the diary of the Goncourt brothers, French, nineteenth century. He has been offered a job building models of murder scenes by the Long Island coroner, a new project. Sonny became interested in art as a child in Sacramento, California. He got on the wrong train once in Germany, likes Europe, lived in Japan. He is generous with his time.

It only takes me three days to forget a face. In three days I have taught, watched television, talked, gotten drunk, smashed my nose into the edge of the elevator door, lied, spent an evening at the St. Vincent's emergency room mumbling, demanding to see different doctors. Spent the long part of a day at St. Vincent's gynecological and head and neck clinics. I have had blood taken, been speculated in the stirrups, swabbed and picked at. I have received prescriptions for a greasy yellow torpedo-shaped suppository, vitamin E, no sex, changes of dressings, and, from friends, vitamin B1, magnesium, yeast, and everything else pertaining to nerves. I fought with Sonny and watched Frank Sinatra on television. I talked on the telephone. Someone told me, "When you get drunk you get really drunk." I guess this means wavering around, stumbling, talking blurry, incoherent, pushing people on the chest, bumping into things, and waking up in the morning with inexplicable cuts and scratches I pretend to remember. This hasn't happened to me before, I know there is something crazy going on.

Today I bought organic cheese, Yeast-plus, coffee with sugar to go, and a fifth of cognac. I've decided not to drink any more. There are two red spots on my sofa. I thought they were something Delfine did. Now I wonder if they are my blood and where did I really bang my nose. I had begun to believe my elevator story. I told the doctor I was high, got up fast and ran into the sharp edge of a counter, hoping the story would correspond with the shape and size of my wound, one centimeter circular on the bridge of my nose. I have vague memories of going back to change my clothes for a reading, the phone ringing, running to answer it and falling, hitting my nose on the edge of the sofa. Jeremy was on the phone. I hung up, my face felt wet. I looked in the mirror at my blurred face bleeding. I decided to take off my clothes, go to bed, and think about it tomorrow. Sonny came in, we were to go out to dinner. I put on my clothes and went to the hospital. I came home, told Sonny I didn't want to see him until I stopped doing these things. I should stay in my loft more, alone, and wonder why I don't since I think I enjoy it more. Drinking brandy alone in my loft at four, sunspots on the floor, sun moving slowly through thin plant leaves, glancing off the thick edges of others, light running in flat diagonals, one white curtain moving slowly. The rule was two shots of brandy before a nap.

Whom should I call on the phone?

Sonny drove me to Provincetown to stay with the Komars for three months. After he left, I had a brandy. The clouds add a third dimension to the sky. A stinging blue on postcards, immutable in Puerto Rico and Provincetown, appearing again in Provençal landscapes, tiny black figures bathing at Saint Tropez. Pale blue envelopes come from foreign countries. Domestic mail includes postcards and first-class letters, stamped dull blue, Eisenhower smiling, moving glossy redwoods, improbable Dakotan hills, Virginian shacks propped up on one log, roofs stove in. Three-refrigerator porch. Lone yellow dog. Empty rocking chair. Two men in a boat float on a thick brown stream, meet lazy catfish or crabs making slow tracks through short gummed water. A quiet division of solids and liquids. Slow motion light, fungoid crystallization of place person thing.

Got up at nine A.M. Glass cranberry juice and swallowed vitamin pill. Urinated. Good Shepherd cereal with milk. Reheated yesterday's coffee, no sugar, drank half a cup in bed. Smoked cigarette. Read Leonard Woolf's *Beginning Again*, read William Carlos Williams' *Autobiography*. Went to sleep. Elise knocked on door. Talk. Talked to Rebecca on the porch, said, "I don't want to go to New Beach, can I use the washing machine?" Asked her to buy me bananas and milk. Brushed teeth, washed face, looked at face, put on lipstick, mascara, black leotard, combed hair. Took laundry downstairs. Upstairs read Williams. Yelled to Linnea about New Beach. Made out shopping list on matchbook cover. Ate bananas, swig of milk from carton. Second load of laundry downstairs, hung up first load. Upstairs, put scarf around my neck to see how it looks. Talked to Rebecca. "It's beautiful today, look at that, it gets light then dark." Left. Turned on radio. Hung up clothes. Cleaned bathroom, cleaned mirror, straightened drawers, put letters in one place, washed dishes, cleaned window sills, put books away, did dance to Vivaldi, did Llewellyn exercises I learned from Delfine. Went to beach. Collected mail. Read letters, delighted, then: maybe they don't really like me. Went for swim, did all strokes with discipline. Lay in sand, reread letters, got cold. Washed hair, vacuumed. Read Williams. Returned vacuum, talked to Rebecca, ate cheese. Took food up, made coffee. Helped mow lawn, fought with Seth about grass cuttings. Read paper. Ate chicken soup at Linnea's. Changed clothes, went to movies. Bought *Jolie Madame* perfume at drugstore. Smoked. Sat in movies, read perfume ad. Bought Williams poems. Had movie fantasy: whom would I invite to the premiere? Home, flushed toilet, urinated, flushed toilet, brushed teeth, flushed toilet. Got in bed, out of bed, poured glass of wine, read Williams, got glass wine, wrote letters, more wine, more letters, wine, read what I'd written.

> *Jolie Madame*, the most sophisticated fragrance in All Paris, created by Pierre Balmain. Luxuriate in mists of totally feminine *Jolie Madame* from top to toe, only shades less potent than the exciting parfum, still superbly lingering to radiate its impressive *joie de vivre* for hours.

Jolie Madame is the cologne I wear occasionally. I use Fresh stick deodorant, Ivory soap, Clinique Sheer Make-Up on my nose and chin, non-allergenic with its own moisturizer. I wear Love Cranberry Glaze on my lips and Love Foxy Gray eye shadow. I used to shave my armpits and legs with a Gillette razor and Gillette stainless blades. I use Crest Blue toothpaste and, sporadically, Pearl Drops, a stain-removing dentifrice developed by a dentist for the use of his own family. I use Protein-21 shampoo with body-building proteins or Fermo Caresse, a shampoo for damaged or delicate hair. I do not file my nails or cut my toenails, I pick them. I have Revlon Deluxe tweezers for plucking facial hairs. I use Yardley Skin Quench as a body lotion—arms, legs, hands. I take no medication regularly, though I took contraceptive pills for six years. I did not gain weight nor did I notice increased depression, loss of libido, dizziness, or eye trouble. I use Fantastik to clean most surfaces, Viva paper towels, Mr. Clean for the toilet bowl, bathroom sink, and tub. I use no particular brand of toilet paper. Comet cleaner for pots and pans and the kitchen sink, Housemaid Copper Wire pads or plastic Tuffys for scouring, Windex for mirrors and windows, plain or lemon-scented Pledge for wood surfaces. A Westinghouse canister vacuum. I do not iron. I use a yellow Oral B 30 toothbrush and Johnson & Johnson dental floss. My boar's hair brush was left in the loft by someone who visited. I use various Ace combs. During my menstrual period I use super and regular Tampax. I don't own a real camera. I have a Polaroid Swinger I rarely use and a Bell & Howell super-8 movie camera I keep in a gray filing cabinet. The doctor measures my height at five feet eight and a half inches, which seems generous. I weigh one hundred and thirty pounds. I do not know my measurements. I have brown medium-length hair, an average complexion for my race, average skin with large pores and few wrinkles for my age. I have gray blue rounded eyes, black eyelashes, and fairly heavy brows. I have a generous mouth, straight, slightly yellowed upper teeth and slightly crooked yellow lower teeth. I have, I believe, gold inlays in all my molars and a mild gum problem around my four lower incisors. My nose is fairly straight with a puckered round scar at the bridge. I wear glasses to see. I am myopic. I have a superfluity of facial hair, my forehead is round and low, my jowls wide with a strong jaw. I have a chin. There is a crease on the right side of my face running from the base of my nostril to the corner of my mouth. It deepens with strain or fatigue. My smile doesn't turn up, it retreats into my cheeks. My hairline is low, my hair relatively shiny and thick. I have broad shoulders, large upper arms, and quite a bit of hair on my forearms. My hands are square and blunt. I have had one tooth extracted, right upper wisdom. My fingernails are short, irregular, with a great deal of cuticle. The skin of my breasts, stomach, and thighs is smooth; I tend to gain weight in my stomach, face, and thighs. I have a mole on the left side of my lower abdomen which gets larger in the sun. I have a triangular scar on my right shin and a heavy growth of dark hair on both shins and calves. My feet are small for my height and thick, the toes short, bent, and plump, with ragged nails. My little toes have almost no nail. My right foot is considerably weakened from a recent accident. The skin on the soles of my feet is rough. I am inclined to alcohol, anxiety, nervous stomach, moods, tentative optimism, and inflammatory infections. I have been analyzed unsuccessfully though we both tried; the same is true of marriage. I have a family and a great many friends. For my work I use Testor Pla paint enamel, #4 sable brushes, 16-gauge steel plates with a baked enamel surface, quarter-inch grid silkscreened on, and Xylol thinner. My rent is $195 per month, I pay a $73 loan payment. I teach for a living. I tend to have more intense orgasms through masturbation than through intercourse. Occasionally I have homosexual fantasies. I have an active dream life. I think I would like to have a child but am afraid of being pregnant. On the whole I consider myself a rather fortunate person although I would like to have had a more classical education.

Delfine overheard a conversation on New Beach, two men and two women with Southern accents. A pleasant-looking woman, forty years old, was telling a story. She worked for one of the Rockefellers as curator of their Oriental art collection. The Rockefellers were invited to an opening at the Museum of Modern Art but were unable to go and gave the woman their tickets. She had a new Indian dress for the opening and took her Afghan hound. She stood in a cubicle at the museum. A man walked up and began talking to her about her dog. He was plump, seemed like a Mafioso, she didn't want to be stuck with him all evening and was curt in her replies. Walking home she realized my God, it was Frank Sinatra. She was furious with herself. She went to the museum the next day on business. Someone said "Hello." It was Frank Sinatra, she almost fainted. He said, "I enjoyed talking to you last night, are you married?" She said, "No," though she had a steady boyfriend. He said, "Would you like to go out to dinner some evening? I'm in New York some, I enjoy your company and have a few pieces of Oriental art I don't think are too good but would like to hear your opinion of." She said "Yes." He said "I'll call you." He did, she was very excited. She was ashamed of the building she lived in and made arrangements to have him pick her up in the lobby of a fancy apartment where she knew the doorman. A huge white Cadillac pulled up, four men got out. She was disappointed. They said, "Come with us." The doorman didn't think she should but she felt she must. Frank Sinatra was sitting in the back seat, he asked where she would like to eat. "I don't know." He said, "My usual hangout is Jimmy McPherson's." Her boyfriend played the piano there. "Why don't we go somewhere else," she said. Frank, thinking she was nervous, took over and made the decision. She walked in, her boyfriend saw her and began playing the piano as loud as he could, she was terrified. Sinatra called the waiter over, "Could you tell the piano player to cool it?" The piano player came to the table and said, not looking at her, "I understand you asked me to cool it?" Sinatra said, "Yes, cool it, sit down and have a drink." He said "No thanks," and walked off, sullen. She was relieved. Sinatra took her home, kissed her on the cheek and asked to see her again. Her boyfriend became more affectionate and wanted to marry her the next day. She said "No." She and Frank went to his New York apartment. The four men played poker in the next room. Everything was white. Frank asked if she liked his place, she thought he'll either hate me or like me and said, "No, I think it's awful." He was mad and then amused. "I spent a million dollars getting it fixed up." His Oriental art wasn't very good. They made out a little on the white sofa. She was there three hours. "What did you do for three hours, you didn't just make out a little," her friends said. She had several other contacts with him, once her phone was out of order, once he wrote a letter. Things are unresolved at this point. Her friends said, "Why you? Maybe he doesn't get it up too much any more."

Sonny and I broke up on the way back to New York from Provincetown.

I first met Jesse in Rochester. Later his face identified itself with a "Hi" at the French Bar. I said, "Hi, don't leave." Driving in his yellow car drunk, kissing him, recalled true love impressions, teenage absolutes. The earth revolves as expected and I react to the repetition of a particular face and body.

I remember first his face attached to the juke box. I remember looking at his pants. "Where did you get those stains on your pants?" "They're not my pants, I found them in the loft." I usually don't like pants tucked into tall boots. He ran his hand down my back. We stood at the tip of Manhattan, watching the water slap wooden pilings. We ate French toast. We said things I can't remember.

Jesse Maxheim is a thirty-five-year-old artist from California living in New York City. He recently had an exhibition of his work which consisted of: two toy trains on a collision course, the collision to take place sometime in the future; some lights on a large field representing his father's last drawing and his daughter's first; a letter from a doctor about his paranoid schizophrenia; and a wall-size slide of the adrenochrome, a chemical found in the blood of schizophrenics. Jesse attended the Oakland School of Arts and Crafts. In high school, he planned half-time activities at football games and swam. He married young and had two children by his first wife, from whom he is divorced. His father, a physicist, died last year; his mother visited Jesse and his common-law wife, Sharon, in their New York loft. Jesse ordered three Minolta cameras in an art-for-goods trade. He received a Guggenheim Fellowship. He feels he is operating at gut level in his work, that he is responding humanly to the people he is involved with. There is confusion in his domestic life, lies, mysterious phone calls, and hysteria. He has a child, Cynara, by Sharon; a red, blue and yellow coat; a fur coat he received in an arts-for-goods trade with a furrier; a yellow Vega which has been stuck in a swamp; long yellow fingernails; bad teeth; curly light brown hair; a full mouth; and deep-set blue eyes. He is tall and owns an Eames chair. He is starting four new pieces. Sharon is interested in real estate but had to quit her job because her boss's wife was jealous and Jesse didn't like her to work; he is sympathetic to the idea of women working and having equal opportunities in life, but doesn't see how this can work in marriage or life. Jesse enjoys cocaine, wants more adventure in his life, and sees some of his friends as potential sources of energy. Jesse believes there is a large general change occurring in society, that relationships can be prototypical, and he would like to preserve the mystique that exists in relationships when they begin. He gave a party for some friends from Kentucky which he did not attend, sitting through four showings of the movie *Asylum* instead. He has spent a good deal of time at art bars and doesn't see why, at this point in his career, he can't put his children's drawings in his exhibitions if he wants.

I went to visit Ed Bryan and Lucy. Neither was home. I was hoping to see Jesse. Jesse was on the sidewalk with a girl with red hair. "What are you doing?" He said, "Wait twenty minutes, I just have to show her some photographs."
"O.K. Can I wait in Ed's loft?"
"If you want to."
I walked through Jesse's space into Ed's, lay down and started to read. I felt pretty good. She yelled, "Oh God, oh God." I thought, "I can't get out of here." Jesse came in, I smelled come on his hand. "Do you want to go for a drink?" "Alright," I said.

E d Bryan is black, a sculptor, with a football player's build and a wide white smile. He taught art at Rutgers and the University of Connecticut at Storrs and has two or three daughters by a previous marriage in California. He was born in

Texas and attended the University of Southern California. He now lives with a published poet, Lynne. Ed makes sculptures of chains and barbed wire hung sometimes from the wall sometimes from the ceiling, loves John Coltrane, and has an easy social manner and mustache. He owned a station wagon which needed a new water pump. Driving from Connecticut to New York with Rose, his car broke down. The area was desolate, dark and cold. A car stopped, two couples were in it. Rose went to the window, Ed walked up, the people drove off saying they would stop at the next service station and notify the state police. Time passed, another car moved slowly by, stopped 300 yards away, backed up, stopped, two men got out and walked towards them asking what was wrong. Ed explained. One man was holding a gun. Ed laughed, "Hey man, you won't be needing that." The man moved the gun around, said, "You never know what kind of trouble you'll run into." They offered to help, offered a lift to the service station. Ed said, "No thanks, some state troopers just stopped and are coming back with a tow truck." The men said "O.K.," and drove off laying rubber. Rose asked, "What did you think they were going to do?" Ed said, "White girl, black boy." State troopers came, lit a bright red flare, they arrived in New York City at dawn. Ed was a football player, one of his daughters wears glasses. He and Lynne went to Africa, brought back cloth, clothes, and jewelry. They thought of moving, the country was beautiful. Ed has received many grants but has heavy financial burdens.

Lucy Singer is a thirty-two-year-old artist with a difficult past who runs two miles a day. Her father is amusing, intelligent, tyrannical, and ill; her mother is tall, graceful, kind, resigned, with a nervous stomach. Lucy hated her grandmother, paternal, who lived with the family. She died this year shortly before Lucy was mugged and shortly after she was left by her boyfriend of five and a half years. Her older sister Ina is emotional, has a seven-year-old daughter, and is separated from her husband. The sisters' relationship has been warm and complex. After joining a women's consciousness-raising group,

Lucy let the hair on her legs grow out, and considered women as a sexual alternative to men. "They're so easy to talk to and so much nicer," she said. She is realizing the extent of her ambition, anger, and desire to please, three elements of her character often in contradiction. Lucy completed an illustrated dictionary: one or two words, some pictures and a usage sentence for each letter. They describe the parameters of her life. The book is called *The Pencil Picture Dictionary*. The pictures and writing were done in pencil and the printing is pencil gray. Lucy and Jim spent a year in Georgia, their house burned down, the cats were killed, their possessions destroyed. She was sick for the following year, upper respiratory infections and migraine headache. Lucy makes movies, admires Fred Astaire and would like an Oscar. She has always had the best personality in any situation, a fact which does not relieve or please her. Her hair is frizzy and black, her features delicate and clear, weighted by large heavy glasses—contacts proved uncomfortable. She has begun wearing eyeshadow, bought a bright silk blouse at Bendel's, is trying to combat her inclination towards dark baggy clothes. At eight years old she wrote a novel about adultery, a word whose meaning was vague and intriguing. Her phone rings constantly, her problems with men are legion, she tried to be gay but can't. A friend of hers who was interested in a gay man who had been living with another man for nine years, complained, "Nothing can work out, he's gay and married." Lucy told her friend, "Gay or straight, single or married, what difference does it make? If it wasn't that it would be something else." Lucy has a profound distrust of rich people, gallery owners, and anyone in power. Her work includes tinted plaster friezes with dancing figures, drawings of piles of yams, a bag lady movie, a movie about teeth, a movie about a song, clay figures standing, bending, lying, dancing. In the movies the boss takes the glasses off his ugly secretary after concluding a business deal. She is beautiful. Lucy knows movies well and can name the hairdressers for different productions. She has seen friends left by husbands and boyfriends for younger, easier women. She wants to change, leaves her phone off the hook, rearranges her loft, and refuses to adapt to loss. Her favorite line at the present is from the movie *Young Frankenstein*. A man on a train comes into the station, music is playing, the man says to a child, "Pardon me, boy, is this the Transylvania station?" She has fallen in love with a man she believes anyone would find beautiful.

I lay on the table, my feet in the stirrups, back of gown open, buttocks pushed down, knees up and spread wide. He put the speculum in my vagina.

"I don't like this, I'm tired of it. I hate it."

He pushed his gloved finger into my vagina, wiggled it around, prodding the outside of my pelvis.

"Sometimes it must be painful for you during intercourse."

"Yes. It's psychological. I'm crazy. When I first started screwing it would really hurt."

"You're not crazy, you have a tipped uterus, your left ovary drops down by your vagina. If someone angles to the left during intercourse they bang into your ovary, which is painful."

"I asked another doctor if something could be wrong, he said absolutely not. Is this something I just developed?"

"You were born that way."

"Is the condition subtle, could it have been easily missed?"

"It's completely obvious, just have people aim right."

"Why wouldn't the other doctor tell me about it? I went into therapy."

"I don't know, maybe he thought it would turn you off sex."

It's like plotting a diagram, the course of my romantic life. I move continually from point A to point B. Nothing distinguishes one from the other. Both are nice, realistic, and rewarding. Neither is primary, but the movement between the two is. C appears, bent on wrecking my course. I break a glass, stop work, moon around. C always belongs primarily to someone else's system. C has a constant glitter, like B when first seen from A. C remains undiminished and remote.

Sonny saw the body of a young man who had hanged himself accidentally in an attempt to have an orgasm. Among his effects were typewritten lists of the women's clothing he had purchased. The lists described each article, name of store, price, whether or not it fit, was kept or returned. There were stacks of photographs he had taken of himself dressed in women's slacks, boots and sweaters, falling on a broken heel, bending over oddly, vague constricted gestures. In photographs he held handmade guns decorated and lettered with the word "lesbian." He wore embroidered masks which could only be read in the mirror. He made hundreds of drawings of women with erections under their dresses, on the verge of being killed, raped, shitting, vomiting or urinating.

I traded art for goods:

Compact Washer and Dryer
Rack
Vent Deflector
Double Pedestal Desk, Charcoal Black
Secretarial Chair, Black
Five-Drawer Blueprint Cabinet
27-Drawer Cole Cabinet, Gray
SMC Coronet Automatic 12 Typewriter
Royal Digital V Calculator
Webster's Third New International Dictionary
SR-T 101 35mm Single Lens Reflex Camera—Minolta
    Camera Case
Carousel 750 H Slide Projector—Eastman Kodak
EZ View Slide Sorter—Logan
Stereo Headphones—Koss
12-inch Color TV—Sony
FM/AM/FM Stereo Receiver with Speakers and Record
    Changer—Fisher
RevereWare Copperclad Stainless Steel 10 Pc. Set
Eureka Two-Speed Custom Vibra Beat Vacuum Cleaner
Northern Riviera Electric Blanket
Osterizer 10-Speed Cycle Blender
GE Automatic Can Opener/Knife Sharpener
GE Dual Power Spray/Steam/Dry Iron
Lady Schick Travel Hair Styler

Friends

Ana Martin is a thirty-eight-year-old high school dropout of Greek-Italian extraction who owns a gallery showing the work of almost-young contemporary artists. Her astrological sign is the last, Pisces, two fish swimming in opposite directions, to the heights and the depths, the sign of the idealist Ana feels she is. Pisces only breathe water and don't touch land except to die. Astrologers maintain that people born under this sign, though having the characteristics of all twelve signs, are incomprehensible to other people. Ana met a Pisces in 1971, likes Scorpios, marries Geminis, and has her chart done once a year on her birthday, March 14, which she shares with Albert Einstein. It is the eve of the Ides of March, a classical moment in history when Caesar, first a republican, then Emperor, ignored fatal omens and was stabbed to death by his colleagues. The study of astrology dates back 5,000 years and hasn't been subjected to scientific methods of examination and assessment. There may be something to it, or nothing. Ana has said there are two things she believes in: her children and art. She attended Pierce College Extension, Athens, Greece; University of Maryland Extension, Munich, Germany; the Sorbonne, Paris, France; Goucher College, Baltimore, Maryland; and the Institute of Fine Arts, New York City. She doesn't have a degree. Ana traveled in Europe, became familiar with the contents of its museums, stayed in people's homes, cheap hotels, hostels, traveled alone and with people, was happy in Greece, happy being sad, lonely and depressed in Paris walking along the Seine and in the Tuileries. She remembers the smell of lemon groves. Ana's father was in the Navy and took her to baseball games. Her mother is an orphan and recently lost weight with the Weight Watchers diet, she has learned to read Tarot cards. They live in Newport, Rhode Island, where Ana's father collects boulders. People find Ana beautiful, reserved, and don't always know what she's thinking. She is five feet seven inches tall, thin, with dark hair, a large mouth, large brown eyes, and a small soft high-pitched voice. She is stubborn, slow to make decisions, and has an erratic, explosive temper. Ana played tennis and wrote sad poetry in high school, married at twenty-two a man of forty-six who owned a company that manufactured scales for weighing meat and produce. The beam scale, or simple balance, originates in pre-dynastic Egypt, and in the opinion of some its invention dates back more than 5,000 years before the Christian era. The self-indicating scales appear to have been invented by Leonardo da Vinci, 1425-1519, as drawn and described in one of his notebooks. Weighing can be a means of counting. A balance is an instrument for comparing the weights of two bodies to determine the difference in mass. The material to be weighed is put on one pan with sufficient known weights on the other pan to bring the beam into equilibrium. During this marriage Ana lived in a townhouse near Hunter College, had a butler, everything delivered, expensive clothes, some jewelry. She traveled in Europe, staying in the finest hotels and eating at first-class restaurants, opened a gallery in the foyer of her home, and was treated like a child. Every morning Ana looked in the mirror and said, "When I get my first gray hair I'm leaving." She didn't get one, left, divorced, and married Alex, who is in the business of commemorative medals. They have two children, Marcus and Damon. She opened the first gallery in SoHo, where many artists then lived, and divided her time between the gallery and artists downtown and family and friends uptown. There are fifty galleries in SoHo now, the artists are moving. She separated from Alex and moved one block from her gallery. Her artists are varied in temperament and aesthetic. Some of the products on view are: large abstract paintings with soft edges and color on canvas; large abstract paintings with harder edges and repeated units on canvas; abstract paintings of medium size intensely colored and thickly painted on canvas; squares of baked enamel on steel dotted or painted and arranged on the wall in groups; large pieces of wood bound together with rope or cut and fitted together; small bronzes of horses and houses; cast-iron abstract shapes displayed on the wall and floor; small wax paintings on lozenge-shaped boards; large piles of cast bronze and aluminum; tee shirts framed by tee-shirt-shaped frames; a bronze dildo, framed; cast colored resin sculptures in a medium-to-large scale; a stack of numbered paper; paintings of dreams on canvas board; torn pieces of paper with notes; things made of beads, cloth, sticks, paint and paper for display on walls and suspension in air; logs shaped or altered by unseen forces; large-to-medium-size paintings on canvas with rectangles in closely valued colors. Readings of written work, performances, dances, and concerts are held at the gallery. Ana exhibits the work of artists she admires even if they are not affiliated with her gallery, tries to make herself and her artists rich, and is always late. She visits younger artists' studios, has friendships with her artists, becomes involved in their work and their lives. She is irritated and concerned when life difficulties threaten their productivity. Ana went to the Spring Street Bar with friends, drank four Margaritas, had heated conversations about the nature of life, Gertrude Stein, space in sculpture and painting, left Spring Street, continued the evening with Bob, discussing the nature of life, different people, the nature of sculpture and painting, they drank another half-bottle of tequila. She woke up sitting in her living room at four A.M. Bob had gone. She slept three hours, made some phone calls, and went to an auction uptown. She has a set of tableware from Thailand which isn't used often because of a tendency to bend due to the softness of the metal. She wonders why she stays out late and if she is losing her sense of humor. Her household includes Light, a cat; Victoria, a strange Colombian journalist with Mafia connections who speaks Italian, cooks, cleans, feeds the children; and Sophia, an art student who cares for the children at night.

John Frank is a thirty-three-year-old artist from Chicago living in New York with his wife Fay, an artist from a small town in Minnesota. He went to the Massachusetts Art Institute and hustled pool. His paintings are made of cotton balls soaked with paint and applied to stretched and unstretched canvas. There is a windmill turning, pushing cotton balls in air currents, tropical birds, fish in aquariums, Greek vases, still lifes, famous ships in battle, two spaceships fighting, one banging into the edge of the painting. John has collected stuffed fish, stuffed birds, figurines of birds, bird cups for drinking. He renovates his loft, watches TV while working, has lost fifty pounds on the Weight Watchers diet, fishes for walleyes and trout in Minnesota backwood lakes where the local people don't eat vegetables. John dropped out of University of Maine in a depressed state of mind. He recovered and entered art school. He decided to quit smoking one day and hasn't smoked since, he continues to lose weight and has an explosive temper and sense of humor. His house is filled with people from all periods of his life who come in and out of town and stay with John and Fay, getting drunk, insulting their friends, having art fights, New York fights. He won't allow anyone in his studio this year: "I'm working hard. Frankly, I don't want people around." When his friends are sick, unhappy, or injured, John thinks and thinks about it. He doesn't like seeing people in pain, doesn't like hearing about it. He caught a 436-pound marlin off the coast of North Carolina and wants a fishing boat, thinks he should have property now, thinks about different ways to live: playing golf in the suburbs, owning a house in the country or by the sea in North Carolina. He can only buy his shoes in Chicago because his feet are so big. Even at 230 pounds John was a good basketball player. He has blond curly hair, a ruddy complexion and wears glasses. When Prudence and Percy the cats' tails were nearly bitten off in the country by a marauding and persistent neighborhood cat, he threatened to shoot it and told the owners, "Frankly I can't afford to continue patronizing an activity of this sort any longer." The owners, a seventy-six-year-old woman and her two middle-aged daughters, thought he meant to shoot them and reported him to the town clerk. John regrets the incident. His father's name is Morris, his stepmother is Beulah, they live in Chicago and winter in Florida. John thinks his father alternates between rage, generosity, friendliness and bitterness towards other people. John's and Fay's car broke down continually on their way back from their summer vacation. John had a good time in Europe but had to carry suitcases full of baby clothes on

Italian trains through Italy, samples Fay was bringing to a friend. He likes Ambrose Bierce, Joseph Conrad, and *Robinson Crusoe*. When he is away, he talks on the telephone to his huge orange cat Percy, and calls Percy "Shortman" or "Short" because of his short legs and barrel body. They play games: John walks by, Percy grabs and bites him.

Karen Dorcas is a thirty-five-year-old artist who ended her first marriage on a balcony throwing bricks at her husband leaving in a Volkswagen, her second by stabbing her husband lightly—a flesh wound—then taking him to the hospital. The first marriage was about leaving Sophie Newcombe College dormitory, the second about coming to New York. Karen is physically and emotionally dramatic, of Greek extraction and from Lake Charles, Louisiana. Art critic Chad Putnam wrote, "Karen Dorcas makes new options in American art—my reluctance to admit this is tied to her extravagance." Karen has created herself. Her hair is dyed red, cut one inch all over her head, her features are Mediterranean and sensual. To one dinner she wore short shorts, a blonde wig and platform shoes; to another, a plain gray jumpsuit and a St. Laurent sweater. Reactions to Karen's work and person are confused and contradictory. She is warm, open, generous, anxious, secretive, suspicious, with a love for intrigue, glamour, the bizarre, the extreme. She has a relatively calm and private long-term relationship into which she retreats. Physically she is androgynous, mentally, a nice girl from Louisiana. She asked Tennessee Williams to write an essay on her show at the New Orleans Museum, he didn't know her work, she showed him photographs, he wrote it, she sent him long-stemmed red roses. She worries about her press, her plans, likes to work with other people, meet new people, seeing how she can use them, where they fit in. She experiments, mixing people, events, friendships, situations, locations, materials, ideas, as if they were chemicals. Karen is interested in the idea of more than one. She has two lofts, one in Los Angeles and one in New York City, with duplicate equipment. She makes sculpture, video tapes, paintings, polaroid pieces, and grows roses. There is little distinction between her life and art. Karen complicates her life, consults astrologers, makes decisions, changes her mind, makes decisions, changes her mind, broods about slights for months, calls her friends from midnight to five A.M., drives, scuba dives, travels, swims, lectures, teaches, plays tennis, takes cocaine, gets drunk, has an ulcer, cooks, entertains, spends money, visits her parents, buys clothes, encourages other artists, makes appointments, changes appointments, works, worries, explodes with anger, with enthusiasm, picks people up, drops them, picks them up. "Complex" means: consisting of parts, composite, containing subordinate clauses, formed by a combination of compounds, containing real and imaginary parts. Karen is making a video tape about a hermaphroditic dog, she plays the carnival barker. "Complex" in psychology refers to a related group of usually repressed ideas causing abnormal mental states. In popular terms a complex is an obsession. It comes from the Latin "complexus," to embrace. Karen did a series of announcements and magazine advertisements mocking the male-dominated art star quality of the art world. These caused some controversy. The first was a black-and-white card announcing an exhibition: a photograph of a child wearing a Greek soldier's outfit. She looks sweet and and pretty. The next, an advertisement in *Arttime*, shows Karen at thirty-two, leaning against her silver Porsche, repainted twice so it would be perfect. She stands in the classic *contraposto* pose, her arm resting on top of the car which is parked in front of a cinderblock California wall, the tops of two houses, the tops of two trees. She looks directly into the camera, has on dark glasses, a print blouse, jeans, and a severely cut suit jacket. She looks successful. Next came a card announcing an exhibition: Karen stands nude in a corner. She is in the *contraposto* pose, back to the camera, face turned towards the camera, her arm raised behind her head, pink-beige ground, red cropped hair, bikini lines, brown smooth skin, jeans dropped to her calves, dropped around high-heeled dark boots—if she walked she'd stumble or run into the corner. She looks appealing. The fourth, a double-page ad, appeared in the fall issue of *Arttime*, which featured an article on her art. She showed the issue of the magazine to her mother one year later. She doesn't think her father's seen it. Two-thirds of the spread is black. The words "Karen Dorcas courtesy of Ana Martin Gallery, Photo Ron Greene" appear in small white letters at the upper left corner. On the righthand side is three quarters of Karen in a three-quarter view: nude, knees bent and spread, right hand on hip, first and little fingers spread wide from hand, right shoulder raised, left arm extended down side, body oiled, left forearm coming from behind the abdomen holding an extraordinarily long, erect penis, a plastic dildo, which emerges from dark pubic hair and presumably her vagina. Her chin is dropped behind her shoulder, lips parted, teeth slightly bared. She wears elongated sunglasses with white plastic frames and diamond stud earrings. She looks dangerous. Reactions were varied. Some thought Karen showed a lack of faith, other a consuming desire for recognition, some felt it was a self-serving gesture gone wrong, an embarrassment, the expression of a vulgar nature, an attempt to bulk up the weakness of her work through sensation. Many admired it. The issue sold out, the largest number of copies in *Arttime*'s history. There were articles in the *New York Times*. A man holding the magazine smashed one of Karen's sculptures in a museum. Six editors at *Arttime* collaborated on a letter published in the magazine:

> For the first time in the thirty years of *Arttime*'s existence, a group of associate editors must disassociate themselves publicly from a portion of the magazine, specifically the copyrighted advertisement of Karen Dorcas photographed by Ron Greene and printed by courtesy of the Ana Martin Gallery in the fall issue of the magazine.
>
> We want to clarify why we object to its appearance within the *Arttime* covers:
>
> 1. In the specific context of this journal it exists as an object of extreme vulgarity to appear in the maga-

zine, it represents a qualitative leap in that genre, brutalizing ourselves, and, we think, our readers.

The letter continues in the same vein. Karen thinks that, at $3,000 (the price of creating it) the ad was a bargain.

Caleb Callahan is thirty-four years old. Three weeks ago he moved to New York from Kansas City where he had gone to a psychiatrist, taught at the Kansas City Art Institute, changed girlfriends, and made soft buildings people would wear and walk in like clothes. His father owns a dry-cleaning business and gave Caleb some sound financial advice before Caleb left for New York. His mother reads detective stories and said, "Caleb, everything I know about geography, food, and politics, I learned there." On the Long Island Expressway a stone blew out of a truck carrying demolished buildings and smashed Caleb's windshield. The truck pulled over, a black man said, "My office is right down the road, follow me." Caleb followed, the man gave directions: "Go to the next road, take a right, then a left, follow it to the end, ask for Bill." He disappeared among the hills of rubble. Caleb drove and drove stopping at office after office, was given the same instructions slightly altered, "Look for the white stucco building, for the wire gate." After driving an hour he went back to the rubble yards and found the truck driver who led him three hundred yards to the office. He hadn't tried to trick Caleb. Caleb went to Yale Art School, Alaska, Japan (where he had trouble driving because he couldn't read Japanese and rarely knew what he was eating), Fogos Island, and England, where he lived near a moor with two friends and had a head-on car collision. He ran into Polly with whom he had been in love, they decided to get married, time passed, Caleb wouldn't become a Scientologist, Polly couldn't give it up, she boarded the L. Ron Hubbard Flagship with a specialty in linguistics and moves through the different oceans and seas of the world except where Scientology is banned. Caleb receives postcards, the names of ports are scratched from their surfaces with a razor blade. He was a track star and suburban rebel in high school, during which time he moved into a local park. His friends visited him with food and beer. In Cuba Caleb was afraid of losing his mind crossing to Florida, crossing a long bridge at night, hallucinating, ending up in jail, terrified. He doesn't like drugs and drinks moderately. His grandmother left him beautiful quilts and old tools in perfect condition, he is always aware of his clothes and surroundings. Caleb and Alice planned a trip to New Mexico with his best friend Ted, a psychiatrist, and Ted's girlfriend Carol, a psychologist. Carol had felt left out of Caleb's and Ted's friendship on previous trips. She felt Caleb didn't like her. He felt she was jealous. There were discussions of motive and intention. The arrangements were elaborate, Caleb and Alice worked hard, Ted and Carol arrived, Ted said, "Let's make it clear that any of us can leave any time we want if things don't work out." Caleb said, not knowing what to say, "Maybe we should all sign statements saying we'll have a good time." Ted and Carol didn't go on the trip. Caleb is generous, slightly suspicious of himself and others, he has a multicolored hand-knit pullover which somebody ruined by washing, a surprise favor. He has a sister and an older brother, likes to be active, reads, is interested in cities, people outside cities, cities around people, food (internal organs, fish, shellfish), and what other people think. Caleb knows when he's said something wrong. He is five feet nine inches tall with brown fine hair and handsome regular features. Rose asked in Southampton, "What is your astrological sign?" "I'm a Libra." "Oh, I have my moon in Libra and Libra rising." They discussed people's signs. Caleb asked "Are you interested in astrology?" She said, "I'm not, I just like reading it in the newspapers and saying 'Oh' when people tell me their signs." The autumn day was beautiful and clear, they went for a walk along the ocean, watching seagulls follow a school of jumping bluefish. After dinner Caleb laughed, "I thought you weren't interested in astrology," waving an astrological book over his head. "It's not mine," she said. "Oh ho," he answered; she said, "Really." They decided to read, he was looking around the room. "Are you looking for something?" she asked. "I just wondered where that book on astrology was."

Caleb bought a building in New York, Alice came, Caleb left, went to Montana to teach and earn money. He has returned and will complete renovations on his loft. He continues his search for isolation and intimacy.

Christopher Tredway is a thirty-eight-year-old native of England, resident of New York City, who recently touched bottom of a black depression. He is socially active, invited everywhere. He lost interest in his social life, preferring to stay home and watch television to stave off melancholy thoughts. As his depression deepened he dreamed nightly of his childhood. The dreams revolted him. He lay in bed trying to sleep, reconstructing each year of his life from 1976 backwards. He reached 1954 bolted from his bed thinking, "My God, what am I doing?" He took a Valium, slept, and woke up refreshed. He enjoys the music of a punk rock group which sings the lyrics:

> I don't want to be with you
> I don't want to be with you
> I don't want to be with you
> I don't want to be with you
> I don't want to be with you
> Then why da ya want to be with me.

He remarks, "It's what all of us want to say, younger people are saying it for us." Christopher is homosexual and has a longing for, but difficulty in achieving, a committed relationship. He has been in love with spectacularly beautiful women and men. He is a painter who enjoyed great success in London and is discouraged by the reception of his work there now that he lives in New York. His last show received no reviews, no attention. This is a change from the past when he was a gifted art student who in the early sixties was the first person at Newcastle Art College to wear Levis. He visited New York, worked for Sandy Newman, met major American artists, returned to London, exhibited his own work, taught, fell in love often, was the object of others' love, entertained, went to movies, plays, ballets, parties, painted, became a resident of King's College, Cambridge, restored a room designed originally by Duncan Grant and Vanessa Bell, formed people's taste, dressed with verve, told hilarious stories, visited New York, and began to lose his hair. He moved to New York City and decided to have the hair transplant operation by Dr. Orenstein. He thinks it helped and was worth the pain, the redness, the swelling of his scalp. Christopher is busy as the designer for the Clay Llewellyn Dance Company and handles the business of American painter Rocky Ross. He travels constantly: Los Angeles, Europe, around the world, Tennessee, and, most recently, St. Barts Island in the Caribbean. He knows many people, some have achieved recognition in their fields. He is interested in what they do. "John and Yoko are nice, they're bringing their baby up on a macrobiotic diet, I don't think it's right. If they want to bring it up pure, don't live in the city; if they live in the city, they should follow a doctor's advice. John has forgotten what he was, he's a regular person now, very sweet, they've become a lovely couple. Bryan hasn't changed one thing, he's still just as unhappy, which reassures me. He says now he doesn't like modern art and doesn't understand it. His girlfriend Jerry is marvelous, like a photograph of a sexy blonde you wouldn't know what to do with if you got her in real life. She plays the naive Texan role to the hilt but she doesn't take me in. I told Toby, call Yukie in Japan and say, 'Get $3,000 in the bank or you'll be in real trouble.'" Christopher's advice is always conservative and concrete. He thought of putting his TV downstairs so he wouldn't wake up in the middle of the night and watch it, but it just makes him think he needs another. "Look at that, isn't it incredible?"—a yellow wall with silver pipes at the side of a bakery—"I'm dreading to hear it's done by an artist." Christopher has an instinctive and educated eye for furniture, dishes, clothes, and other design products. He is specific and absolute in his tastes. He feels the snow was deeper in New York City in 1960, now New York looks the way Europe is supposed to look, dirty, decrepit, run-down, filthy. His father owned a textile mill where Christopher worked after graduating from a Quaker boarding school and before deciding to go to art school. At nineteen he went on his first trip alone, to a music festival in Edinburgh. He heard Janos Starker play the Bach Unaccompanied Cello Suites, met an American boy, Stanley III, with whom he had no sex but corresponded with for years. At that time he didn't like classical music on principle and now likes rock music on principle. At twenty Christopher insisted that his family go to the play *Five Finger Exercise*, written by the author of *Equus*. "I wanted them to see it because I thought the family was identical to ours. After the play my mother said, 'Why, Christopher, they aren't like us at all, your father doesn't even play golf.'" He is worried about aging. Christopher says about his drinking, "I have more fun when I do." Within one year his mother died and his father married his mistress of twenty years. Six months later his father died. Shortly after, his stepmother died. Thinking about his family Christopher said, "My grandmother, like me, was the only one in the family truly committed to saving things. She had a big painted Welsh dresser in the kitchen. There was a drawer full of corks, a drawer full of pieces of string, a drawer of paper bags, one of tissue, and perhaps one for lids. During the First World War my maiden aunt started knitting for the troops. She finished one sock. My grandmother put it away. During the Second World War my grandmother got a new housemaid who one day happened to mention that her father had lost a leg in a coal mining accident. My grandmother said, 'I have just the thing,' ran upstairs and came down with the sock as a present for the maid's father."

Gavin Frazer is twenty-nine years old, an artist from England who nearly died of hepatitis. The doctors misdiagnosed him; delirious, he jumped through the hospital window. Gavin looks like a satyr, has a slim body, an orange jumpsuit, several leather outfits, and thick wiry hair. He spent two years in New York on a Boxer Fellowship and now lives in London, committed to the idea of an indigenous European art distinct from that of America. He has a quick mind and a broad range of interests, his acquaintance is varied. He knew he was homosexual when he fell in love with his roommate, who didn't reciprocate his feelings. He lived for some time with a woman who became a lesbian. His work is analytical. He enjoys anonymous sex in movie theaters and on Hampstead Heath in the afternoon. He was a resident artist at Hull College, fell in love with a member of the Gay Alliance Association who had a very butch, domineering boyfriend. Gavin planned to make contact with him through the GAA and offered to have their convention in Hull. The boy wasn't able to be there. Gavin takes color snapshots and usually carries a camera. He likes postcards and is interested in architecture, particularly tall skyscrapers and towers. He exhibits regularly in London and sells his work. His homes are usually painted white, including floors, with few knick-knacks. He comes from a lower-middle-class family and is the only child of parents who live in a London suburb. Gavin had one great love he nursed through meningitis, who later rejected him. They remain friends but Gavin is never sure how well the other is psychologically. In New York Gavin listened constantly to records or radio station WBAI and went out every night for drinks, dinner, and gay bars. He always lives alone. He thinks that maintaining his masculinity is important. He always has close women friends, relationships with sexual overtones. Socially Gavin is ebullient and enthusiastic, always ready to do something.

Meredith Ridge Slade-Ryan left London and a twelve-year marriage. She moved to New York, lived with friends, then took a small loft on Grand Street. She is thirty-six years old and was born near Boston. Meredith and her husband Robin traveled with her parents in Europe. Her father, Frank, thought Robin should get a haircut. "Bob," he said, "you look just like . . ." words wouldn't come, "you look just like an Egyptian." Meredith says her parents believe speaking louder and slower in any foreign country will make them understood. "Wa-ter, wa-ter," her mother shouted, pointing alternately to her mouth and a glass. As they left the restaurant in France, Frank said to Robin, "Bob, did you see the tip I gave that little waitress?" "No I didn't, Frank." "Well, Bob, I gave her a Kennedy half-dollar, and you know, Bob, tears came to her eyes." Meredith was dressed extremely well as a child. Her Shetland sweaters came from Scotland and her shoes from England. She was sent to boarding school, ran away, went to Massachusetts College of Art, made many friends, modeled in Provincetown summers for the Hans Hofmann School of Painting, bicycling to work nude under her raincoat, and told everyone she was a lesbian. During her graduate career at Yale she had an orange cat, a basement apartment, and an affair with Robin, an undergraduate art student. They decided to marry, Meredith got pregnant, Robin graduated from Yale, they left for a honeymoon in Europe. Meredith occasionally shows a picture. She and Robin are standing on the deck of a ship against a powdery sky. Meredith is wearing a large blue dress, her red hair piled on top of her head and on top of that a great blue cartwheel hat, she looks like an Irish cleaning woman with a young charge. She screams with laughter. During drunken marital fights Meredith would shout at Robin, "You just married me because I was pregnant," forgetting they had gotten engaged before the pregnancy. She has visited both Mexico and Russia. Though politically to the left, she talked at length to the FBI about her visit to Russia. They were the only people who showed real interest in her trip. Robin and Meredith went to Peru where Robin's parents lived. His father is with the World Bank. They ate at a good restaurant, had servants, and went to Macchu Picchu where Robin made a film. Their daughter Virginia was born in rural Vermont at a progressive school where they were teaching. Robin entered Yale Graduate School in painting and their home was filled with a group of art students who considered themselves the best. Meredith loves to cook, there was never too little to eat. She followed a mathematical plan, if there are two, cook for four, if there are four, for sixteen, and so on, geometrically. They had lunches, brunches, dinners, and parties. When she smoked marijuana her tongue would get big, filling her mouth, she couldn't speak or breathe and had to go to the health service where she was seeing Dr. Wiggins, a psychiatrist. Meredith and Robin fought, once she appeared at a friend's house some distance from home at four A.M. carrying a knife. Virginia and Robin picked her up in the morning and stayed for breakfast. Once Robin knocked her down with a car, once she tried to push him over a balcony. Meredith is a receptive, appreciative audience, she has a quick temper, a sense of humor, and a mind of her own. Her mother feels she has great administrative abilities, a subject which came up recently when Meredith, discussing the possibility of opening an art gallery, said, "All I need are two very good French suits." Meredith bought or was given in the middle sixties the complete line of products from Design Research, a store specializing in goods for the home. In the early seventies these were augmented and sometimes replaced by furnishings from Habitat in London, whose design ideas were advanced for that time and place. At Yale her friend Nadia gave people gifts, took them back, had a nervous breakdown, was hospitalized, taught art at the hospital, started living with a man whom she loved, gave small dinner parties, everything exquisitely prepared and served, each course served in a different room, fixed up a house and told a story about each object in it, searched for and found the fourth of a set of rare ruby-red glasses, and hanged herself in California. Meredith and Robin decided to go to England, bypassing the New York art scene. Their friends gave a party in the Park, everyone dressed up. Vincent played the flute, Ted the recorder. The evening was gold, pink, and warm, the grass smelled, they drank champagne, ate pâté. Meredith, Robin, and Virginia sailed. Meredith was afraid to fly. In Corsham, Wiltshire, England, Robin and Meredith fell in love with the same student, Bran, a young boy committed to an extreme evangelical faith which involved speaking in tongues and being moved by the spirit. His friend Greg, recently converted, made a pale fourth to their threesome. Bran attempted to convert Robin and Meredith. Robin resisted but became desperately unhappy. Meredith took long walks in the fields with her Bible, clutched Bran's hand in the back seat of the car, spent hours lying on his bed talking about faith and morality. Greg, Robin, and Meredith all received zip-up Bibles for Christmas from Bran. Bran went mad, left school, went to a psychiatrist at home, dug ditches so he didn't have to think, eventually returned to school and lost the fierceness of his faith. The friendship remained but was altered. Bran gave his virginity to an American art critic on Meredith's and Robin's couch in their front room. Meredith has distinctive taste concerning home, food, clothes, art, and people. Meredith visited Toby in New York, became pregnant, returned to England and made the painful decision to have an abortion. Robin brought flowers and champagne after the operation. They decided to separate. For eight years Meredith liked everything parallel and perpendicular but now she likes to introduce a diagonal. She arrived in Southampton as a weekend guest at eleven P.M. and by twelve-thirty A.M. was rearranging the living room furniture which remained that way until her friends gave up the house. Meredith's recent work has been felt tip drawings of objects on 9½ × 11 paper with carbons of the drawing process. She is now painting and making clay objects from her paintings, a flower pot becomes a painting of a flower pot which becomes a clay flower pot. She has several boyfriends, likes young men and the Japanese, whose attention to detail intrigues her. Meredith takes everyone seriously.

Reid Gibson is thirty-three years old, five-nine, attractive, a funny and moody artist who was a hockey player. He has a banana nose. In grade school he teased another student about the size of his nose, the student said "Look at your own," since then Reid has been self-conscious about his looks. His work includes video tapes with and without his dog Duchamp-Villon, a blue Weimaraner, drawings on typing paper in faint pencil or brush and ink, photographs and audio tapes. Reid has a dry sense of humor. He sits on a stool or at a table with a few props and does and says things suggesting the irony of life, the foibles of human nature, or makes up tests for his dog. Reid sits on a stool in a white tee shirt with a fang coming out of his mouth, gestures to a small stick leaning against the wall and says, "I guess you're wondering how I got this stick and this tooth." He took his clothes to the laundry, a woman stopped him on the street and said, "Which do you want, this stick or this tooth?" He said, "Both." "You can only have one." He said, "I'll take the tooth." He delivered the laundry and went home. Later he went to pick it up, a woman stopped him and said, "Which do you want, this stick or this tooth?" He said, "The stick." Other tapes are devoted to how much Reid likes water; the copyright dates of the *Webster Abridged Dictionary*; a discussion with a pianist about concert dates and Chopin; how to buy a house for $40,000 when you only have $30,000; his dog licking milk out of a glass, pushing a ball, making faces, and learning to read. Reid's photographs are numerous: his dog on four legs, three legs, two legs in profile; his red-haired beautiful wife, Elaine, dressed in an ice skating costume on ice skates ironing, while Reid with a suitcase and dark trenchcoat, collar up, slips out the side door, captioned "Housewife with ice skating as a hobby and a husband who travels in disguise." Reid writes very short stories, some only a sentence long. A drawing has the penciled heads of a sad-looking woman and man divided by a line between them. Under the man are the words "All I talk about are aesthetics," under the woman are the words, "All I talk about is how I look." Another says at the top of the page, "Two equally unpopular people." There are the heads of two men, a line between: Under one, "I always talk about terminal illness"; under the other, "I don't care about nothing." Reid plays chess, spent the summer at Lake Placid, New York, as a guest of the Pearlmans, a couple who own a SoHo art gallery, where he met their son's many friends in the ice skating field. Elaine and Reid flew to St. Maarten, a Caribbean island, for their October wedding anniversary instead of going to Houston, Texas, for dinner. Reid sat on the beach and was jealous of Elaine swimming with young brown men possessing perfect bodies. Reid wears plaid shirts and used to sleep in an attic in Massachusetts. He was scared to walk down the stairs at night to urinate, so he put a kleenex over a grating in his closet and urinated through it. He was always caught. The grating was directly over the kitchen table. His sister is married to an Italian. Reid attended Massachussets School of Art, each of his roommates knew about a different period of music. Reid admires Glenn Gould. He taught in Minnesota, first saw his wife standing in a College Art Association conference line in Cleveland, Ohio, followed her everywhere and said he couldn't be alone. She was annoyed but married him. Reid is flirtatious, enjoys women but doesn't formally date. He takes a fair amount of drugs and drink. He is happy during the day and gets depressed at three A.M. until Elaine talks him out of it. He doesn't meet many people he can't handle now, his video tapes are the most in demand at Caswell Gallery's tape center. Reid says about video, "Some people have a heavy touch, some a light touch, but heavy or light they're all boring." Reid doesn't smile in his tapes, which rent for $60 and sell for $250. He has a truck, takes his dog out on Sundays to swim in the Hudson River, is interested in books, and thinks many women beautiful. Reid is very popular now and did a color drawing of trees. He is concerned that the interest in his art is losing momentum, that he is losing momentum, he takes some coke, works twenty-four hours trying to decide in which direction to push his work. His separation from Elaine is final, she is in California, he remains in New York with Joan, his red-haired girlfriend. The dog visits Elaine in Los Angeles but spends most of his time in New York with Reid. Dogs have long been known among the domestic animals as man's best friend. They are absolute in their loyalty and devotion yet seem independent by virtue of their boundless cheerful energy and good health. They demand constant care, but the owner is rewarded by displays of affection, need, and startling, amusing behavior not seen often in human beings.

Dick Bitts is a thirty-three-year-old man with a delicate frame who moved from Chicago to New York. His twin sister was stillborn. His grandfather helped build the railing around the Grand Canyon. Apples saved Dick's life when he was stationed in Thailand. The Army serves the same meals the same day in all parts of the world, a soldier in the Arctic will eat what a soldier eats in Thailand. Dick couldn't eat slabs of hot roast beef, steaming mashed potatoes and gravy in the humid Thailand heat and ate only the apples served after meals. He was popular in the Army. Crouched in a muddy pit, looking up and out at targets, Dick, who had never fired a gun, closed his eyes, squeezed the trigger and shot blindly. He was awarded the rank of sharpshooter. Though not interested or gifted in athletics, Dick is a fine underwater swimmer. A group of men stood around the blue Olympic-size pool at the Nuclear Defense Edgewood Arsenal Service Club. Dick took off his shirt, folded and placed it on a chair, dove neatly into the water, dropped to the bottom, swam slowly the entire length of the pool, surfaced, climbed out and put his shirt back on. A tall black man said, "What do you know, the rock can swim." Dick's Army nickname became The Rock. He was stationed at a nuclear research lab in Maryland and never understood his job, which was classified and involved putting dots on papers at specified intervals as they passed by him. He was a talented art student, his painting of many small chairs was purchased by the Chicago Art Institute and kept in their basement. His family is close and Christian Scientist. His father died, his mother became a real estate broker, his sister married a Proctor & Gamble executive from whom Dick receives free samples of Sure deodorant, deodorant soap, and Crest toothpaste. Dick moved to New York City, went to a party. He returned at three A.M. and he walked to the front of his loft, looked out and saw that every floor in the building opposite was brightly lit and on each was a painter painting. He became depressed, left New York for Chicago, and moved in with his mother. He considers himself lazy, likes Brooks Brothers clothes, dresses with care, and is fastidious by nature. On the top floor of Marshall Fields department store is a house, Trend House, which is open at the front. Its decor changes seasonally. Dick said the people last living there were a family of three, a man, his wife, and their son who was taking a course in interior design. The couple turned over the job of decorating the house to the son. Each room was done in a different style, the living room Mediterranean, the family room ranch. He selected a semi-double bed with hard cylindrical cushions and a canopy for the bedroom, sunburst clocks, orange and purple wallpaper for the dining room, and white and gold furnishings for the living room. Things were shifted, changed, adjusted, readjusted, never comfortable, never done. The father came in one evening, tripped on the long white shag rug, slipped and fell, becoming impaled on a sharp crystal obelisk which decorated the coffee table. The mother stopped talking to the son and, after the funeral, moved to the back of the house into the only room not decorated. One afternoon they met in the vestibule, the son said, "Things are all wrong," the mother thinks he's come to his senses, he says, "That occasional chair has to go." The son moved to Albuquerque after a course in hotel management and now has a position at a Holiday Inn. He works the night shift, front desk, and is trying to figure out who owns the tangerine Oldsmobile parked at the motel entrance. The keys aren't in the car. Dick worked with Burr Tilstrom, who created *The Kukla, Fran and Ollie Show*. The Kuklapolitans or puppets were frequently in Dick's care. Kukla, Ollie, Beulah the Witch, Fletcher the Rabbit, have distinct and separate personalities; when they have stagefright they look out through the lens of the camera into a friend's home. Dick has had two affairs, one with a man, one with a woman. He much prefers the woman and when asked why, said, "The conversation after is better." He feels that two men aren't that interesting a combination. Puppets are jointed figures which by various devices are made to move in mimicry of persons or animals, usually for dramatic performances. The stage has no floor, a curtain or three-sided screen with an opening for the proscenium arch is required. Painted or dyed scenery is suspended behind the dolls. Puppets must be held high so that the operator's head is invisible. The stage lighting (floods or strips) shines upon the puppets' faces, as well as upon the scenery. Humorous lively plays are best for this grotesque, intimate type of theatre. As a child Dick kept to himself. One day the teacher asked everyone in class to write about their favorite classmate. Dick was troubled, he hadn't spoken to anyone during the term, the papers were collected, he still didn't know whom to put down. The teacher looked through them, then at the class, and said, "This is very interesting, everyone seems to have written about the same person, Dick Bitts." Dick is about five feet seven inches tall, with tiny bones, small sharp features, and blue eyes. He is anxious to begin and complete a self-portrait as his hair is dropping out at such a rate it won't last six months. His work includes paintings of dancing eyeglasses, fragile miniature balsawood rooms, among them an office called *Newwork*, the corner of an art gallery, a motel room, and the living room of a suburban house in which one chair is overturned, its placement suggesting that the person who occupied it sat with his back to the fire and the other three people. There are paintings of a Palm Springs pool and, most recently, a picture of the Pfaff brothers, Edward and Otto, both looking at and away from a piece of blank paper. Dick is pleased with his decision to leave Chicago and live in New York, he needs to get an air conditioner for his compact skylit apartment on Tenth Street as he can't bear the summer heat.

Felice Canifer is a twenty-six-year-old member of the richest minority group in the United States, the Agua Caliente Indians whose reservation is Palm Springs, California. She is a millionaire born in Palos Verdes, California. Her sister wants to be a veterinarian. Felice's day starts at seven A.M. She feeds her dog Sabi, her cat Tonka, walks Sabi in Washington Square Park below her seventeenth-story apartment with parquet floors, returns and does the Erno Laszlo morning ritual. Laszlo is a series of preparations for the skin of the face and neck developed by a Hungarian doctor dead five years and used by, among others, Jacqueline Kennedy, Arlene Dahl, Liza Minnelli, and the Duchess of Windsor. Felice uses the series of products for one-o'clock skin, slightly oily. In weather above 40° she fills the bathroom basin with water as hot as her fingertips can stand, dips a bar of Black Sea mud soap into the water and rubs it on her wet face and neck, rinses her face and neck thirty times in the same hot soapy water. The dirt sinks to the bottom of the basin, the natural oils float to the top of the water and are splashed back into the open pores of the skin. She dries with a towel and saturates a cotton ball with Light Controlling Lotion, applies it on her entire face. She saturates a cotton ball with Regular Normalizer Shake-It, well-shaken, applies on face and neck and blots with tissue. Fingertips pHelitone Cream under her eyes and smoothes gently blotting with tissue, applies Controlling Face Powder generously with a fresh cotton ball to face and neck, removes the excess and buffs the skin with another cotton ball. She finally applies a powder rouge with sponged puff anywhere on her face that needs brightening. Felice has asked Miss Flower, the Laszlo consultant at Bergdorf Goodman, if it isn't possible for the company to make a shampoo, there is none on the market she can stand. Felice worries about her mother, who eats and drinks too much. She's an accomplished businesswoman who gets little pleasure from her wealth or from her social, civic, and political activities, and little comfort from her marriage, which could be called stable and happy. Felice loves her stepfather and wishes he could help curb her mother's self-destructive tendencies. She doesn't know how to make her mother do anything, even if it's good for her. Felice goes to ballet lessons, singing lessons, lunch, manicure appointments, acting classes, and then out for dinner. Returning home she performs the Laszlo nighttime ritual drunk or sober. On Friday she leaves for her four-bedroom house in Southampton with two fireplaces, gray wall-to-wall carpeting stained by Sabi's urine, color and black-and-white televisions, regular and microwave ovens, toaster broiler, gray green walls with white trim, executive dining set, butcher block kitchen, land, double garage, trees, studio, grape arbor, rose trellis, and hammock. She doesn't use baggies or plastic waste disposal bags for ecological reasons. She tries to always get household goods on sale or at a discount. She advised a friend who recently acquired some money, "Don't get too generous, you'll get yourself in trouble and get mad." Felice visited New York City as a teenager, her stepfather gave her a ring from Tiffany's, she wept with joy at the Waldorf Astoria and wanted to return to New York as a high school graduation present. She went to Chadwick School which she despised and was jailed for running away. Felice was tall, thin, red-haired and beautiful, her best friend, the bock beer heiress, was tall, thin, blonde and beautiful, they picked up boys on the beach though both were going steady. She came to New York City at eighteen, enrolled in a fashion design school, quit and moved into a loft on Greene Street with one of her instructors, Robert, an intelligent graduate from Yale School of Art and Architecture. She came into her money at twenty-one, $50,000 a year, tax-free. They moved to Two Fifth Avenue, overlooking the square, bought a dog and saw little of people living below Houston Street. They joined a dream-oriented therapy group. Robert wanted them to concentrate on mental telepathy and shared dreams. The relationship lasted five increasingly difficult years. Robert's therapist thought it was Felice's fault. Felice failed to take Robert's temperament seriously enough. The therapist felt artists, being special people, should be treated specially. They broke up. Felice began affairs with the unhappily married son of a man dead, rich, and famous, and Parker, an attractive divorced architect. She played the field, it didn't work. She established friendships with artists eight years her senior she had met through Robert. She gave one of the use of her Bergdorf charge card for Laszlo products when the artist was broke, lent another money and gave her a studio in Southampton for the summer in exchange for pet care, light gardening, and grocery shopping. Felice considers herself intellectually weak, she'd like to be committed to something. She is emotional and direct. Parker, Dick Bitts, and Jane came to dinner, Parker said, "I don't like the salad, Felice," she threw it at him and ran upstairs, leaving them watching *The Great Escape*, starring Steve McQueen, on television. Parker finished his steak and left the table. Jane and Dick watched the movie and analyzed the situation. Doors slammed, they heard noises overhead. Felice and Parker came down an hour later. "We're going out for ice cream." They returned. Parker sat down, began eating, said "This is a rotten banana split." Felice takes holidays seriously, is an excellent dancer, and likes a song by the Stylistics, "What Was I Before You?" The house in Southampton came on the market after a woman named Ruth died, it was a bargain. A different woman named Ruth died, in New York. Her apartment in the Pulitzer Mansion, between Madison and Fifth, designed by the notorious architect Stanford White, who was murdered by his mistress's husband, came on the market. Felice bought it and began renovations. Parker designed the interior. After discussing tiles they walked to the corner. A girl came up who had dated Parker, they flirted, Felice stood there, Parker finally said, "This is Felice, I'm designing her apartment." They decided to have a baby. Felice had her intrauterine device removed and became pregnant. They married on June 25 in Southampton. Parker will pay half the New York rent, give Felice a household allowance, assume financial responsibility for their children, and see to the upkeep of the Woodstock house. Felice will share expenses in New York and take care of the Southampton house. The wedding was under the rose trellis. Both sets of parents agreed it was the loveliest day of their lives. Felice was happy to say, days later, "This is my husband, Parker Boyd."

Harry Walter is in his forties, an architect and collector of contemporary art, of Russian Jewish extraction. He lives in London and spent nine days of the past Christmas season in Egypt. He was deeply moved by the land, its people, their architectural and artistic heritage. The Pyramids would change, would appear different, at different times of day, different in different weather. Once they shimmered every stone vibrating in light in front of Harry's eyes. They don't sit heavily on the land, their form is active and transcendent. Egypt is essentially a thin green strip of land six miles wide bordering the Nile, a river of a peculiar green color. Eau de Nile, the name of a color, is the river's color. In Luxor the women aren't allowed to eat with the men and the nights are cold in January and December. Harry slept on dirt floors in huts, on beds in palaces, and ate freshly baked bread. He would rise at seven A.M., take a taxi to the City of the Dead, spend the day looking, return at dusk for his meal. A home can be bought for little money in the small villages surrounding the City of the Dead. The best guidebook for Egyptian antiquities was written in the 1930s. Harry didn't notice the war. The people were the most sophisticated he's met traveling, it's not a permissive or accepting society, it is one in which certain judgements have never been made. The entire country, part of the Gondwanaland foreland, is underlain by a crystalline basement complex which occasionally crops out at the surface. The 750-mile length of the Nile is a relatively narrow groove, flat-bottomed and sinuous in outline. In some parts the valley is fourteen miles wide, in others it narrows until the enclosing steep bluffs are washed by the waters of the river. It is surrounded by deserts. Lizards are numerous and include the desert monitor, which attains a length of four to five feet. The crocodile, hippopotamus, lion, giraffe, and ostrich depicted on ancient Egyptian friezes have vanished and probably retreated south to the tropics many centuries ago. Butterflies are rare but there are numerous moths, wasps, hornets, grasshoppers, and praying mantises. Harry's mother lives in a manor house in Hampstead, wears gilt boots, and paints. Each room of the house is filled with her paintings, which often have a flower motif; the surfaces vary in thickness from a quarter of an inch to one inch. There is a brochure of the work, her Christmas card was a reproduction of one of her paintings with the words "a painting by Tanya Walter" inside. Another card is a reproduction of her painting with the frame reproduced also and on the back a sticky substance to fix it to the wall. She sent each of her children a case of assorted spirits for Christmas. Harry has a brother Simon who runs the family business (vacuums), and isn't mentioned often by the other brothers; a sister whose husband committed suicide; a rich brother, Sebastian, who has gone bankrupt, is married to a ballerina, and retains occasional use of his chauffeur. Carl, the youngest, writes for *The*

Economist, has married twice and is in analysis. Tanya served tea for five: Harry and Carl, and two women of Russian Jewish extraction, one of whose sons is a doctor in New York; the other woman's daughter is married to someone rich and investing in gold. A three-tiered tea trolley was wheeled in by a woman. Carl asked, "Who's that, mother?" Tanya answered, "She's Polish." The tea trolley was covered with plates of small decorated sandwiches, many of which had to be eaten immediately to make room on the trolley for the teapot, cups and saucers. Harry lives in a large apartment in Belgrave Square, the kitchen has curved walls, recessed lighting and resembles the interior of an airplane. There are many German appliances, including several meant to knead dough. Harry goes once a year to Harrods department store and buys twenty bottles of Brasso, ten boxes of Brillo pads, a dozen of Fairy Liquid dish detergent, tins of imported sardines, soups, pheasants, quail eggs, bottles of honey, salad dressing, and other staples. He spends five hundred to a thousand pounds and doesn't need to worry about these things the rest of the year. A bomb recently exploded near his flat, it was intended for the Prime Minister who lives a short distance away. Harry's flat shook from the reverberations. There are spring locks on the door and usually four sirloin steaks and five sirloin roasts in the freezer. Harry keeps his new bicycle and color television in his bedroom. He bought dozens of wire bins to hold and organize his shirts, underclothes, and socks. There are three ten-foot shelves holding the bins, each shelf holds shirts divided into categories: white, dress, sport, long sleeve, short sleeve. Cecil, who worked for a titled lady now dead, comes in every day at five P.M. to clean the apartment, shine Harry's shoes, sponge and press his suits, take out the laundry, and fill the ice bucket. He has never used the dishwasher, which frightens him. Harry's acquaintance varies from aristocracy rich and poor to businessmen, architects and artists known and unknown. He knows some novelists but hasn't read their work and owns many books about art. He has a large diary for daytime appointments given him by his brother Carl (he gave Carl a salami from New

York), and a small diary for evening engagements. He has been involved with Minya, a woman with a title from a country like Czechoslovakia, who wore Yves St. Laurent clothes and went off with a French woman who drove a motorcycle and wrestled. He spent a great deal of time with Monika who has the time-consuming responsibility of caring for a large fortune. He's participated in orgies. Harry spends at least a month of each year in New York, he finds the energy and passion of the people much greater than in London where his work is. Harry is generous with his friends, about five-seven in height, round but not fat, wears glasses, doesn't get mad often and when he does, deals with it efficiently and quietly. He's impatient with people who don't do anything and admires people who take chances with their lives. Belgrave Square is curved and white; nightingales sing in the park.

Marshall Tate is thirty-one, six feet three inches tall, an art historian and art critic with a passionate interest in the Baroque. His attentuated hands and head cause him to resemble a figure in an El Greco painting. For Rose's birthday dinner he made a Moroccan carrot salad, roast tomatoes and peppers, cucumbers and cumin, a stew of lamb, almonds, prunes, and honey, oranges sliced thin with a special serrated knife from France and layered with orange water, powdered sugar, and cinnamon, one hundred dates stuffed with crushed almonds flavored with orange water and rolled in powdered sugar. Everyone remarked on the excellence of the meal. At Delfine's, Marshall cooked fried chicken, corn bread, green beans with bacon, gravy, mashed potatoes, and pecan pie. After dinner he put on a Gladys Knight and the Pips record and tried to teach everyone the new dance steps. Last summer his favorite club was a Puerto Rican one in New York whose habitues dressed and danced flamboyantly. *The Cobweb* is one of his favorite Vincente Minnelli movies, he's trying to see every movie of any importance that has been made, and has strong opinions on what is good and what is bad. This decisiveness carries into the area of art, literature, and music. He feels

Robert Ryman is the most important American painter since Pollock. Marshall agonizes in his search for the correct phrase, the establishment of logical order when writing criticism. He brings venison, huckleberries, smoked fish, and turquoise-studded Indian jewelry from his parent's home facing a lake in Idaho. His parents are upper-middle-class and drink heavily. He was forced to break with them during the summer of his thirtieth birthday over money. They have become reconciled. He has an older sister engaged in divorce proceedings and a younger brother who travels. Marshall's fine, thinning blond hair gives clear definition to the lines of his skull, he took to Southampton red flowered corduroy pants and tight colored tee shirts but as a rule doesn't dress extremely. He is preoc-cupied with a painting, *Las Meniñas*, by Diego Rodriquez de Silva Velasquez, the most important of Spanish painters and one of the world's greatest artists, who was born in Seville and baptized on June 6, 1599. In *Las Meniñas* he has created the effect of a momentary glance at a casual scene in the artist's studio while he paints the king and queen. Only their reflec-tions are seen in a mirror in the background, accompanied by the Infanta Margarita with her ladies-in-waiting and other attendants. Velasquez's last activity was to accompany the king and queen to the Isle of Pheasants in the summer of 1660, the year of his death. Marshall visited Morocco for the first time in the winter, swam in a pool looking at the snow-covered Atlas mountains. He loves the sea, travel, and members of his own sex, which doesn't exclude warm friendships with women, heterosexual men, and couples. His love affairs are often difficult and frequently with foreigners. Marshall and a friend were playing in the upstairs bedroom. Marshall tied his friend nude to the window facing the street. When someone walked by Marshall released the shade, the resultant crack drew the passerby's attention to Marshall's naked friend spreadeagled and pressed against the window. He is writing a book on famous historical transvestites, a Moroccan cookbook, cata-logues for exhibitions, and the introduction to an extensive survey of recent art.

FRIENDS

Lina Antonelli is a thirty-year-old art dealer from Genoa who always wears black clothes and doesn't eat meat. She will never marry, a decision she made at sixteen. Her father drinks, which causes him heart trouble and created a need for open heart surgery. Her mother, who died four years ago, ran a beauty salon then quit to help her husband run his driving schools, one of which she left to Lina. It was worth ten million lire. Lina's father was in the military for eleven years, deserted during the Second World War because of his anti-fascist sympathies and is now emotionally a fascist. Lina has long black hair she washes once a week, large brown eyes, creases from her nostrils to the corners of her mouth, a tall slim body. She is quiet and self-contained. Her apartment is ten years old, has five rooms, bedroom, study, bathroom, kitchen, living room, and a rowing machine. The doors of the study and living room open onto a narrow terrace where she has a small bed to take the sun. The foyer has a yellow marble floor as does the study, the kitchen floor is brown and white marble, the hall, bedroom, and living room floors dark green speckled marble contained by a white grid. The floors shine and reflect in their surfaces the contents of the apartment. Saman Gallery is located on a tiny street going up a damp hill paved with irregular blocks of stone. The name Saman is the first word, before man before woman, when there was one thing. She doesn't care for Rome, one must be defensive on the street, it is the city of the Italian lover. Lina is friends with Primo, an art critic who always wears black, eats little meat, and resides in Genoa. Lina hasn't spoken to her father in years, he wanted her to do things she didn't want to do. Four years ago she received an obscene telephone call every day for four months. It was the first time she had lived alone. After school she wanted to become an actress, wore the décolletage, became involved with a beautiful rich man, a situation which she found boring but safe because she knew how to handle the game. She thinks the position of women in Italy is very bad. She quit the theater realizing that it was a way for her to be not real. Lina's father was of the Italian lover type and very beautiful. Her apartment is all white, two white tables, two white sofas, tan rug, two white hooded ashtrays, a double bed with a pink wool cover. She doesn't like the country or the mountains, only the sea, and isn't able to go this Christmas because she has no money. Many women in Italy are antifeminists, this is normal. In Milan, Giovanni said, "You're doing nothing." Lina didn't answer and opened her gallery two weeks later. They had been to the Alessandra Castelli gallery named Man and His Art, Giovanni saw a woman ran it and he said, "Oh no, not another, this is too much." Lina hasn't had a good meal in Rome, she doesn't want a child, is sympathetic to the writing of Simone de Beauvoir and not to that of Violette le Duc. She says Pirandello tried to write a novel a day for a year and got tired after two hundred. She has friends who have friends in customs and likes to deal only with people she likes. People in Italy are curious about her relationship to Primo, it is their problem not hers, she says. Genoa is old, the walls buckle and blister from the damp, trees grow from their sides. Lina sees herself in life as in a play, and doesn't know yet what to do with her self-consciousness, she thinks she may be too old or too new. Lina prefers one very good thing to several things which are not so good.

Primo Avanti is a thirty-four-year-old art critic in a state of change. He lives in Genoa, goes to the United States in fall and spring, to Milan once a week, and to Rome occasionally, wears black, has black and gray hair, long sideburns, a rounded face, round eyes, and wears glasses. Primo travels light and is interested in human rapport. His parents are alive, his father is in the import business, fish, and lives with Primo's mother on the third floor of the same building Primo lives in. He has a white Renault and an eight-room apartment. During his first trip to New York he stayed in a midtown hotel and took bus tours, the guide spoke Italian and said this is a Gothic church, there is a copy of it in France. He eats little meat and enjoys good food. It is not the custom in Italy to tip but Primo does if he intends to return to the restaurant. He finds the food of Rome too heavy and says each Italian city is different and their people different. Traditionally, the Florentines are liars, the Genoese tight-fisted and insular, the Milanese greedy, the Romans, the Southerners, all different. In Rome the wife of an artist said we need you in Rome, Primo. He wants to write about whom he wants to write about and deal with people he likes. He likes American artists, whom he finds open in person and in their work. His relationship with Lina, an art dealer who wears black, excites curiosity and interest among his acquaintances in Italian cities. He travels alone and has many meetings about publications, wants to remain independent, laughs a lot, and likes the privacy of Genoa. He'd never been in the cupola of San Pietro before he was thirty-four and finds Venice beautiful, water and gold. He likes much art work, his taste is changing, he's interested in dreaming, and how one thinks. The Milanese are very elegant, the Romans elegant but more vulgar. The Italian lover is a bender, he bends women with his eyes and acts. Primo was lost once in a German city and found himself through reconstruction and deduction. He explains the fascist architecture around San Pietro as an effort to make it more powerful, more imposing, he feels the weight of his Italian past. He is the only child of parents with whom he has good relations. They have a country house in the flower district, near a small restaurant which sits on top of a broken hill looking down on clouds and mists. In the sun, Primo drank new wine, ate peppers, potatoes, fresh bread, salads, prosciutto, artichokes, carrots, green pasta with wild rabbit sauce, wild rabbit roasted in white wine, wild boar roasted in red wine, roast veal, fresh lettuce, zuppa inglese, tangerines, walnuts, apples, and drank a tumbler of clear grappa. In summer, the normal road to Santa Margharita and Portofino is blocked with cars, the tunnels cut into the rocks are filled with fumes, the waters of the Mediterranean are polluted. He doesn't care for France, it's just hills and flat, dislikes Germany, and likes people who tell the truth.

Giovanni is in his thirties and homeless. He used to live at the Fuseli Gallery in Milan. He's a sculptor or not an artist at all, talks continuously, moving from one end of the table to the other, from one end of the room to the other. He claps his hands loudly, abruptly in large groups of people, says, "Everyone go now, it's over," they look at their feet and laugh. His legs are short, he moves like a monkey. Dancing at the Arizona Club he dropped on one knee, sprung up as it touched the ground and kicked up his other leg. He said in English, "You are beautiful, your laugh is good, I tremble with love for you, more wine for Giovanni." He said, "Tony, I do a work with you, let's us three go home and sleep together, my teacher was . . ." He stopped talking and asked Giorgio for the English words. "He was a great god." Everyone laughed. He can control four rooms of people. Some say he isn't crazy but that other people think he is because he says the truth. He does complicated things with language. People become nervous as he approaches, he kisses women's hands, some say he's a sex maniac. He stroked the pale blond-hair of a beautiful woman saying, "Tony, I show you how to touch your woman." To Salvatore, behind him, eating cheese left over from lunch, he said, "You look like a rat." He continued moving his hand rhythmically from the top of the woman's head to the nape of her neck saying, "I love your brain, she has a beautiful brain, I touch her brain." Giorgio's girlfriend danced many times with a man in a beard. Giovanni said, "Giorgio, if I were from the South and that man danced with my woman I'd kill him." Giovanni is from southern Italy. He goes to Fuseli and says, "Marco gave me ten dollars." Fuseli gives him twenty dollars. He returns to Marco and says, "Fuseli gave me twenty dollars." Milan is a north Italian industrial city made of gray stone: buildings, streets, arches, courtyards, fitted together piece by piece. It has wide and narrow streets, piazzas, bars, and a thin yellow winter light. Five nights a week a dense fog fills Milan, nothing can be seen, planes can't land, it's impossible to drive. The people are elegant, interested in money, thin, and eat well. The land is flat, the Alps rise from its flatness, there are few trees. *The Last Supper*, a fresco by Leonardo da Vinci, can be seen in Milan between two P.M. and four P.M. A couple in an open sports car drives through the sharp cold wind. Some restaurant bathrooms are holes in the floor.

Eric Ullman is a twenty-four-year-old, blond, tall, slightly stocky rich boy from Sweden with a ruddy complexion. He works as an apprentice at the Ana Martin Gallery in New York. He receives no pay and is cheerful and competent in performing various tasks. He lives uptown with his girlfriend, also blonde and Swedish, who models for the Ford agency. She doesn't like it but makes good money. Eric can recite some of Max von Sydow's speeches from *Virgin Spring*, in particular the one where the father is yelling in the smoky room while his daughter's murderers sleep. In Eric's apartment is a long curved lamp, a table, a sofa, and a large Lowell Nesbitt flower painting. He collects art and is thinking of purchasing a bridge of milled iron by Elias Shaeffer for about $2,200. He will go to Elias' studio before finally deciding, to see if there might not be something more fun. His collection includes a small Sol LeWitt sculpture of three cubes, an Otto Haig, a Rodney van Keller, three Picasso drawings (one of museum quality), a Giacometti sculpture, Warhol and Stella prints, a Tom Wesselmann painting. One night drunk in Sweden he told the manager of a club to shut down unless he could provide nude ballerinas. Eric invited Harriet, who also works at Ana Martin's, and Elias to dinner. They ate cold marinated herring, drank aquavit and beer, they sang and enjoyed themselves. Eric keeps a diary. He writes advance comments about his appointments, whether or not he is going to have a good or bad time depending on whether or not he likes the person. Someone asked, "If you had a bad time with someone you liked or a good time with someone you didn't, would you change or amend the entry?" The problem does not come up. He has a Ferrari in Sweden, purchased three years ago for $10,000. It has been driven eighteen miles, to and from the license bureau. He has invested another $10,000 in making it perfect. He keeps it under a white sheet on blocks with the battery out. It has a record player and a bar. Eric has a pair of khaki pants, pleated with an elastic waist;

a leather coat midcalf length, ripped; shirts and matching pullover sweaters. Having nothing to do for a time, Eric went to work as a laborer in his father's factory in an effort to make contact with the working class. At the end of seven months he learned they talked primarily about the number of girlfriends they had and the amount of liquor they consumed. Eric found himself talking about the same things. He married, invested in a large building in downtown New York—each floor 10,000 square feet, his with seventeen skylights—and has fathered a child.

Nico is a diminutive for Nicholas Pickworth, the youngest son in a family of three boys who attended the distinguished Winchester Public School in England. Nico graduated from Oxford University with a degree in economics and philosophy. He enjoys reading *The Economist*, Maynard Keynes, and the philosopher Berkeley. At Oxford he bought a house in an old working-class district called Jericho, renovated and furnished it with beanbag chairs, cardboard furniture which his father designed, and pictures by contemporary artists borrowed from his brother Toby. He let a room to an American, Miss Lightbody, who became sexually interested in Nico. She was slightly overweight, Nico called her Miss Heavyweather. Near term's end she began to throw orgies and would come downstairs nude with her friends and invite Nico and his friends to join them. Once a friend of Nico's went upstairs, stayed a while, came down fully dressed, and said, "I couldn't really get into it." Nico had an exhibition and sale of his father's cardboard furniture in the Jericho Parish Hall. He served sherry and wine. Nico gets caught up in things he regrets and usually has someone he is meant to marry. He is twenty-five years old, wears scarves, works for the World Bank, lives in Washington, D.C., down the block from Jacqueline Onassis's old house, travels to underdeveloped countries to assess their needs, makes a good salary, has purchased a sports car, flies to New York, saves love letters, dates a twenty-five-year-old lawyer and loves to sail in the Scottish islands. He is close to his parents.

Gilbert Quince is thirty and appears in a movie with Stacy Keach. He has a role as a dope dealer in California, where the movie was filmed. Acting is not his profession. He is working on a book about the effects of television on children, his research involves travel, sitting around pools in Los Angeles meeting with television producers and directors. In Washington, D.C., he met Shirley MacLaine, Warren Beatty, and Julie Christie. He enjoyed talking to Julie Christie, who had rented a house in New Jersey and spent much of her time making Christmas presents for friends. Gilbert writes poetry, reads a great deal, and carries in a briefcase a book, a notebook, and the *New York Post*. Gilbert makes phone calls from public booths near subway stops. He's rarely home and has an answering service. His brother is a psychiatrist married to a psychiatrist, they have two boys and a marriage which has survived much upheaval and a commune. Gilbert attended Yale, and after graduation began working for a community improvement association, primarily in the black Hill Neighborhood of New Haven during the riots. He visited a gifted friend in Long Beach, a junkie writer living in a garage, married Anne, moved to New York City, traveled to ranches in Colorado, California, New Mexico, separated from his wife, entered therapy for a limited period of time, and worked for NET television. One of his shows was about a young model who had come to New York to make it. Gilbert doesn't drink much or take drugs, is always on the move, doesn't bite his nails, his voice is soft, he's a good listener, five feet eight inches tall, of medium compact build, dark curly hair, tan complexion, with brown eyes and a cleft chin. He looks good in suits and recently split up with his girlfriend. He keeps in touch with old friends in all parts of the country and manages to see them once or twice a year. He's always alone. He likes to find out from people how they manage to do what they do.

Cliff Dunn is a quiet artist from Newport Beach, California, who, when asked, answered, "No, I wasn't popular in high school." He works with fiberglass, slats from orange crates, pigments, neckties, drawn upon, cut up, reformed, attached, connected; the result is admired by many artists, among them Rocky Ross, who owns a piece previously displayed in the Whitney Museum Biennial Exhibition of American Art, which occupies two or three floors and shows the work of several hundred artists. Cliff is self-contained. Trying to describe a piece made by another artist, he said, "You know, it was right across from mine at the Whitney." He has a private source of income and doesn't teach, his hair is blond, he is attractive, rarely smiles socially, and stands by walls. He has a few best friends, drives very fast when drunk, and reads Herodotus.

Affair

Alone in my loft tonight, drinking white wine, I transcribed a song by Smokey Robinson and the Miracles. It took an hour and a half of lifting the needle on and off the record, playing and replaying sections of the song.

Oo-ooo-oo-oo-OOO-ooo-ooo-oooooo
Saw you there!
And your laughter seemed to fill the air
Ah-h Baby, a scent like perfume from your lovely hair
A scent that I-I-I do-oo-oo, adore
MMMM-Mark said to me, e-e-e-e-e-ee don't walk o-on-n-n
    into misery
Hey! with your eyes wide open can't you see-ee
A hurt's in store, just li-ike before-or
Oh-Ho oh, But here I go again walking into love,
Here I ago again never thinking of-f-ff
Danger, and my Defense
Disregarding all-l-l of this just for you-oo-ooo
I could know the dangerous si-ide
I won't stop until you're mine
I'm past the point of no retur-urn
Ba-aby
You walk by-y-y, and I said to Me, Myself and I-I-I
Now we've got to give it one more try-y
I know somehow, time is no-ow, right no-ow-ow
Oh-h-h, Here I go again walking into-oo, love
Here I go again walking into love-ove
Here I go
Here I go
Here I go
A-a-again.

Saturday, September 29, I watched the Stones on TV, took the train to Easthampton with Karen Dorcas. Hangover, alternately depressed, exhilarated. Ran, etc., sat in ocean, walked, wanted to move around. Couldn't read, couldn't sleep.

Sunday. Easthampton. My hair is falling out. I am thirty-two years old. I've had a thyroid blood test and one for cholesterol. I've been to Don Lee, a scalp specialist, and had a treatment. He says he can cure it, it's seborrhea. The first treatment, so much hair fell out, then it got a little better on Wednesday, today it was coming out by the handfuls as I washed it with Don Lee shampoo, hairs twisted around my fingers as I combed it coming out in clumps of three and four. It's terrifying me. Now it's beginning to look different, flatter all over my head. I've had a nice time here. I got drunk with Karen on the rooftop looking at the very tops of trees and the sky bent by the corner of the building. Drunk, I smashed my elbow, it's swollen up funny. The opal in my ring is smashed, a chunk fell out. Is this bad luck? Opals are strange stones, I've read, and dangerous, but in what way I can't remember. I hope this won't cause me bad luck, maybe it's just a warning. Dieter telephoned, I said, "Hi, I love your house, why don't you bring Ron Liner up with you?" "Ron Liner!" Dieter said. "Yes, I met him last week at a party, he walked me home, he's cute." Dieter said, "Well, I'll talk to you tomorrow." I handed the phone to Karen and thought about Ron. The circumstances under which we met are as follows: I attended a party for Ed Barr with Ana Martin and Alex. There was champagne and a live band with a saxophone. Ron was standing at the drinks table. I said, "Is your last name Liner?" He said something. I said, "Well, is your last name Liner?" He said, "Yes, what's your last name?" I said, "Elliot, I met you about three years ago with Allan Jerome." He said, "Let's run away together." I said, "No." He said, "Why?" "Because I want to stay at this party a while, then I want to go home and watch *To Catch a Thief*." He said, "Can I go and watch TV with you?" I said, "No." He said, "What are you saving yourself for?" "Nothing, I've just begun to enjoy myself exclusively." "Do you want to fight with me?" I said, "No, do you want to fight with me?" He said, "No." I said, "Good." He smiled. We talked to Dick about his boat, eighteen-inch hull, twelve feet wide, thirty feet long with one mast. That's a weird boat, I thought. I put my arm around Reid and danced with him. I put my arm around Marshall whom I didn't know very well. Ron danced with several women, he had on a black leather jacket, it may have been quilted at the top. I returned periodically to the drinks table, saying things. Ron did some-

thing I didn't like, then he kissed me on the neck, I didn't mind
that. They ran out of liquor. There had been twenty-four
magnums of champagne. Someone was going out for beer. I
said "Hi" to many people, I sat on a stool. Ron came up and
said, "Let's go." I said, "What I'd like to do is go to the French
Bar and get one brandy, a package of cigarettes, then go home.
Would you walk me all the way home? I don't like to walk alone
at night in the dark." He said, "Yes." I said, "You won't stop at
your house and say I'm too drunk to go any farther, leaving me
the choice of coming up to call a taxi or walking home alone?"
He said he wouldn't. Someone gave me a beer. I said, "Ana, I'm
walking home with Ron." She said, "Ohhh." I said, "That's all."
We walked home. We talked, I finished the beer. Ron said
"Why?" a lot. He put his hand on my buttocks. I said, "Don't do
that." He said, "You're supposed to like it." I said, "Well, then
you're doing it wrong."

We got to my house, I started across the street towards the
Spring Street Bar which I call the French Bar. Ron said, "Why
do you call it the French Bar?" "I guess because they serve some
French food." He didn't want to go there, he had to piss. I said,
"You can piss at the bar," he said, "No." I said, "You can piss in
the street," he said, "No." I said, "O.K., you can come up but
I'm going to act as though no one is there but me." We went up
in the elevator. I made tea, he lay on the couch. I knocked my
tea over with my foot. He giggled. I didn't pay any attention
and wiped it into the rug with my hand. I put on Smokey
Robinson's last concert and sang along with the record. I
changed my clothes and stepped in the ashtray, said, "Oh shit,"
and put the butts back in. Ron looked like he was asleep, I
brought a blanket out to put over him. His eyes were open. I
said, "Your eyes are open, I'll use this," and laid the blanket on
the floor. I put on a Beethoven quartet, number 15 in A minor.
"Do you always listen to chamber music before you go to bed?"
"No, sometimes I listen to Erik Satie." I put on Erik Satie. I may
have attempted to do a staggering imitation of Eugenia
Onslow's piece to *Gymnopédies*. We talked about San Francisco.
Ron said something about San Francisco eccentrics. He said,

"Can we sleep together?" I said, "No." Later he said, "Well, maybe I better go home to my own cabaña." I said, "Yes." I didn't move. He said, "Hand me my jacket," I couldn't decide if it was quilted at the top. In the elevator he said, "Call me." "No, I won't do that, you can call me." Neither of us were listed under our own names. He said, "What's your number?" I wanted him to write it down he didn't, he said, "I'll remember." I didn't hear from him during the week. On Friday I told Ana and Karen about Ron. We discussed it. Ana and I agreed that Ron was quite beautiful, Karen didn't.

This is the information I got about Ron:

1. He is very funny.
2. He was with a woman named Jill for a long time.
3. He is quiet.
4. He was recently living with or is living now with someone named Sue, an artist who looks like Jean Shrimpton.
5. He was with Jill a long time; she was funny, talked a lot and was very devoted to him. "Ron was her man and she did everything for him," Karen said.
6. He and Sue, with whom he may be living, have gone on sailing trips.
7. He doesn't hang out much.
8. He doesn't talk.
9. He is stoned a lot.

I began fantasizing about Ron:

1. Sex. Conventional lovemaking in a gentle affectionate and wholly satisfactory manner. The only deviation was, we would screw at his place rather than mine, a thing I don't think ever happens unless I am a guest in a foreign country.
2. Long deadpan conversations in which Ron and I ask each other outrageous questions, prefacing each one with "Jane (or Ron), do you . . ." "Well, Ron (or Jane)" and answer. This takes place on Dieter's East-hampton rooftop at lunchtime. We eat clams. We go for a walk and kiss. We don't make love, there's no privacy.
3. Fantasies in the city: Not as good.

The fantasies are shattered because Dieter didn't ask Ron to come up. Now I'll have to call him, which spoils everything. That and losing my hair. Another hair just blew away over my right shoulder onto the beach. "What's Ron's number, Dieter?" "431 something." Now we're on the roof in late afternoon, drinking margaritas and reading the *New York Times*, which describes the effects of a frontal lobotomy as the blunting of the higher sensibilities such as intelligence, abstract thinking, and the ability to fantasize. Fantasy actualizes desire, the brain can see desire but not admonitions. The current lobotomies involve a surgical technique called orbital undercutting: the surgeon delicately peels off only a thin sheath of the white matter at the base of the frontal lobes without touching the underlying blood vessels. One doctor performs about twenty-five such operations a year. Eighty-five percent of his patients are returned to normal living. He claims his greatest success is with obsessive neurotics such as the handwasher. One patient washed in carbolic acid until the skin came off and gangrene set in. The brain operation removed his obsession.

I learned the following from Dieter:
1. Ron is of Philippine, American Indian, and possibly Spanish extraction.
2. Dieter took a museum curator to visit artists' studios. The first artist they visited opened the door at eleven A.M. and said, "Oh hello hello, I'm drunk, I remember you were coming." Once inside they listened to him talk about his work for forty-five minutes and apologize for being drunk. The second artist they visited was having a fight with his wife. She wouldn't let them in. The last studio they visited was Ron's. He opened the door, wasted, his eyes incredibly bloodshot, said, "Hi man, there is the work," and disappeared. The museum director asked if that was the way he always was.
3. Dieter has a feeling that Ron is no longer living with Sue because he used to write out Ron's check to Sue, now he writes it out to Ron.
4. Ron is always dry in his sense of humor.

5. Karen doesn't think Dieter has Ron's right phone number, Dieter thinks he does.

I don't think Dieter wants to give me Ron's number or is embarrassed by my asking. Read Suzanne Langer, *Symbolic Logic*.

Back in the city I saw: Dr. Orenstein, Dr. Clemans; called Dr. Goldman about tests; went to Reid Gibson's show; called John Frank to change date.

Monday I called Ron. John Frank had given me his number. I had been to Don Lee's for a hair treatment with Caleb. Caleb took my opal ring to be fixed, his gift to me two Christmases ago. I went home and called Ron at five in the afternoon. I said, "Hello, may I speak to Ron Liner," "This is Ron Liner." "This is Jane Elliot." "Jane Elliot?" I said, "Do you remember me?" "The girl at the party?" I said, "Did you get home safely?" "Safely, yes, but I got sick sometime between dark and light." "I'm calling to ask you for a date." "A date?" "Yes, I thought we could go to the movies or out to dinner or for a walk." He said, "Yes, in two hours," took my name and number. He called and came over. After some discussion we went to the movies. He talked about anal suppositories, I ate an apple, it was cold walking home.

October 3rd—my father's birthday I think. I'd have liked Ron to call. I couldn't call him. I called him first, he should call me. I don't want to call. I think I'll read. The hair doctor said I won't go bald. Eight P.M. worked purposelessly. Messed up plate, mistake in first line, smeared it out with thinner, let it stay that way, first time I'd done that. More hairs all around. One on pen. Lots in work area.

Things to remember:
1. Lucy's advice.
2. It's only the second day after I saw him, I don't know him, I'm making this happen, it's confusing, as always.
3. Thirty-two years of living deny that a state of well-being is to be derived through association with another human being.

4. Stop trying to figure out why certain people like me better than I them and vice-versa.

I watched Katherine Hepburn on the Dick Cavett show. Katherine Hepburn put her leg on the table, second-guessed Cavett's questions, and laughed a lot. She finds herself fascinating when stone sober. She said, "You can't have everything, no one can have everything." She learned early that "anyone who thinks they can have everything is stupid. If you choose your work it's full-time, do it or quit it." She has no regrets. She's enjoyed her life, her nature is uncomplicated. Things are frightening but you do them. No one made a pass at her in Hollywood. Now no men in Hollywood are interested in women, if you get her meaning. Cavett asked, "Why is that?" "Overpopulation," she said, "the women get more masculine, the men more feminine." Cavett: "The men blame the women." "Women are blamed for everything, that's what they're trying to change." Concentrate. Total concentration is the key. She thinks Spencer Tracy was a better actor than she but he felt that it wasn't quite the job for a man. She always had money enough to say no. She swims, rides, plays golf, runs, works, washes dishes and cleans sinks like everyone else. She has time to read. "Fame is something behind you."

Karen called to invite me to a goat dinner. I had her read the guest list of one hundred to find out if Ron was on it. Hope I don't have trichomoniasis. Katherine Hepburn spoke of the possibility of improving one's own character, the impossibility of improving another's. I haven't wanted to talk to anyone else since Ron and I fucked. I can't think of a good joke. I feel put down. Maybe a joke about being celibate because of infections. I used that already. Doris, allegedly the best palmist in New York, warned me not to be afraid. "You're afraid of your animal sexual instincts which are unusually powerful." I'd had six stingers and agreed with everything. She thought I was right-handed, I'm left-handed. She said, "You're a twin, you have a double life line." I'm not. What does this mean? Pulling my thumb, forming a right angle with my thumb and my palm, making the lower palm bulge, Ron said the more sensual the bulge of flesh formed by bending the thumb the more sensual the person. "Do you have hair on your big toe?" he asked. "Yes, on my right big toe." He said that indicates sexual prowess. I found some on my left toe too.

The worst time for not getting a phone call is between five and eight. After that it's all right. There are questions I should ask myself:

1. Do I like Ron?
2. What do I know about him that I don't know I know, that makes me like him?
3. What does Ron have in common with other crushes involving a certain degree of rejection?
   a. Handsome, slightly sullen, slightly passive or recalcitrant.
   b. Actively seductive in manner.
   c. Mean or insecure in a deliberate, charming way, closed not open, lets people fall into traps, manipulative.
   d. Verbally sexual, irresponsible.
   e. Funny, intelligent.
   f. Knows more about something than I do and is able to imbue it with a great deal of value.
   g. Uses sex to reassure himself about friendship.

Katherine Hepburn said go for what you want, if they offer less turn it down.

To Tell the Truth with Garry Moore: three women claim they were captured by the Red Chinese. Bad food, dysentery, viruses, captured by junks, no response from American consulate, friend died in captivity. Number three says she was captured by family junk, number two by a fishing junk, number one told her family she was going on trip, ten miles off Hong Kong shore she was captured. Where did she land, what charges were made against her, did she sign confession, was she under duress to sign confession? Number two said there were other women in prison, not as we know prison here, number three saw only cook and interpreters. One, two, or three? Panel of stars must guess real prisoner, $50 to prisoner for each wrong guess. One vote for two, one vote for three, one vote for one. One is a sportswear buyer. Two is a co-producer of Casino

Rouge, a nightclub act. Three spent forty-four weeks in a Chinese prison camp. She wears glasses.

I liked sleeping with Ron but it hurt the third time. Did he know he was hurting me? Yes, because I said I wanted to change position, that it hurt. He didn't. Was he cruel, indifferent, angry, insensitive, helpless, confused? If a man said, "You're hurting me," I wouldn't persist. I probably wouldn't do anything to get in that position in the first place. I was afraid he was going to do something mean.

Monday I called Ron and asked him out. He said yes. I took a Valium. Called Ana to say I had asked Ron for a date, she was amused. Took nap. He called when he said he would. This pleased me. He asked me to meet him downstairs. I usually throw the keys out the window. I went downstairs. Later he said, "Take off your heavy-duty jeans." I said, "These are summer-weight, I haven't been sleeping around." I'm not taking this lightly. He came up, I had coffee he had a brandy. Decided to see *Deliverance* and *McCabe and Mrs. Miller*. Walked to the theater, I suggested a diagonal route, he countered: "Straight with three turns." I said, "I'm putting myself in your hands." I put brandy in a thermos. We went Dutch. We sat in the smoking section. We both wanted our arms on the armrest. We held hands. Hands sweating, chatting, pleasant, mild anxiety when he didn't touch me, tried to suppress it, not interpret it or him. Left movies, bought cigarettes and an apple. Spring Street Bar, saw Sonny, ate. I got five dollars out, Ron got out ten, I looked at Ron, pushed my money across the table, he pushed it back, I pushed it out, he pushed it back. I said, "Really?" "Yes." "Thanks." He said, "Let's try out your box," I call it a cube, where I sleep. "O.K." Went home, he smoked some grass. I drank a shot of brandy, we went to bed.

Make love, screw, coitus, fuck, sleep with, which word? Don't know. He said "Pussy." I hate it. He asked, "What do you call it, then?" "I don't know." "You don't talk about it, then?" He had me confused. I call it my vagina, clitoris, uterus, labia, pubis. He was needling me, I was furious. Leaving the next morning he said, "Take care of your pussy."

I combine pain and pleasure flatly but I can't reconcile them in reality or fantasy. The negative is easier. The positive is fugitive and waning. The positive: examining bodies, jokes, laughing, asking questions getting answers, answering questions, listening to someone else's musical selections, talking about palms, feet, loss of hair, keeping moist, wearing hair back, tones of voice, tension, stopping talking about work, feeling amused.

He said, lying on my back me on my stomach, "Can I piss on you?" "No." "It'll be warm and nice." "If you do, I'll kill you." He said, "O.K." I asked, "Right now?" He said, "You can leave me in this box." "But you'll rot and smell." "You can seal it up like a tomb."

I'm deciding to have an idea. Katherine Hepburn said being an artist is lucky because an artist can use the pain she experiences in life. "That's why their characters are suspect," she added, laughing. She also said don't worry about how things change as one grows older—talking about the new space between her toes—just be thankful they work. Finally called Ron, he was out with someone else. A feeling of slowly coming out at the seams.

I think there is something about life here, there's no backstop, catcher, or shortstop.

Friday, Dr. Waxley called, no trichomoniasis. Decided I wouldn't have it, didn't. Caleb gave me back my opal ring he had fixed, a new stone with more fire. It scared me, I couldn't wear it on the same finger. At Spring Street Bar told Caleb about Ron. I looked up: "Hi, Ron." "Hi." Couldn't concentrate on the rest of the conversation with Caleb. We started to leave, I got cigarettes, Ron came out of the bathroom, "You have a haircut like mine." In the drugstore I thought of different answers to that. One was, "Yes, Ron, I want to be just like you."

I thought I'd call him. I call everyone else and ask them places but they're either people I don't want to go to bed with or they are in love with me. I wish I didn't think I was the only person in the world. The phone rang it was Ron, I was happy. Ron came over, I was high. We watched television, then went to his loft. We looked at his paintings, drank a beer, ate cheese on bread with no mustard, looked at about two hundred drawings and watercolors—he said I could have one—went to bed, he put gray black and white patterned sheets on the bed, drank coffee with milk. Got up with hangover. He put Visine in my eyes. Went out for breakfast. Saturday, the streets were empty, the first restaurant closed, the second closed. He said, "We could get our shoes fixed." There was a place open. I followed with my hangover, we caught a cab, ate at the Pink Teacup, I didn't eat. It was a holiday. We walked back to my loft, had coffee, orange juice, went to bed. Ron left.

He has an arch in his loft which relates to the square. He has walked through the Himalayas, lived in Barcelona, lived in Rome for a year with an actress, tried out for the movies but didn't get a part. "What did you do when you tried out?" "Stood in an office and turned around." He thought Marcello Mastroianni was nice. He's no longer interested in Europe.

Monday I was mad at myself, furious. I had dinner at the Spring Street Bar with Meredith. People joined us I didn't know. Caleb and Ana there, we joined them, arguments. I got too high and came home at eleven-thirty. Called Ron. We had some kind of conversation; I thought, he's not dealing with me any more, I feel bad I hate him. I knew I shouldn't have called. This is true in any situation. Still had the impulse to call back, wouldn't have if I hadn't been high.

The next day Ron called. We decided to go to the movies. Ana, her mother and a friend came over to have a drink and look at my work. Ron didn't call back. Ana said, "I just saw Ron at Fanelli's looking all clean." He called from Fanelli's. I met him there with Meredith and Dick Bitts, who was drinking vodka. Ron had had his hair cut. We went to Luizzi's, everything I ordered they were out of. Meredith left with fruit for her bats, Dick decided to go to 42nd Street movies, Ron and I went to Spring Street, drank cognac at the bar. He said, "You have a Kurt Weill mouth." A German came up to borrow a pen, we talked to him. We went home. Laughing hard in bathtub.

Thursday, went over to Ron's. Took vitamins. Ate caviar

paste. Drank champagne. It was someone named Michael's birthday. Caught cold, went home, they went to Shannon's. Ron came back at midnight, said, "You should have come. We drank brandy and champagne and sang. She has red hair is a real heartbreaker. She is a Pisces too." "Whose hearts has she broken?" I asked. "Michael's and Ramon's, everyone's." Ron said, "Shannon will give Michael everything." "What?" I asked. "Everything." Went to Spring Street had steak for strength. Meredith there. Ron grabbed my hand over the table, "Jane, did you think I went over there just to shoot up?" "No"—it had never occurred to me—"Did you?" "No." Ron said he was deciding whether he liked me or not. "Do you?" He said, "You have a particular objectivity." I laughed all through his comments. I was flattered. We drank Irish coffee, Meredith poured what remained of a double tequila in Ron's Irish coffee, drank that. Meredith was there with table of tall thin people. I told Ron. He said, "You're just like Reid—always talking about tall thin people." "I'm not like Reid." He said, "Yes, same middle-class Southern California background, snobs." Went home, took bath. In bathtub he said, "You have a back like a Navajo woman, strong, you'd make a good mother." Ate at Fanelli's with Ron, he walked me to taxi, said, "She's running away." Got on bus for Provincetown.

Back from Provincetown, I called Ron. He came over, brought tequila, a new record, and his ex-girlfriend's ex-husband. Meredith stopped by. Ron handed me the album. "I'd like you to consider this record a gift, Jane." Ron and I sat on the couch, drank tequila. He said something about his date for the weekend, they were going to Shelter Island. I asked "Who is your date?" "Ana." "Ana who?" "Ana Martin, Otto and I are sharing her." "That's nice." "It's not true," he said. "Oh." "It's an important time for me with Pisces."

In the bathtub in the morning Ron didn't know how long he'd be away, it depended on how he liked his date. I asked "Who is your date?" "I just told Otto he'd better have some dates or I wasn't coming." He said something more about dates.

AFFAIR

I asked "Who?" "You don't know her anyway, what's all this about dates?" I said, "Nothing, you keep bringing it up."

October 24, I had lunch with John Frank, picked up cleaning and clothes. Heisenberg's Uncertainty Principle: looked it up. Ron left last Thursday for Shelter Island. I thought:
1. He's fallen in love on Shelter Island.
2. He's totally indifferent.
3. He is in town and has fallen in love.
4. I hate him for one reason or another and imagine I see him at a party. I'm waiting for a friend from London. It turns out to be Mick Jagger who's very interested in me but I'm not so much in him. He brings at least four bottles of a good champagne.

I called Ron, someone else answered late afternoon yesterday. Today during the sensitive hours of five to eight I painted and was saved from calling Ron by Karen Dorcas calling. Can't nap because my heart beats too fast during fantasies negative and positive. Only allow myself to have negative fantasies, rehearsals. This is ridiculous. If I'm going to use a certain amount of my time this way I might as well get some pleasure from it.

I have talked to six depressed people today:
John
Rose
Harriet
Karen
Reid, well five, and me makes six, Janet seven.
Two nervous people:
Karen
John
Meredith, three.
One normal person:
Ula, maybe Delfine, maybe Marshall, three.
This is interesting; how many people have I talked to today:

Rose:	1 hr. on phone, 10 minutes in person.
Caleb:	10 minutes phone.
John:	1½ hours his place, mine.

Karen:	1 hr. Spring St. and Rose's.
Meredith:	15 minutes gallery.
Ana:	3 minutes gallery.
Christopher:	5 minutes phone.
Felice:	10 minutes my place, phone.
3 people in store:	10 minutes.
Dick Bitts:	4 minutes his place.
Ula:	5 minutes at Fay's.
Reid:	1½ hours his place.
Elias:	10 minutes phone
Faith:	3 minutes phone.
Delfine:	40 minutes phone.
Marshall:	30 minutes phone.

18 people total.

Seven hours and twenty minutes were spent in social intercourse. I got up at eight A.M. and I'm awake at eleven-thirty P.M. Seven hours and twenty minutes out of fifteen and a half hours, roughly half of my conscious time. This does and doesn't surprise me. A very interesting program is on television. David Frost and the MacWhirter brothers, twins, who wrote the *Guinness Book of World Records* and the *Dunlop Book of Facts*. Frost has some of the record-holders on. 2,078 centimeters or eight feet two inches is the height of the world's tallest man. I'd be depressed but he's cheerful. I'd probably act cheerful on television too. His philosophy is when in Rome, people are getting taller I'll wait until you catch up with me. Driving is difficult, he sits in the back seat to drive, there are special adjustments to the car. I'll probably have two more fifteen-minute conversations. The tallest man in the world is American. A woman screamed as he walked down a hotel corridor his head visible through the transom of her room. He isn't married but he's looking. He has gray hair and glasses. His suit doesn't fit it's gray. He's singing the song with the world's longest title, by Hoagy Carmichael. The two heaviest twins weighed thirty-five pounds between them at birth. One woman in Brazil has borne thirty-two children. Her eldest is thirty-seven, her youngest, four. She was married at fourteen, raising thirty-two children was tiring but now there isn't as much work, they all help at family gatherings. The husband is ready and willing to have another child. She is not. He was married once, within the marriage he has fathered thirty-two children, has had relations with four women outside marriage, fathering ninety-two children, a total of one hundred and twenty-five children.

An American man has been married nineteen times. His first was at nineteen years of age, he was madly in love, he is sixty-five now. He hopes to get married again. He doesn't look for anything it just comes, happens. Every marriage has left its mark on his home and mind. He never has to smoke, take a pill, or drink, he just closes his eyes and reminisces. His shortest marriage was thirty days. She is in the audience, he married her a second time which lasted three and a half years. They are in business together. If he behaves she will marry him at eighty. He has thirty-three children. One from the fourteenth marriage is in the audience. Highest priced escapade $300,000, has spent a million, what's money for but to enjoy. Another wife in audience too. All his wives similar, there are seven basic colors and you can only have twelve different idiosyncrasies then you repeat. Love at first sight or two it's just like making jello, you may put in too much water once, the next time you don't put in so much.

I have told:
  Delfine
  Karen
  Ken
  Ana
  Lina
  Primo
  Marshall
  John
  Meredith
  Caleb
  Janet
  Mom
  Sonny

Christopher
Felice
Dick
Lucy
Gavin
Harry
Gloria
Rose

that I might be in love and not to tell anyone. Twenty-one
people, over a period of four weeks, about four per week. Four
more:

Rebecca
Reid
Ellison
Ellison's friend

I haven't told Ron. I tried to call Rose, but I don't know what to
say about the Ron situation. The world's record knitter uses
7,000 ounces of wool in a year, sheared from fifty-seven sheep.
Called Ron and Ted last night, didn't get them, thank God. Had
conversation with Rose about Heisenberg's Uncertainty Principle and two ways of looking at things: *in vitro*, under glass,
microscope; *in vivo*, in life, regular size. Does the instrument of
vision seriously alter the thing seen? If you look at something *in
vivo* you can't isolate it. No absolute. Everything can be split,
you can't get to the absolute particle in looking at nature.
Layers. A man speaking the fastest in a foreign language, a new
record. These red shoes I just bought are the first new shoes
I've really liked even though they're too small. *Tales of Hoffman*,
"The Red Shoes," she dies, feet in rags, dancing, can't stop.

Harry Walter arrived Thursday morning. Started Diol, pills.
I hadn't seen Ron since he left for Shelter Island. I called. He
got back on Monday. I told him about my red shoes, the choice
I had, too large or too small, the twenty-four-hour urine test I
discarded, my art depression, my health which was good, my
new record Johnny Hartman and John Coltrane. "When can I
come over to hear it?" "Now," I said. "Good timing." Ron told
me about driving around in Otto's boat drinking brandy, doing
water colors, catching porgies and singing "I loves you Porgy"

to the fish on his plate at dinner. I asked, "Do you want to go to a concert at Ana's?" "Yes." The lady came over and told us not to smoke. I put my cigarette out, Ron continued smoking. Ron mentioned his date frequently. "I made my date laugh through a whole concert on Shelter Island." On Fire Island they looked at a mural, the dates walked through the door in the mural. I got mad, snarled, "If you have something to tell me about your date wait until after the concert, don't spoil the concert for me." He made a face, stuck out his tongue, I did the same. A woman played a Bach chaconne. We were invited to go to Max's, I didn't want to. "You go if you want I don't feel like a crowd." We didn't go. Walking past the bodega I yelled and gestured, "Do you have something you want to tell me about your date, just tell me don't tease, be direct." He had nothing to tell me. We went to eat. He said, "How do you feel?" "About three-quarters worse than I did before the concert." He said, "Everything works out." He was attentive, solicitous about my welfare and state of mind at the Japanese restaurant. We went to Spring Street, sat at a table, had brandy, I explained why I was mad: contradictory messages. "Look, I have never made the assumption you've fallen in love with me, that you are faithful. I have, on the contrary, always assumed that you see a lot of women. So all your allusions to dates are irritating and stupid. If you've fallen in love, or have something to tell me about, something you think might affect me, say it directly." He understood what I meant. I felt happy again. At my loft we listened to Johnny Hartman, smoked some grass. Ron said he'd like to see me get really stoned. "What if I have an anxiety attack?" He'd put his arms around me. I got stoned.

Monday, October 29, I arranged complete Jane Austen and incomplete Simone de Beauvoir at the foot of my bed in two piles. No one travels more than sixty miles in a Jane Austen novel, they are constantly on the move in Simone de Beauvoir. Ate well, bought a bottle of Rémy for $13.50. I am giving up on Ron. Sat in studio on secretarial swivel chair. Depressed enough to work, mooning around playing moody records. I thought: I will say to Harry when he comes in, "Harry, I'm so miserable."

Had to stop and think if I said the same to him in London
moaning about Gavin Frazer while I was staying with Felix.
Felix was throwing trash cans and yelling in windows at me. I
distinctly remembered telling Felix I was miserable. This is a
pattern: having drinks with people who are in love with me
during the unrequited periods of my loves. Evidence of my bad
character and selfishness. On the phone I told Rose how Ron
and I were sitting in the dark at my loft. I was stoned. We
listened to a song, "Under My Thumb." We danced. Ron said I
was really perverse. I told him I was not. Rose agreed on the
phone that I was perverse. I said perverse is moving away from
the truth. She read me the definition:

perverse-fr. *pervertere* to turn the wrong way, destroy,
corrupt, pervert. 1 a : turned away from what is right
or good : CORRUPT, WICKED (the only righteous in a
world perverse—John Milton) b: Contrary to accepted
standards or practice : INCORRECT, IMPROPER (Or a
verdict : contrary to the evidence or the direction of
the judge on a point of law) 2 a : Stubborn, obstinate,
and persistent by temperament and disposition in
opposing what is right, reasonable, and correct or
accepted : WRONGHEADED (a dual nature, one half
positive, and passionate to. . . .

I had to get off the phone. It sounded like Harry had just
vomited in the back of the loft, I hope not on my painting. Yes,
I think he did, I can hear wiping up sounds. No, he might be
looking at books. I'm sick of my waspy girlfriends, Ron Liner
said.

Later that week I gave a dinner party at my loft for the
visiting Italians. I had called Ron in the morning to ask him to
the movies: he didn't know; Dieter walked into his loft as the
phone was ringing, I talked to Dieter. Ron called back, we
arranged to go to *Day for Night*. I said, "The movie's at three,
come by at two, I'll leave the elevator open." Time passed, I
wasn't dressed, the phone rang, Ron asked, "What happened?"
He had tried to get up in the elevator, couldn't, my landlord
thought he was a break-in junkie. I hadn't turned the elevator
on, I thought it was one. Ron said, "No, it's two, meet me at the

subway." At two we arrived uptown; I was right, it was one before. Ron forgot to set his clock back: "I haven't been home nights." We had a brandy at an Irish bar, killing time until three, the waiters had brogues. At the theater the man said, "This movie doesn't start at three today, only on weekends, it starts at four." I'd gotten the time from the Sunday paper. Ron and I went to La Crêpe, the waitress spoke French. Ron said, "I'm not staying at my loft at night." We went to the movies: our shoulders didn't touch, we didn't hold hands, we didn't talk. The movie was about making a movie. Jacqueline Bisset played a beautiful actress, her husband is a psychiatrist who gives her pills, talks to her in corners and pats her shoulder. He is older, has bright blue eyes, white hair and wrinkled tan skin, the whole cast likes him. She is kind. Jean-Pierre Léaud is a baby. The director uses the lives of the actors in the movie he's making in the movie. Driving downtown in the taxi I knew everything that would happen and started to cry. It was raining. Ron came up for a brandy, eight people were coming for dinner. We sat on the sofa. "Are you having a romance?" "Yes." I cried while talking about the music playing, answering questions Harry asked from the kitchen, throwing down the keys to Jeremy, complaining about the stains his blueberry pies made on my cutting board, laughing, water came out of my eyes. I don't remember the conversation. I said to Ron, "I feel bad," he replied, "Nothing's final." Something crashed in the kitchen, Harry dropped some beers, they cleaned it up. Ron left. I went to the back of the loft with the bottle of Rémy, cried harder, my body shaking, making inarticulate vocal sounds. I gasped, my face and clothes were wet. I told Jeremy I couldn't stay for my party. John and Fay said I could stay at their place; I packed and left, still crying. Ate dinner there crying, drank Rémy, felt good. I went back to my loft with John and Fay, my face red and puffy. Drunk. I danced with Dan Polakoff, he kicked over some thinner on my work. Jeremy, appalled by my behavior, wrote to a friend, "Jane is still finding new ways to torture her friends." Delfine had a black eye from a fight: in anger, Dan had kicked a box which flew up and hit her in the eye. She didn't know why no one noticed it. The Italians sat in the corner, drank mineral water, and smiled. I changed my clothes and went to bed. I remember Liner said, "Don't be sad." I said, "You have to allow for other people's feelings." He said, "Here's to feelings, keep vulnerable," and clinked my glass.

The next day was Halloween. Liner called. We had dinner at Spring Street with Meredith. Meredith ordered many different things, eating only a little of each. We drank brandy. I disagreed with Ron and Meredith about women. Ron said, "The worst thing is hitting a woman." This made me furious, "You shouldn't hit anyone." I don't think they understood. Meredith and I talked the most. She said she thinks men are great; I don't, necessarily. Ron told Meredith she was snarling, that her lips were drawn back from her teeth. I said, "She isn't, she's just talking about something." He said, "We love you, Meredith." According to Ron, people need to be told they are loved, frequently, and touched every day. I didn't know what was going on. Ron said, "We're just getting to know each other." He made a phone call, returned, and announced, "I have an infection on my dick, I have to go see someone about it." I left the table to pay, Ron disappeared. Meredith and I couldn't find him, went to my house, drank wine and talked. I tried to call Liner to see if he was all right, I was furious, but his leaving with his infected dick, disappearing, made me want to apologize for something.

I called Ron Friday to see what had happened to him. He offered to fix me lunch. I had a hangover. We ate tinned salmon and looked at pictures from his sailing trip to Haiti. I left after twenty minutes to meet Rose. Didn't tell him I was mad because he told me Meredith and I were competing the whole evening. He made a good case but it's wrong, even if right, because he wanted it to be true.

Someone has to cooperate with me. Not give me their love or answer my demands or refuse me. Surely a triangle has the possibility of more than two dimensions, it doesn't, four points needed, then pyramid. My sphincter muscle contracts at odd times, the middle of a sentence, from couch to toilet in the

middle of a cough. Saturday, Ron said, "Jane, let's get married."
"Yes Ron, what are you doing this weekend?" He replied, "I
want to get married on a Monday in August." "I want to get
married in March." He asked, "Are you divorced?" "Yes."
"O.K., if you're divorced, then a year from tomorrow." This
was Ron's style. I am a literalist, he is not. Someone told John
Cage if you're lost in the woods stay in the same place, you'll
become a magnet drawing the people searching for you to you.
Casual remarks uttered casually rivet me. Cage asked himself
about a great artist: does he live in the confusion and terror we
do? Cage never mentions terror and confusion. A friend told
him, if you find one morel in spring, call me, I'll drop
everything and come and cook it for you. Cage found two
morels in spring, called the friend, who said, "Do you think I'd
come all that way for two mushrooms?" Too neat.

On Tuesday, November 6, Ron made lentil soup at my house.
We talked, took a nap. He had trichomoniasis, was taking pills.
Came with me to deliver painting. We decided to go to the
movies, had cokes at the Americana Hotel. He told me stories
about his date: they went to Woodstock, they ran out of gas on
the freeway, there were two levers attached to the reserve tank,
he was pulling the wrong one, left his date on the freeway,
walked for gas though he had a full reserve tank. He laughed, I
smiled. He talked at length about a party he invited me to, for
Betsey Johnson, on Wednesday. All different kinds of people
would be there. I accepted happily. Before the movie he asked
if I thought we were compatible, I answered, "Yes, but those
things take a long time." I asked him the same question. He
said, "Yes." The movie was *The Long Goodbye*. We got out of the
taxi, he walked home.

I got dressed up to go to the party. Ron didn't come.
Meredith called, said she was going to same party. I said, "Call
me if Liner's there or tell him to call." She didn't call back. I lay
on the sofa dressed up, leaden, depressed, looked at the ceiling,
and thought, "This is the first time I've really been relaxed in a
long time." Changed to studio clothes and painted.

Called Liner the next day. He said, "I should have called

you." "Yes." He said, "I apologize, it was really awful of me." I can't stay mad, and told him that, and that I wished I'd talked to him when I was furious.

Friday, November 16, I taught Karen's class at Hunter College. Started period. I called Liner, wrong number, didn't call back. Mother called, she has arthritis. One operation is possible, if it doesn't work she would to have her leg amputated. She's not going to try. Read *Emma*, drank champagne.

Monday, Liner called. I went over, took Matisse catalogue and Bach Cello Suites for comparison with his. Reid Gibson was there. He held up the catalogue, comparing it to Ron's painting. I lay on bed. We compared the Bach Cello Suites, Ron's by Starker, mine by Casals. Ron said, "What's different?" "Yours are thicker." Reid looked at Ron's painting, brought the tips of his fingers together, released them, and said of the painting, "It's like perfume." They both smiled. I continued reading a book written by someone who had disappeared in the Caribbean. Ron said he's never seen Reid act like that. "How?" I asked. "How he acted," Ron answered, "people act funny around you." We took Reid's truck, bought beer, drove to Brooklyn to buy olives, cheese, caviar paste, spinach pie, and sweet pie. I dislocated both thumbs opening or closing the truck door. The button was stiff. We ate at Ron's loft I asked if his girlfriend was Shannon Garcia. "Yes." I was hurt, but proud of my ability to identify her by clues in conversations, directions in which Ron walked, intelligence gathered from friends. Ron said there really had been nothing between us, why was I upset? I said my experience was different than his, that I'd like things to be opposite; him breaking into Shannon's day for lunch and coming to me at night. I felt increasingly depressed, said, "I'd like to go home." He said, "Let's exchange Bach Suites for a while." He's always with people, I'm not. In the truck he said, "I can call you, you can call me." "O.K." I got out. I asked, "What's Shannon like?" "A beautiful sensual woman who loves music." Ron lisps, hitting his tongue against the back of his front teeth, he thinks it's sensual. "Shannon is not like a new lover, she's more like an old friend. Everything was more complicated than you thought. Not just you and Shannon, but lots of people." Sunday, November 25, I went to lunch with Nico. Sat on sofa, drank wine. Ron called from a bar and asked to come over. "Yes, in about half an hour." Nico left, Ron arrived. "You have arms like a swimmer," he said. "Why did you like that movie?" "What movie?" I asked. *The Way We Were.* I said, "I told you you'd hate it, why did you go?" "To see what it was like," he answered, "they should have stayed with their own types." "That's what they did at the end and that's as boring as the other way around, maybe more so." Something was wrong, I asked what. Ron wouldn't confess. He was acting strange. I felt strange, "Does it affect me in any way?" "I'll have more time for you now but I don't want to live with you," he answered. I yelled, "That's not what I want anyway." I was nervous, we talked about Ron's chances for a dancing career, I told him he can't deal with strong women. He asked, "What am I doing here?" "Just touching base to tell yourself you can." He left. I changed clothes and looked down at my opal ring: the new stone had split in half.

Monday, December 3, called Liner, light conversation, etc. . . . asked if he was high the last time I saw him? No. He was depressed about his status with his girlfriend, and didn't want to lay it on me. I asked, "Is it cleared up?" "Yes." Ron asked had I fallen in love with anyone? "No." Mom called, told me her bones are aged, doctors at St. Mary's Hospital said so. She told me my first art teacher died on my birthday last year. Had dinner with Caleb and fought.

Pearl Harbor Day, Liner called. "Have you ever stuck to something for a long time?" Surprised, I said, "The painting I'm working on now." We went to Spring Street, sat at bar. "Brandies are good for upset stomach," Ron said. I had one, he was right, it went away. John walked in and said, "You have the same haircuts." Ron looked at me, "I told you." John had been a hairdresser in Chicago. Ron talked to someone who lives in his building. At my house I said, "I'm hungry, do you want to get something to eat?" He said, "I'm sort of expected for dinner, it's my modern relationship, we love each other but don't live together." "You mean you eat dinner there and spend the night? That doesn't sound so modern to me." I went on: "O.K., I'm getting dressed and going to eat. Do what you want." "What are you doing after dinner?" "Going to a concert." He said, "I don't have money for dinner." "I have some if you don't eat much." He said, "I'll come." We ate. At the concert, in the first dance the woman wore a white leotard and black satin pants, did something with one of the structural columns of the gallery. She wore mud for the second dance and lay on the floor: it was improvisational. There was a drumming piece. We laughed a lot. He said, "Maybe I made the wrong choice."

Tuesday I twisted my ankle doing ballet while drinking tequila. Liner called, came over, examined my foot, bought an Ace bandage and wrapped my ankle. He told me a story about being drunk, falling, then running on a badly sprained ankle. He woke up to leave for the sailing trip in Haiti. Because of his black cane, they were suspicious of him at the airport. He doesn't know where the cane is now. Ron left after we each took Darvons with milk. "Always take pills with milk," Ron says.

Next day, Liner called. "Hi Janey." "Hi Ronny." "You hypnotize people into calling you." "How?" I asked. "By being charming." He's calling just to keep in touch, that's what he's going to do. "Will you be around later?" "Yes," I answered. "Maybe I'll come over for a beer later in the afternoon." I said to Delfine, "If Ron says he'll do anything in advance he won't." Ron called back and said he'd gotten settled into his place, didn't want to go out. "O.K., see you later."

The Friday Ana's Christmas show went up, Ron came by for breakfast. He made good eggs, toast cut in triangles, and said, "Doesn't that make you feel better?" "Yes." The eggs and toast were neat on the plate. Ron had a Darvon with milk. He said, "You should have a steady boyfriend."

Ron came over at lunchtime Monday. We talked about work. I thought I was being mean. Meredith continued working, and said, "Your conversation isn't going anywhere. Stop it." I asked Ron to make some soup. "O.K., I'll do it for you." I hesitated, then said, "O.K." I asked him if he liked my hair pushed back from my face, he replied, "You have a good face, I just don't know about the rest of you." He went shopping, bought wine and Armagnac. Meredith and I started drinking while I painted. Ron said he'd go to his loft and come back later.

By six or seven Meredith and I were very drunk. She told me to call Liner, I didn't think it was such a good idea, I was too drunk. She told me it wasn't nice of me to paint while Liner was cooking. I called, he said, "There's people here, a friend from California." I asked if I could come over, saying I was drunk and might just go to sleep on his bed. "Someone's already sleeping here tonight," he said. "I don't mean overnight, just while I'm there. Shall I bring a bottle of Armagnac?" "Sure." I put on a fox jacket over summer pants and halter, sandals over Ace bandage and bare feet, and took a cane. The ground was covered with thick snow, the bare spots with ice. I took Meredith's arm so I wouldn't fall. We parted at Broome and Crosby, she said, "We'll pick you up, just call." I walked upstairs, in the door. Ron said, "Clive Arts, Jane; Jane, Shannon." I was shocked. I tried to be nice in the way I am when I'm drunk. I interrogated Clive about the derivation of his last name; what he was doing in New York, etc. He mumbled. I asked Shannon what she did. She was thinking of going into fabric design. It's a rough field. She went to school in Minnesota, one of her teachers was Jeremy Gideon. I said, "He's a friend of mine." Everything was hazy. I said, "My first date with an artist was with your ex-husband when I was in college." King Pleasure came on the radio. I ordered, "Turn it up." It was "I'm in the Mood for Love." Shannon said, "King Pleasure." I said, "Yes."

I kept trying to get Caleb and Meredith to pick me up, they said "Yes," but didn't come. I felt more and more foolish, scared to walk home alone this drunk on ice, with a hurt foot. I went in the other room to look at Ron's painting. He came in. "Why did you let me come over? I think it's mean," I yelled at him. He tried to give me the drawing he said I could have before. "I won't take art under these circumstances, you're just trying to placate me." Ron went upstairs with Clive to look at Reid's drawings. I was left with Shannon; she decided to go upstairs. I left, then came back to get my Armagnac. I poured everyone's glass back in the bottle. I fell down, ended up sitting on the stairs. Shannon asked, "Are you alright?" "Yes, thanks." Shannon extended her arms perpendicular to the sides of her body, shook her shoulders, snapped her fingers to the music, and smiled at Ron across the table. I left, walking in the snow in blue pants, orange jacket, sandals and bare feet. The streets were deserted, snow white, buildings black. I looked up, didn't recognize the buildings, I was not on my street, lost, my feet were frozen, parts hurt, parts numb, frightened of frostbite, kept walking. Saw Fanelli's sign on Mercer. It was open, walked in, asked if I could warm my feet, I knew they thought I was crazy and drunk. They gave me coffee, I drank it alone at a table. "How much do I owe you?" "Nothing." I got home.

Woke up humiliated. Ron called to see how I felt, said he was worried that I'd be embarrassed. I was, I said so, apologized. He said, "Everyone thought you were pretty weird." "I imagine so, I was very drunk and upset." "Don't feel bad, Shannon thought you were really strange because of the things you did." "Oh no," I answered, "I don't want to know what I did. What did I do?" He told me about the Armagnac. I remembered that. "I was angry." "You yelled at me and wouldn't take my drawing." I explained why. He said he was just trying to make things smooth. "I'm sorry I spoiled your evening, I'm embarrassed, I apologize." He said, "Don't apologize, they're very nice people, you'd like them." "I didn't like them." He said, "I didn't realize you were so limited in terms of people."

Gilbert Quince came over, Ron came over. We ate onion soup and watched television. Liner was furious at me, wouldn't admit it, Gilbert Quince was mad, because of the way I act around Liner: subservient. Gilbert said, "I've never seen you act that way." Liner said again, "I really didn't realize you were so limited about people." I apologized. He said, "You don't need to apologize," I answered, "We all have our limits, there will be people I like and you don't, that you like and I don't." He pointed to Gilbert, "Yes, I don't think I like him." "I don't think he cares what you think, Ron." Ron poured a drink, "If you hadn't acted so badly it could have turned into a nice orgy." "I wouldn't have liked that." "Yes you would, you don't know," then, "I guess everyone acts silly sometimes." "Yes," I answered. He and Gilbert left together.

The next day Liner again came over, took a blue Valium, saying it put him in a different space. He got up to leave, I didn't walk him to the door. He said, "I'll have Cliff Dunn call you about the loft." I said, "Don't bother, just have him get in touch with my landlord." He said, "You should meet him." "Why?" "Because he's much smarter than the people you talk to." I got up from the sofa fast. "At least my friends don't do this," I yelled, wiggling my arms stretched out from my sides, snapping my fingers. Ron stared at me, he didn't know what I was doing, because I couldn't do it right. I did it again, repeating, "At least my friends don't do this. I haven't seen that since the seventh grade." He said something. I yelled, "Get out of my loft!" He said something I couldn't hear because I was yelling, "Just get out!"

Death

I called California. Jenny answered. "Dad got drunk and didn't go to his doctor's appointment, he had more pains. He wants to stay in Long Beach for the open heart surgery, he hasn't stopped drinking or smoking. He's still driving to work in San Diego. All the doctors at the golf club are really concerned about him. He wants his friends and family around. Last time, in Texas, it was so cold and impersonal. You come back when things are settled like the date of the operation. I'll call you, then you come back." I prepared to leave New York on Tuesday for Dad's operation.

My first day home, I got up at nine A.M. and ate cantaloupe. Fought with Mom. Didn't want to, but did. Making coffee, we argued over the grounds in the pot. "It looks so disgusting, Jane." "But it tastes so good." Paid bills, worked, but work seemed dull. Time dislocation, difficult to do things consecutively. Finished work, didn't have sit-down chili lunch, crammed cheese and bread into my mouth, standing over the sink. Went upstairs to argue with Mom. Pubic hair was sticking out of my bathing suit. "Tuck yourself in, Jane, cut those off!" I had thought about doing it, didn't, wouldn't tell Mom. Went to the beach, read Simone de Beauvoir's *Woman Destroyed*, which drew me into some sort of hopelessness. Tried to focus on beach and sand. Forced myself to go in swimming. The water was nice. I stood on hard, fine sand, water buoyant, tossed myself around. It was completely familiar and made me cry. Dad came home, bantered, he looked good. Mom and Dad got high. I went with Jenny and her boyfriend Ivo to see Karen Dorcas' movie. I had huge fame desire, envied Karen, was also bored. Someone thought I was Karen's sister. No one knows who I am.

Next morning, I got up late after Cold Duck with Karen and called Rose, who reassured me about my work. She sympathized with envy feelings, desire for fame. Worked. Sorted drawings, depressed, nothing there. Jack came over, nothing there. Went to Glider Inn with Mom, Dad, Jenny, and Ivo. Dad flirted with the young waitresses. Fight between Mom and Dad. I asked Mom to take yoga lessons with me, she refused nastily because she was mad at Dad for kicking her under the table.

Ivo had said, "Sex is through at 55." Mom answered, "So what else is new?" Dad kicked her hard under the table. It hurt. He yelled, "You're so insulting." I turned to Mom, "Do you know what you said?" "Yes, I know what I said," her face squeezed up like a rubber ball. I asked again, "Do you realize what you said?" "Yes, 'So what else is new?'" I snapped, "Then you know why you were kicked." In the end she didn't know why she was kicked.

On Sunday Mom asked, "Did you hear the earthquake, did you feel it, you didn't, I did, just sitting at my desk, didn't you feel it, didn't you hear it, 7.4 on the Richter Scale?" I revisited the Bay Side. Thirteen years ago was still going on. Tan bodies, eighteen-year-old brown-haired teenagers lying sprawled, reading or talking to friends, on the beach. I walked along the water, looked at the lifeguard, I was either invisible or noticed, couldn't tell which. I was amazed by the number of perfect bodies with long shiny hair, groupings of two, five, six, many small children. A blond swimming teacher talked about the five-hundred butterfly. The beach was zoned by age: Laguna to 57th Place, women and small children; 58th Place to 60th, teenagers, large groups of girls, some looked like stunted adults; 60th to 61st Place, some new houses, mixed ages 30 to 50, both sexes, hipper, probably from 62nd Place apartments. I was moved by the dark smooth water in shadow underneath the small marina, old pilings, mussel clusters. The Seaside Inn had been repainted; Scotty died an alcoholic, Merle still ran it. The buildings most recently painted are olive green. They used to be pale blue, pink, mint green, aqua, and desert pink with white trim. 62nd Place, Marge Hubbel Realty painted olive green was still in business. Her daughter committed suicide in 1959. She shot herself through the head with a revolver at Stanford, her grades were low. I heard about it in the shower on a sunny day, or I heard about it and took a shower crying. When my grandfather died I cleaned my white buck shoes on the back porch and cried. My mother cries each time she sees the spinnaker Judith painted, sailing on Wet Wednesdays or Thirsty Thursdays. Judith was a recent suicide, pills and drink.

She was an artist. I didn't ask about it, though I thought her husband was unfaithful. They found my first art teacher this year dead, killed by smoke, huddled at the foot of the stairs in her burning house. She probably dropped the cigarette she was smoking in bed late at night, drunk. Lenore Sherwood said she was ill, had to enter a home and couldn't paint any longer. Her hair was dirty, Lenore put it up in the familiar knot, and stuck the two tortoiseshell chopsticks in it. It was dirty but Lenore didn't feel up to washing it. Wondered how old I looked to people as I walked by. Shadows fell across the sand from a tree. Reassurance from the Alamitos Bay market. Prices had gone up. I charged notebooks, mushrooms, cherry tomatoes (coat with oil, salt, pepper, bake at 350° for ten minutes), ½ gallon Gallo Hearty Burgundy, two black Bic pens medium point, and peaches with bruises.

Mom brought up Betty Fraser and Mrs. Monroe. Betty liked my hair, remembered I was always trying to push it in directions it wouldn't go. I said I never mastered the California look. We reminisced about John Tate. Betty said, "What a crush you had on him, you were dying from it." "Yes."

The sun reflected off the slow-moving surface of my Bloody Mary. I could hear tinkling ice cubes on the stairway. I looked at my legs, a scratch was bleeding. The cat did it, I hadn't noticed. During Mom's stroke Jenny brought her a book of Charlie Brown cartoons. She lay on her bed in the hospital leafing through it, staring at the oil wells pumping. The days were all gray. She didn't know if she was afoot or on horseback. The nurses taking her down for a brain test treated her like a slab of nothing. I petted the cat in the broad five o'clock sunlight. She groaned, squeaked, hairs drifted up, hairs drifted up caught and shining in the late afternoon sun.

Today I ate: provolone cheese, nectarine, glass milk, glass milk, swig apple juice, coffee with milk, mushrooms on toast, glass milk, peppers, cheese, ½ peach, chile relleno, taco, guacamole chips, and coffee.

For dinner we went to Bacas, a Mexican restaurant where the old Corsican Room used to be. None of us had eaten there. The menu was limited, the dishes reasonably priced. Mom wore a white pantsuit and looked handsome, white hair at her temples, brown skin, she limped, her knee large and stiff with arthritis. She thinks about acupuncture. Jenny wore pale pink pants, pink halter, and a short sleeve pink and white cardigan. Ivo was sunburned. Jenny drove. I thought, we all have on pants. A man in a short red jacket wanted to park the car. We got out, sat down. A mariachi band was playing. Mom said, "It's nice to be close to home." Jenny wanted to go to Don José's. I didn't care, I wanted to eat. All day I lay on the bed hungover and jealous of rock stars, reading about them in *Rolling Stone*. Darkwood booths, menus. Mom ordered a martini, drank it down fast. She had forgotten her glasses, so I read the menu to her, she drank and didn't listen to me. "If you ask me to read to you, at least you can do me the courtesy of listening," I said after she had pointed to the largest bloc of writing and said, "No way, that's too large." I said, "Yes, we've already discussed it." She said, "We'll have more than we can eat, we always do at Mexican restaurants, don't we, Ivo, you'll have more than you can eat, just wait and see." "I only ordered a taco and a chile relleno," I said. "Well, wait and see, they put all those goodies, beans and Spanish rice, on the plate." Jenny and I were taut and anxious at table's edge, waiting for the guacamole. Salad with roquefort arrived at Jenny's place. I watched nervously, Mom got another drink. Ivo was pleasant. I suggested to Jenny that we put the salad in the middle of the table and eat it simultaneously. I speared a large piece of lettuce, too much dressing, Jenny's fork came down and ripped the piece in half. "Jesus, Jenny." She giggled. Ivo said, "Jenny, help me with mine." The guacamole arrived. We began to eat mechanically, perfectly paced. Tortilla chips were too greasy, too cold. Mom said "I love Mexican music." Mariachis came around. Ivo said, "'*Mujer*' for her," pointing to Mom, "'*Cielito Lindo*' for her," pointing to Jenny. Jenny and I sat hunched over, embarrassed and awkward. I looked at Mom, she was grinning beatifically, bobbing her head at the singers. She turned to my blank face, her eyes looked oiled, dark brown, her lips flattened against her teeth, her eyes

filled with tears. "I don't care," she hissed, "you can go to . . ."
Her voice broke. She turned to Jenny and Ivo. "I love it, I love
the music, and Mexico." The song continued. I continued
eating a disgusting greasy chile relleno like a sponge oozing
watery oil, thinking how graceless Jenny and I were. I attempted looking at the musicians, turned again to Mom with a
try at a pleasant expression. Her face tightened up, her eyes
filled again. "I don't care." Her voice broke, she turned away. "I
love it," beaming defiantly, "I love the music, I love Mexico."
"*Mujer*" ended, "*Cielito Lindo*" began. Jenny moved closer to her
plate. The word "*morena*" was sung. I was laughing silently, out
of control, remembering Jenny asking a small boy in Baja
California where the beach was, using the word "*morena*" for
beach. The boy stared, turned and ran in terror. *Morena* means
brunette in Spanish. My mother bobbed, lifted her hands
beside her head in a gesture of abandon, and quickly dropped
them, saying "I love it." The musicians left. Mom snapped to
Jenny, "I don't care I love it." I said, "Mom, I didn't say
anything." She said to Jenny, "She," indicating me, "sits there
like a huge phony sophisticated I-don't-know-what." Everyone
broke in. Mom said, "I don't care, my food was delicious and I
like the music, don't you agree, Ivo?" Jenny and I were stuffed
into silence. We had finished the twelve-inch platter of tortilla
chips. I asked, "Did you tip the musicians, Ivo?" "Yes." "How
much?" "One dollar." "Oh." "The other table didn't tip at all,"
he said. I noticed the musicians, two booths down, had begun to
tap their feet and smile. They hated our table. We drank coffee.
I got up first to leave. The man in the red jacket couldn't start
the car. Jenny hit the steering wheel in front of our house. She
said, "I hate Mom." I asked, "Mom, are you sure you don't want
to go to the movies with us?" "Well, I will go, why should I sit
around here alone?"

The movies are *Child's Play*: possession, suicide, presence of
Satan; and *A Separate Peace*: adolescent envies, competition,
love, and death on the operating table. In *Child's Play*, James
Mason is a severe, aging Latin teacher with a dying mother. He
makes crazed, incoherent accusations against Robert Preston, a

colleague. Preston is an English teacher loved by the students, whom he calls "my boys." The school is Catholic. There is a new gym teacher, a former student of Preston's. James Mason's mother receives lewd phone calls during the day, accusing Mason of perverted behavior. Mason gets pornographic magazines in his letterbox at school as if he had a subscription. His gums look infected, his flesh green and unhealthy, his jowls sag. Preston is fit, with a mustache and hearty red face, he stands up straight, Mason slumps. The gym teacher looks like he has adenoids. There is a bright sarcastic young priest named Father Penny who is thinking of leaving the Church. There is inexplicable violence in the school. The boys attack each other, one has his hand banged repeatedly in a locker door, another has his face ripped to shreds and an eye pulled out. They will not tell anything. School may have to close down. There are bad notes going around about Mason. He's getting crazier. He says Preston is sending the notes. "No!" says the headmaster, "I got them from the boys." They think Mason's strictness in the classroom has upset the boys and created this evil. He won't change, they fire him, he breaks down, his mother dies, it has been Preston all the time. Mason yells to Preston, "You won't win, I'll give you what you want: me," and jumps off the roof. The gym teacher is horrified, he now knows how evil Preston is. School closes. He overhears Preston making arrangements on the phone for another job, he yells at Preston who says, "My boys love me, they're in class right now at ten P.M. waiting for me." They run down three flights of stairs. He's right, the boys sit in the classroom like zombies. The gym teacher tries to convince them that Preston is evil, that he has betrayed them. "When trust goes it can never return," he says, or something like that. They quote Latin back at him, conjugations of the Latin verb "to trust." He's lost. Preston leaves the room. The students have red-rimmed eyes, frozen green faces, they move towards the gym teacher, throwing their books at him, chanting. Preston is in the chapel telling his beads, watching the flickering flame that signifies God's presence. If God leaves the church, the flame goes out. Dark figures move in around

Preston, slowly blocking him from view. The flame goes out, Preston's expression ambiguous. Credits to chanting.

The booths were square with curved padded benches, dark brown. The posts were carved. There were curtains separating the booths, made of cut-up serapes, flounced. Jenny wished she had bought serapes in Baja. The waitress wore a Mexican miniskirt and said, "*Buenas noches*, my name is Robin, would you care for a drink before your dinner?" Jenny said, "My name is Jenny, Robin, I knew you at Wilson." Robin left with Mom's drink order. We wondered if Jenny had insulted her, she didn't seem to recognize Jenny. Robin brought the drink. "Do you remember me, Robin?" Jenny asked. Robin said, "Yes, very well, Jenny Tauber." She seemed embarrassed. She said, "We have to say that, '*Buenas noches*.'" Ivo thought they should say "*Buenas tardes*." He speaks Spanish fluently, having lived in Argentina after fleeing Czechoslovakia with his family. I said, "Fine, we didn't think you remembered Jenny and we thought you thought she was being snotty." Mom said, "This is Ivo, this is Jane Elliot, Jane Tauber Elliot, and I'm Jane's and Jenny's mother." Robin put Mom's drink down. Mom said "*Gracias*" with the Castilian "th" pronunciation. Ivo had salad, iceberg lettuce, each leaf completely covered with Roquefort dressing, refried beans, a taco; a tamale, bad; and an enchilada, good. Jenny had a taco, bad; enchilada, good. Ellen, two enchiladas ranchera, rice, and refried beans, delicious. Jane: chile relleno, bad; taco, bad; guacamole, fair. The tacos were supposed to be beef but were really half chicken. The hot sauce was hot. Service was slow, food greasy and cool. Ambience good. The busboys wore black pants with serape waistbands. The mariachis wore white silver-buttoned pants, black jackets, black flat-brimmed hats with dangling balls. One had a 12-string guitar. Mom said they were real Mexicans, people just wouldn't pay money for anything else. California guacamole is a pale fungoid green, the flesh of avocado mashed with garlic, mayonnaise and chili powder.

It was the thirteenth year my parents had lived in the same house. Everything looked old. Olive greens, dark and light, the aquas, dark blues, and golds had faded, the cushions were frayed, the furniture had become late fifties/early sixties modern. The water heater had failed, there was trouble with the plumbing. The washer was on the blink. There were worn tracks upstairs in the white wall-to-wall shag carpet, paths from chair to chair, room to room. The room I stayed in was once Jon's and Jenny's, then Jon's. I put the large glass boot in the closet with my clothes.

Today there were five dishes of cat food in my room: water, milk, Purina Moist Tidbits, dry cat alphabet food, canned Friskies. Jenny bought a kitten to take the place of Ping, one of her two Siamese blue-point cats, who was killed last week when Mom and Dad, and Dan and Joan Corwin, left her out after dark. We could not tell Mom until Pong, the surviving cat, had made friends with the new kitten, a seal point. After Ping's death Mom said, "No more cats, no way, I can't take it," meaning the worry about Dad's operation, her arthritis and high blood pressure. Jenny and I walked across the beach to swim, the sand blew in fine white clouds four feet from the ground. We carried towels. I was scared Mom would open the door to my room, Pong would skip in, hiss, and attack the kitten, and my mother would have a stroke.

She likes to keep things the same. The cushions, though old and faded, were lined up on the white curved naugahyde sofa in precisely the same order they were thirteen years ago. She makes arrangements against time. She arranged for Jenny and me to donate blood, keeping levels constant. My father would need seven pints. Seven pints had to be donated to keep all the blood in the world even, that inside, that outside. Bess Fitzgerald, who barely knew the family, had offered. The Red Cross gives you doughnuts and coffee after they take the blood, to help you regain your strength. My stomach seized up, thinking of the ordeal was like flying. I thought about my father going into surgery, and envied him his drugs.

I drank all day, cautiously. Four Bloody Marys. Restraint. I tried to make phone calls. I called Lucas, and we arranged to meet at Randall's. Talked intensely and was physically affectionate to Mom. I explained everything to her, why we are so mean, why she is. Then went to Randall's with the half-gallon of Hearty Burgundy. They were watching television. I breezed in, keyed up. Looked at *TV Guide*, changed the channel. Kept talking, changed radio station, laughing. Randall didn't want me to. He was furious. He hit me and cut my lip. Randall sat on a chair with me to his right. I insisted we talk about it, he didn't want to. I insisted. Lucas said, "Let's go," and took the wine. I wanted to go to the beach. Lucas wanted to go to his house. Lucas showed me his writing. I was too drunk to really read it, said, "I want to go home." In the car, Lucas did something about sex. He wanted to go to bed with me, I didn't with him. Then it was morning, night was blacked out. Lucas knocked at my window, I looked out at him and three different kinds of plants. He came in. I laughed, told him my memory is punctured, whole transitions, scenes, clauses have leaked out. He said, "You should give it as much importance as a grain of sand. I remember everything perfectly. I'll tell you what happened." "Yes, I'd like you to do that." That scared me even more than forgetting, accepting his reality. Went to the beach. He said, "I don't want any sex hassles with you." "Then don't." I wasn't sure what he was talking about. I didn't want sex with him. He said, "O.K., you're not my cup of tea but I enjoy you, or would like to know you for what you are." I covered myself with mud, with wet sand, packing it all over my thighs. I was wearing a black leotard, the sand was white, bright, the sky was blue. I felt like a sieve. Huge seagulls. One dove from fifty feet, wings clamped to its body. Lucas said he hadn't seen one do that before. It couldn't have been a seagull, it wasn't a pelican. I suggested a tern.

I dug holes in the sand. Read article and stared at pictures of vampire bats. Read about primitive tribe where women aspiring to the fourth highest female tribal rank must have a tooth knocked out by members of the tribe. They hold her head and gouge the tooth out with a sharply pointed stick of green wood, blood covers her face, they apply a white chunk of white root which stops the flow of blood but not the agony. A rite that has to do with dreams of women, women dreaming of teeth crumbling, falling out, extracted, shattering like panes of glass or turning to dust in their mouths. Lucas remarked that women tend to lose teeth the more children they have.

I dug holes in the sand, smoothed the surface over, punched holes in the sand. Everything in my body was moving around much too fast for the landscape. Large body movements, lifting an arm, spreading both arms, hauling sand to my chest with my arms, these movements were slow, and bore no relationship to the movements of cells, neural impulses triggering chemical reactions, sweat bursting from my pores. A Balinese girl comes of age. Joyous tooth-filing ceremony performed for both sexes protects against Asdripu, the evil in human nature. Priest rubs gold rings on girl's lip then wields his tapered file, metal screeches against enamel; white dust flecks the priest's hands. He grinds down the six upper front teeth until they are all even. Every Balinese must undergo tooth-filing to qualify for eventual cremation lest the gods mistake him for a fanged demon and deny him entrance to the spirit world.

Mom and Lee had drinks before dinner. Mom said, "I kind of like you-know-what but I'm never going to get any." A friend of Lee's and Franklin's has a house in the desert. His wife died. He is fantastically rich. Lee was having fantasies about him. Mom said to me, "Look at you, your cigarette is on the thing, that's wrong, that's how it will fall over and start a fire. Change the cat box. It's in your room and it will smell."

Dad came home today. I had gotten a haircut. Both of us deplored the recent murders: twenty-three or twenty-four young boys sexually molested, tortured for up to three days and killed in Houston, Texas, by an employee of the Houston Gas and Electric Company. He was helped by friends, seventeen-year-old Wayne Henly and someone named Brooks. Services were held today in L.A. for a young couple who were murdered while hitchhiking to Las Vegas to be married. Their bodies were found in shallow graves by the road in the desert. The girl was raped, shot twice, and stabbed seven times, the boy stabbed twenty-seven times. A young Air Force recruit, clean-cut and pleasant, has been arrested for the crime. The police believe he just went mad, he wasn't drunk or on drugs.

Attention was drawn to him by a man who helped him remove his car from the sand where it was stuck. My mother said, "They were hitchhiking, you just can't do that." Dad and I yelled, "That's not the point, we're talking about why so many people are going mad and killing other humans." The Houston murders might have been the record for mass murder. At that time, the record was held by a California man who had killed twenty-five farm workers the previous year. That may have been a political set-up, though.

Joan and Dan Corwin were coming over to go with my parents to dinner at the country club. Downstairs Mom said, "Do you like my dress?" Sleeveless, white ground, small navy blue circular pattern, drop waist, pleated skirt. "Yes," I said tonelessly. She continued, "It has a kind of neat long-sleeve jacket and it's so comfortable." I stuffed my quesadillas down. I said to Mom, "It's really a nice dress," sounding unconvinced out of habit. She said, "I wear it here, below my knees, because of this," pointing to one arthritic, swollen knee, "Otherwise I'd wear it here, above the knees." I said, "But the length you're wearing it is very fashionable now. I have two dresses that length." "That's what's so great, you can wear any length now, I have some winter dresses even longer. Remember when skirts had to be one length? I'm really glad they've gotten over that." Joan Corwin drank vodka. Their daughter Linda, a graduate student at Berkeley, died several years ago in a sailing accident in the San Francisco Bay. She fell off the boat, her boyfriend panicked and lost sight of her. Joan said two days after Linda's death, Dan fell down, breaking his ankle, and was brought home in a hip-to-foot cast. After the cast was removed he fell again and returned from the hospital in a hip-to-foot cast. The authorities were still dragging the Bay for Linda's body. Two weeks later, Dan woke up in bed screaming, he was taken to the hospital. They found two blood clots in his lung. A short time after this, Joan's cousin, who has fished all his life, drowned. Her sister had a stroke and died. A few months later another member of the family died of a stroke. Her older sister had cancer and had been receiving radium treatments. She was seventy-eight years old and was leaving in August for a trip to the Caribbean. She planned to take a forty-two-day cruise the following year. Another sister aged seventy-four shot golf in the eighties, played bridge every day, and looked younger than Joan. Once, at the country club, a man approached Joan and asked, "Will you marry me?" He was one year younger than she. He said, "I've looked all over, dated. Would you marry me? I own half of Texas. I'll take you around the world." Mom laughed, "I wish someone would say that to me." I asked, "Why didn't you just take the trip?" Joan said, "Believe me, if I were asked tomorrow I'd go." A boy called a year after Linda's death, he'd been on a trip. Two days ago a letter came in the mail. The handwriting was Linda's, Joan clung to Dan's arm. The "g's" were made with a separated downstroke, the "w's" peculiar. She knew Linda was dead. She opened the letter, it was from Susie, Linda's roommate at Berkeley, who had just married. Joan got out Linda's letters, the writing was identical, she had never seen Susie's. Joan asked me what she should get Susie as a wedding present. I suggested a large dictionary. She said, "I have some absolutely beautiful decanters. Everyone drinks. We bought the decanters in England and they would cost over $150 here. They have silver labels around their necks saying Bourbon, Scotch, Gin, whatever." Mom said, "Even if they didn't drink, they could keep them out as decoration."

I went downstairs. My father was sitting at the table with Dan. Dan is his lawyer and best friend. My father explained the terms of his will to me. The four children, Jane, Rob, Jon, and Jenny, were the trustors of the Hartwell Corporation, which owned two peninsula properties, stock, insurance policies, and the Oceanside Construction Company. Dan was trustee, the trust was in favor of Ellen Tauber, our mother, in the event of Henry's decease, upon her death it would revert to the children. In case Ellen predeceased Henry, the favor returned to Henry. It was fine with me. I asked if Jenny's college education was at Mom's discretion. It was. She had no obligations to the children, but she couldn't touch the principal. This was true in the event she remarried and would be true, too, of my father. The Hartwell Corporation was to be kept separate from the Oceanside Construction Company. I asked, "Can Mom make the decision whether or not the business is to continue operating?" Dan and Dad said, "No." Dad said, "I've given Dan some instructions about that. I think we have a damn good promising organization down there and have suggested putting the company on a profit-sharing basis which would work well for all of us." Dad said, "The children's stock has no voting power. You, the children, own 90 percent of the stock; 10 percent is kept out and is the voting stock." Dan shook his head. I said, "What happens to the 10 percent?" Dad answered. "That's a good question. Dan, she should have gone to law school. The 10 percent is in Bert's name. He will sign a paper saying he lost his stock and it reverts to the trustors, Jenny, Jon, Rob, and Jane. The plan is irrevocable, in case any of you marries someone who would want to take all the money. Dan would rather have it a revocable situation." I said, "Why can't you keep this document revocable and have a binding contract the four of us would sign, like a coda or amendment." He answered, "We couldn't get away with it. It would probably be interpreted to make the whole thing revocable and too fluid."

Joan came downstairs, she thought it was time to go out to dinner. She told Dad that Dan should have always been his lawyer, that she prays for Dad every night, and that she knows he's going to come through it alright. I said, "It's like taking an umbrella out when you think it might rain. If you take the umbrella, it won't." Joan snapped around, "No, your father is just trying to straighten everything out." Dad said, "I was just giving Jane, the senior child, all the information, Joan." I went to the kitchen and fixed myself some orange juice and rum, there were tears in my eyes.

Dan, Mom, and Joan hugged Dad a lot, and talked about what good friends they were. Dad said, "I've known Dan forty years, he and Joan used to bundle on our sofa before they were married." Joan said to me, "Have we aged much?" "No, I think you look marvelous." I mentioned that Nellie Springer looked ten years younger since she lost so much weight. Joan and Mom discussed Nellie. I asked, "What about me, have I aged?"

"Well," Joan said, "you haven't aged but you're very tall, aren't you?" "Yes, about five-eight." She said, "I didn't remember, I remembered you as so thin." "I've gained ten pounds since I've been back here." This wasn't true. She said, "Well, you'd probably lose it all in your face. I've gotten fat in the stomach but I have no hips." She turned around, pulled her white and flowered dress against her invisible bottom. "Isn't that marvelous," I said. They left.

This morning I visited Nana nervously, briefly. She told me she doesn't like her weekend nurse, Mrs. Clark. I picked up a book with interest because of its inappropriateness, *Gil Blas* by Le Sage. Nana said, "That's Mrs. Clark's book," like it was something weird. I put it down. "You know, Jane," she said, "I have to whisper, Mrs. Clark has ears like a ferret, I'm not having her back here again, she just sits behind me and rocks back and forth all day. My Lord, I'm a nervous wreck." I told Dad that Nana didn't like Mrs. Clark. He said, "Oh, I know, all your grandmother does with me is complain, that's why I don't go over so often, I could write down the whole conversation from beginning to end. She talks to you kids, though."

I read the paper.

PRESS-TELEGRAM Long Beach, Calif.,
Thurs. P.M.

July 19, 1973
For information on crimes
SUMMARY OF SECRET WITNESS REWARDS
   —Rewards totaling $4,000 including $2,000 guaranteed by the *Independent/Press-Telegram*'s Secret Witness program and $2,000 offered by the Compton City Council, will be paid for information leading to the arrest and conviction of the murderer of 55-year-old Compton City employee Raymond Adams. Adams was shot to death by an unknown gunman as he was operating a city street sweeper at 4:45 A.M. Sunday at the northwest corner of Compton and Long Beach Boulevards. Officers answering a call of shots fired in the central Compton area found Adams slumped over

the wheel of his sweeping machine which was standing at the corner with the motor still running.

—A $2,000 reward is offered for information leading to the arrest and conviction of the murderer of 21-year-old Joyce King, of 5221 Courtland Ave., Lynwood, slain in the early morning hours of January 1, 1972. Miss King left her home shortly after midnight to walk to a nearby drive-in restaurant. Her partially clothed body, slashed by forty to fifty knife wounds, was found approximately eight hours later in an alley behind the 11600 block of Louis Avenue in Lynwood.

—Rewards totaling $4,000—including $2,000 each from the Secret Witness program of the *Long Beach Independent*, the *Press-Telegram* and the Santa Monica *Evening Outlook*—will be paid for information leading to the arrest and conviction of the murderer of Kathleen Ann La Chance, aspiring Long Beach 24-year-old actress. Miss La Chance was last seen alive at 5 P.M. on Nov. 15, 1972, when she left an actors' workshop play rehearsal at the apartment of a friend in Los Angeles. Her nude body, arms bound by leather straps and mouth stuffed with sand, was found late that night near the pier on the Santa Monica beachfront. She had been raped and stabbed repeatedly.

Jenny and I made waffles for the family. Jon and Shawn came over. Waffles, bacon, fruit salad. I told Mom to go upstairs if she was just going to nag. The waffles were limp and dense from staying in the warming oven. I shoved my food down, nervous and grouchy. Dad was grouchy about Mom forgetting to put the coffee on. Mom was grouchy at me for not getting more maple syrup. I said, "The waffles lie like a cloud on our stomachs." The kitten jumped up on Dad's lap, trying to eat his waffle. Dad and Jon watched the Russian and American track meet on television. Jenny asked Dad if he wanted wop, greaser, or chink food for lunch. He wanted a sandwich. He had bologna and cheese, potato chips, and cherry tomatoes. Jenny and I went to the beach, asked Dad if he wanted to go swimming. "No." We came back, got dressed to take him to the hospital. I wore a brown dress with red and white check collar and cuffs. Mom wore a gold and white pantsuit. Jenny wore a pale green, figured halter top. Dad wore a pink short-sleeve shirt, white belt, slip-on white shoes, light blue cotton pants finely striped with dark blue and light red. He carried a duffel bag. We went in Jenny's car. Stopped at Nana's. She had fired Mrs. Clark. My mother complained and worried loudly to Mrs. Starr on the couch. We got up to leave. Nana remained in her chair because of her broken hip. Mom said to her, "You can't be alone on weekends, you have to have someone here." Nana was crying because of Dad. I pushed Mom, clenching my teeth. I whispered through them, hissing "This isn't the time for that." I almost pushed her over.

We went to the hospital. Mom worried about how she would find the parking lots when she visited the hospital. The parking lots were closed. We got out in front. Yesterday, Dad, before getting dressed for dinner, kept asking, "Does this look all right?" He had on a pale blue seersucker suit and had to strain to button the pants. I said, "Yes." "Really? Oh God, it looks awful, I wore it when I weighed 180 pounds. It will probably be the only thing I can wear after surgery." Dad held the entrance door open for us. He gave his name. We sat in a waiting room waiting to be called. Jenny and I ate Red Hots, Mom tried to make jokes about Jenny eating chocolate chip ice cream on potato chips while I was eating a bologna and cheese sandwich with mayonnaise, mustard, and green taco sauce. Dad filled out a form about his different illnesses. He asked Mom if he had ever had sodium pentothal. Jenny had had it, they said count backwards from 100 to 1, she didn't get to 100. Dad asked Mom, "When was my last anesthetic?" Mom says, "Your angiogram? I don't know." The admitting nurse said, "Mr. Tauber." We got up. The nurse warned us, "There are only two seats in my booth." Jenny and I remained in the waiting room. I finished reading about the Oregon coast which, due to far-sighted planning, extends naturally and ruggedly from California to Washington State with no commercial development. I looked at some rock formations. Jenny and I discussed not leaving Mom alone, and whether or not she was psycho.

Mom came and got us. We went to the third floor, couldn't
find Dad's room. The hall diverged: one way, labor and delivery
room; Dad's room was the other way. There were a gold shag
carpet, two French Provincial dressers, one tall and thin, the
other wide and short. A TV hung high from ceiling; green and
gold brocade upholstery on both the swivel occasional chair and
the rocker. There were double layered curtains and Venetian
blinds in the two windows. The nurse was confused by so many
people. She asked for Dad's pills because they had to be
checked. We left. Dad had an EKG. We returned. The bed was
rolled down. Jenny fixed the TV I read the *TV Guide* and
planned programs for Dad. Dad said, "Don't be surprised if I
get scared and take a taxi home." We laughed. Dad talked about
nervousness causing him to have angina on the way to the
operating room. He told his doctor, "I can't stand to see the
operating room any more." We wondered about his dinner. He
suggested that Mom run out and get some vodka and tonic
after I complained, "It's too bad you can't get drunk." We left.

We stopped at Ivo's to let Jenny off. I didn't have my glasses,
Mom didn't have her license. Jenny had to drive us both back. I
got my glasses and drove Jenny back to Ivo's. I was mean to
Mom about a Mexican dinner. She had wanted to go out. We
ate at home. I said, "Don't you really want to go out?" "No."
Dad called to ask us to bring his Right Guard anti-perspirant
tomorrow. He called back later to say Dr. Irving wanted to talk
to us at eleven-thirty A.M., then told Mom that after he saw the
doctor he had had a tightening in his chest.

At the hospital there was a man on the sun porch whose robe
was open over his legs. I thought he was exposing himself.
Another man was hunched over, and stared. Mom told me
about a cardboard box of shoes in her bedroom. "I have to put
these away, Jane. The last thing I saw of my mother's was a
cardboard box of shoes, they had stolen everything else."
"Who?" I asked. "The people at the home, you know, that's the
hardest job, working in a home for the mentally disturbed, so
they just steal everything. But they couldn't use the shoes."

I dreamed:

Jane Johnson secretly going out with
    John Lane, doesn't tell me till very
    last moment, until I've been down
    there to visit.
John didn't like my visit much.
Missed things he wanted to see.
Turkish show?
I live in a funny house, sort of made of
    carboard in garage or hangar but really
    outside or half outside.
Jane's snotty, sort of, about John Lane.
I get info out of her because I say she's
    been deceptive.
Earlier, Stephie Blair there.
I leave wine in elevator.
Earlier, Jane J. and mother visit, they
    let me talk about my plans to go down to
    visit John Lane.
They act enthusiastic and don't tell truth.
Something, half of disease I have.
In patio.
Mom says that's all your stuff, then, what
    are you going to do with all of it.
Take it back to N.Y.
It's not even that messy, books.
Not messy like food and clothes.
I'm late for school.
Still live in cardboard box, with Rob and Jon.
Get to school, students have made suggestion
    boxes shaped like skull, nose falls out of it,
    I say it's O.K.
They worked hard.

I hit Jenny on the ass as hard as I could with my notebook.
She wouldn't speak to me. I apologized several times. Jenny's
car had stalled in the driveway. We were supposed to be at the
hospital at eleven-thirty. Jenny and I pushed it out. Mom said,
"There's no power steering, I can't steer it." Jenny answered,
"The motor's not on." We took Mom's car. Jenny picked the dirt

from her comb with a pin, Mom objected. Dad was wearing red pajamas with paisley blue and red robe, black ballet slippers. He was talking business on the hospital sun deck with a man named Charlie. They wheeled a surgery cart by. In the car we discussed cars. Mom asked Jenny to turn on the air conditioning. "You don't have air conditioning, Mom," Jenny said. The conversation on St. Mary's Hospital terrace was interrupted last night by the sound of a police helicopter with a brilliant searchlight, cruising.

Morbid interest; trapped; choice:

suffer vb suffering / (ME *Suffren,* fr. OF *souffrir,* fr. (assumed) VL *sufferire,* fr. L *Sufferre,* fr. Sub − up + ferre to bear − more at SUB − , BEAR) vt 1 a: to submit to or be forced to endure (martyrdom) b: to feel keenly: labor under (thirst) 2: UNDERGO, EXPERIENCE 3: to bear up under: ENDURE used chiefly in negative statements not able to bear pain 4: ALLOW, TOLERATE vi 1: to endure death, pain, or distress 2: to sustain loss or damage 3: to be subject to disability or handicap syn see BEAR − Sufferable Sufferableness
Sufferably Sufferer

die
Death/deth/ n (ME, fr. OE *deāth*; akin to ON *dauthi death, deyja* to die − more at DIE) 1: permanent cessation of all vital functions: the end of life 2: the cause or occasion of loss of life 3 Cap: the destroyer of life represented usu. as a skeleton with a scythe 4: the state of being dead 5: Destruction, EXTINCTION 6: CIVIL DEATH 7: SLAUGHTER 8: Christian Science: The lie of life in matter: that which is unreal and untrue: ILLUSION

death bed
1: the bed in which a person dies 2: the last hours of life

Got up four-fifty A.M., washed hair, at hospital by five-fifty

A. M. Saw Dad. He smoked a cigarette, had oxygen, they gave him a shot that didn't really take. I started crying. The nurse said, "Don't let him see you, if you do you have to leave." Dad wheeled out on the gurney. Drank coffee, played Casino. Crazy Eights. Ordered patty melt, added pickled beets, pickles, blue cheese, ate all day. Dr. Irwin came down. He performed three bypasses. At night, Dad talked.

Casino Scores:

Jane	Jenny	Rob	Ellen
17	6	2	23
Jane	Jenny	Ellen	Rob
16	5	6	17
Jenny	Rob	Shawn	Ellen
17½	20	8½	9

I went to Venice to visit Karen Dorcas. Sunset glared in my eyes, intense orange red yellow. Sun went down farther, saw two planes, jets, coming in over freeway, four lanes, to land. Two broken-in small houses side by side. Roofs covered with birds, wires covered with birds. Grocery store had all kinds of fresh vegetables, Chinese and Japanese not just American. Ocean in Venice, little chill on the water, fresh hissing. Tiny popping seething of white water foam. Tumbled in wave, getting drunk, losing memory.

> The terror of being judged sharpens the memory: it sends an inevitable glare over that long-unvisited past which has been habitually recalled only in general phrases. Even without memory, the life is bound into one zone of dependence in growth and decay; but intense memory forces a man to own his blameworthy past. With memory set smarting like a re-opened wound, a man's past is not simply a dead history, and outworn preparation of the present; it is not a repented error shaken loose from the life; it is a still quivering part of himself, bringing shudders and bitter flavours and the tinglings of a merited shame.
>
> George Eliot—*Middlemarch*

Three men fishing. One has a granddaughter who is also

188

fishing, her rod is bowed, no, it's his, the sun is glinting off the deepest part of the curve. He's wearing striped Bermuda shorts, a navy blue jacket and a straw hat with the brim turned down in back and front. "He caught a fish this big," says a girl in an orange bikini sitting to my left ten yards away, facing the ocean which moves back and forth continually, cresting in small jagged waves breaking on shore. One of the men bends over, looks at whatever has been caught, hidden from my view by a rise of sand. Another man stands to my right, hands on hips, in front of his rod held perpendicular to the sand by a metal pole with cleats, he's wearing a white hat, khaki Bermudas wet from the bottom to groin in a jagged line, a white brown aqua dark blue shirt with squares. A man further down in a blue and white windowpane shirt, white hat, and khaki Bermuda shorts casts, standing in knee-deep water. They group and regroup, gathering around one rod and then another. The rods are parallel to the water's edge and perpendicular to the sand.

People walk by, some rub their chests, stoop and look at what has been caught. The men and the girl bend over frequently to pick up bait, they rebait their hooks and walk between the rods. The man in the center walks to the water to cast, he turns to the right, his left hand uppermost on the pole, he twists his body from the waist up, feet solid, pointing forward, the pole follows, he whips himself forward, once more facing the sea. The line loops arcs tosses plummets glides out over the water, is pulled out by the weight and the momentum of his movement, into the water, drops sinks becomes invisible, the part of the line closest to the top of the rod is obscured by the color of the sea.

This is the fishing club, they fish every Sunday and cook what they catch immediately afterwards in the Gallaghers' back yard. They eat fish and drink Almadén wine. Franklin Gallagher says, "I'm about ready to wrap it up any time you are." Peculiar long narrow-beaked birds with spindly tall back-jointed legs. Four sailing boats in a line, equidistant from each other. People swimming, running, standing still, lying on their stomachs or backs, sitting at variously inclined angles in beach chairs, riding on rafts, holding each other up or down in the water, walking back and forth along the water's edge on the wet hard-packed sand. They talk, smoke, look out to sea, read, construct shelters with umbrellas, towels, and blankets. They are of different ages but not very old or very young. There are no dogs. If a dog comes on the beach a lifeguard yells over a loudspeaker from one of several lifeguard shacks, "There are no dogs allowed on this beach, please take your dog off the beach, there are no dogs allowed on this beach."

There is a strong offshore breeze as there was yesterday, luckily, when sulfur gas leaked from a tank at the chemical farm, forming a cloud that extended twenty-five miles, moving east. Some people in small power boats are fishing one hundred feet off shore. The people fishing on shore are preparing to leave, their movements are slight, reeling in the line, turning to gesture, taking the bait off the hooks, wetting a bag, staring, locking their reels. They are virtually motionless. Something pops in the air. Something honks. The power boats offshore are rocking.

I changed glasses, corrective to dark, put down my pen and lit a cigarette. Got it lit on first match. A man jogged by. People are always jogging, some by the water on wet sand, others at dusk down the middle of the beach in soft sand, and others at night down the boardwalk in tennis shoes. People ride their bikes up and down the boardwalk, the wheels on the loose boards make a repetitive hollow wooden sound. Not many people wear shirts during the day but some do, they are usually over forty or have very fair skin. One man did a combination jog and stride, jog and stride. During the phase in which he strode he looked at the ground and dropped his arms down free, while he jogged he looked straight ahead chin up and pumped his arms in right angles close to the sides of his body. Some men passed, about the same height, in navy blue boxer trunks, jogging fast. They passed a woman with sunglasses cocked back on her head, red sunsuit, walking slowly in the opposite direction. The water was blue and green and yellow and white. There were many yellow beach chairs—I had one—

and several yellow bathing suits. The fishing club was still fishing.

Jenny woke me, she was going to school. The Siamese kitten purred and vomited on my bedspread. I watched him, sleepy, slit-eyed, he was like a dream, bunched up and vomiting on the edge of the bed. Got up, dressed, went to travel agency to pick up my train ticket. They wouldn't take a personal check. I was angry. "I've never had this happen before," I said. (A lie.) "What am I supposed to do, carry cash around to buy tickets? I've traveled by Amtrak all year, have paid by check in New York, Chicago, last week they took my check in Oakland." (A lie.) "How would one travel?" I asked. "They don't demand cash in London, Paris, or Morocco." (I'd never been to Morocco.) "Long Beach must be a pretty special place." "It is," they said. I left. Straightened out ticket, lay on the beach feeling sad: the day was white, wide, clear, with hot sun. I thought about the things I hadn't done. The water was cold. I walked. The beach was deserted. I looked at things with a last-look look. Picked up ticket at another agency.

I thought my mother was going crazy. I hated her when she apologized. I should have flown, I thought over and over. Visited Nana, she was going stone-deaf and blind. She gave me twenty dollars for the trip. My eyes felt tight. I said, "I'll have a steak and champagne for dinner on the train and drink a toast to you." Shopped for Mom. Saw Jenny, we ate quesadillas as a goodbye. Jon and Shawn took me to the train. Jon talked about his life. I went, "Uh huh." Rob brought dope the night before and left in a rage because I was too busy, and didn't pay attention to him. I was doing things wrong. Regretted decision to take train.

On the train I cheered up, read, got coffee, ordered coffee for morning, silent, drank brandy and coffee looking out on things I couldn't identify. Bleached white cliff filled the window. I couldn't guess its color or substance in the sun, it was white sand with dark plants growing over it. I couldn't see if the roads were cut and hard, or soft and rounded like sand. The shadow of the train was geometric, rectangular, and notched in a medium shade on the sand. Read *Pale Gray for Guilt* by John MacDonald. I should write letters, swim every day, walk twenty minutes or one mile, get on schedule, enjoy life, pay bills, get job, push work, be nice to friends, cut down fantasies, listen more to other people, use dental floss, stay out of the sun, go to face cleaner, lose weight, not clench teeth.

Dear Mom,
On train, I'm glad I decided to do it. I think you'd really enjoy it. Am having a brandy and coffee in my room looking out at a very beautiful but totally unidentifiable landscape. White hills, etc. Thanks for everything at home, I started out with the best intentions but realize I made things hard for you and the apologies shouldn't all be on one side (yours), so, sorry for being grouchy, irritable, and so on. I think it's hard for me to come home and hard for people (you, Dad, Jenny, and so on) to have me there. I'm sorry you're going through such a difficult time. You seem to be worried a lot about getting old, your arthritis, etc. . . .
I want to tell you though, small consolation I know, that you look marvelous and it's very hard for me to think of you as being as old as you say. I hope fervently that I look as good in my forties as you do in your fifites. I'm going to say something that might make you mad, but ignore, if you want. I think with the strains you've been under that it might be good for you to just (gasp!) see a psychiatrist once a week or a couple of times just to let some steam off. It was very helpful to me through some pretty rugged times and I think what you're going through now is more difficult than anything I've had to face. Jack Komar's wife Rebecca went to one this summer, against all instincts, and found it very helpful just to talk to someone outside the family situation. This advice or whatever, comes out of my feeling that you and Dad seem so active and young to me that I can't take your argument of being "an old woman and not willing to change," or not wanting to get into new things, very seriously. Dad

apologizes for not thinking clearly after open heart surgery and I'm amazed that you both have the grace and awareness to do that. I think you're both too hard on yourselves. At any rate I'm glad I was able to come back this summer, it was a very important time for me, even if I sulked my way through half of it.

Sharp points of light, artificial, long low land, lights dim, train slowed. Turned on light, all lost. Just a horizon and low curves and bushes.

Three days ago Henry Tauber had his sixty-second birthday. He's a Libra in the pipeline construction business, sewage and water mains. His passion is money. He enters the hospital on Halloween for his seventh major operation, six have been for vein and artery transplants in the leg and groin areas, for open heart surgery to replace valves, and for exploratory purposes. This one is to remove a polyp from his lower colon which necessitates going through the lower abdomen. He knows Richard Nixon's doctor in Long Beach. He has made and lost a lot of money. At one point he owned a construction company; a pipe supply company; a popular steak restaurant, Reilly's; one half of a golf course (which was opened officially by David Nelson, his wife, and Wally of *The Ozzie and Harriet Show*); two oceanfront homes; a carpet company; and one half of a quarter-horse, Little Deano. His uncle Lloyd, a Catholic convert and president of the Bank of Hawaii, said before dying (he was dragged over a cliff in Hawaii by his electric lawn mower), "Hank will be the first millionaire in the family." After making a million (valuation based on all holdings and properties, including equipment) Henry was elected the youngest president of the Associated General Contractors. He went to Washington, D.C., to speak to the Senate on behalf of this group and found out shortly before speaking that he was being sued for bankruptcy. With great sadness he resigned his presidency, got a bank account in Nevada, and started his business over. He can't stand working for others. He is now reduced to being his only employee besides a secretary, and says, "I do about everything except sweep up, I have a man in once a month to do that," and laughs. He has $400,000 worth of bids out and is respected for his honesty. Henry was born in Idaho Falls. His mother and father moved to California. He quit law school during the Depression. He values education and allowed his four children to attend any college they wished as long as they maintained a good grade average. He has a younger sister Barbara, a lesbian who was seduced by her high school English teacher with a book of poems by Sappho. She moved to the East Coast, is a computer expert, and lives with a woman and two chimpanzees in the woods outside Boston. Henry had been married to his wife Ellen for over twenty-five years, they had a silver anniversary. A few days later a van pulled up to their house at eleven A.M. and stripped it of every item of value: all the family silver, the gifts of silver, Ellen's jewelry and mink stole, the televisions. Henry says that the Tauber family crest is a horseshoe upside down with all the luck running out. He has had, with Ellen, four children: Jane, B.A. Mills College, B.F.A, M.F.A. Yale School of Art and Architecture; James Robert, "Rob," honorably discharged from the Army and student at several colleges, who plans to re-enter school in pre-law, then go to Harvard; George Jonathan, "Jon," All-American swimmer, B.A. UCLA, M.A. USC; and Jenny, a senior in graphic design, University of California at Long Beach. A year ago Henry believed there was a strong possibility he would die during heart surgery. He arranged his affairs, had his children speak to his lawyer, who made them conversant with the terms of the will. He entered the hospital and tried to get Ellen to sneak in a bottle of vodka. He smoked a cigarette before his preliminary anesthesia, seven hours later he emerged from surgery in good condition. His first day home he asked for greaser, chink, or wop food. He continues to drink and smoke heavily. His father was an alcoholic whose last years were constructed to allow mornings at the stock market and early afternoons at the Pago Pago Bar. Henry's mother broke her hip on her eighty-fourth birthday and tried to crawl towards the phone but couldn't make it. "Lord I was weak as a kitten," she said, having lain there through the night until someone from next door broke in to help. She said she was able to hold it until the ambulance came, but as soon as they moved her she soaked her gown. Henry says she is fine, alert, and happy except when he comes to visit, then all she wants to talk about are her funeral arrangements. Henry supported Richard Nixon but no longer talks about politics except in general terms, lower interest rates, etc. He looks younger than his age, has a homely, attractive face. His nickname is Potsy. He has blue eyes, a fair complexion, graying hair thin on top, very small neat feet, and severe burn scars on his leg from a firecracker explosion in childhood. He watches television to unwind, trades in his Cadillacs every year. He fell off his ten-speed bike when he tried it for the first time, at night while drunk, and injured his elbow. At Christmas he irritates Ellen by asking the children to bring empty boxes from the garage to bulk up the number of presents under the tree so that when neighbors walk by they'll feel they've been out-yuled. Henry supervised every aspect of the house he built for his family: two living rooms, upstairs and down, built-in vacuum, two kitchens, a complete intercom system. He kept the intercom on to hear people's comments about the house as they walked by, and would frequently intone through the system, "Please don't muss up the sand in front of the house." He doesn't read much, enjoys Harry Belafonte and golf. He stopped smoking and drinking for ten years, only taking a glass of champagne at his daughter's wedding. He started again after being ill, and because his social life was boring when everyone drank but him. He broke off a twenty-year friendship because a friend of one of his friends embezzled money from Henry, and Henry's friend continued to speak to the embezzler. He has close relationships with his employees. Henry felt tired, went to the doctor in August, and immediately entered Community Hospital on Termino Avenue for treatment of leukemia. There are three courses of therapy. He had no remission on the first and began the second. "We know it will be all right," Ellen said. "He's in isolation, his arms are blue from taking blood, he has boils around his mouth, on his arms, on his whole body from the drugs." He ran his business from his bed, received chemotherapy, began losing weight and sought comfort in the religion he had abandoned as a child. Franklin visited: "How are you, Hank?" "I've never been so sick. Help me out." Phil visited: "What can I do for you, Hank?" "Get me out of this." Remission began, he'd lost forty pounds, the doctors were confident. He died. Jane flew from New York, Rob from Berkeley, Jon and Shawn drove from San Diego, Jenny and Ellen were there. He had written fifty pages for Jon about his life and business experience. The nurse threw them out while cleaning up the room. Ellen had seen the priest giving the last rites but thought it was just a prayer, her background is Protestant. His death was a shock. His mother was told, his sister notified, the obituary was written for the paper. Services were held at St. Luke's. Jenny hated the coldness of the ceremony. The office staff, foreman, and field workers came from San Diego and Tia Juana, Mexico. The family left so fast no one had a chance to say what a wonderful man he was. The phone rang and rang, flowers came, Ellen asked for donations to the leukemia fund. Jon took over the presidency of the company. Rob thought Henry's secretary had stolen his color TV. He thought Henry wanted him to have it. Jane accused Jon of taking everything over. Jenny and Rob were mad at Jon for keeping the Cadillac. He felt he needed it to take clients to lunch. People brought food. Ellen was mad at Jane for not cooperating and for making an appointment with Henry's lawyer. His sister Barbara never called. Ellen's brother Jim said he'd never speak to her again because she didn't invite them over after the funeral. No one went to the cemetery, the casket was closed. Jane, Rob, Jon, Jenny, and Ellen looked at each other and cried. "Lord, I'm just a good-for-nothing heap of bones," his mother said, and refused to take her medicine, or eat, and couldn't sleep, lying awake all night picking at her quilt, listening to the news, staring out the window at her neighbor's wall. They planned the family business, percentages, long-term strategy. Jon would buy them out eventually, he wanted to be independent. The lawyer said, "There are

$500,000 in outstanding debts we know about. The insurance is borrowed on. The bank has frozen the money in all accounts." Rob thought Jane was causing tension and stirring everyone up. Rob and Jane went to All Souls Cemetery and Mausoleum. The man wrote on a card: grave twenty-eight, block forty-one, tier T, section B. "Count it out by graves," he said. "There's no headstone, it hasn't been paid for." They couldn't find it. A crying woman said, "Is it in the cheap or the expensive section?" They didn't know. The cheap section is near the fence separating cemetery from freeway. They found the grave, opened a bottle of champagne poured half on the ground, not knowing which way his feet pointed, drank the rest, cried, didn't know how to leave, and stood in the dusty sun listening to cars on the freeway speed by. Rob took his clothes, returned to Berkeley. Jenny moved into an apartment. The house was sold to the mother of a high school friend of Jenny's, who had married a rich man. The family got comfort looking at the ocean. They said they loved each other. Ellen worried about arthritis, high blood pressure, and the expense of her Naples apartment. Jane assured her grandmother she could die at home, took Henry's bathrobe and calculator, and left for New York. Jon and Shawn took care of the business and had a baby, John Henry Tauber. The doctors wrote, "We don't know why your husband died." Rob and Jenny remembered his IV wasn't connected the last three days. Jane wanted an investigation. Rob thought she was causing trouble. Ellen thought it was nice of the doctors to write a personal note. She said, "He'd be driving up from San Diego now." They talked to each other: "What did he say to you?" "Did he say anything about me?" "How did he look?" "Was he sad?" "Did he know?" "What did you do?" "Who saw him last?" "What did he say?" "Did he take out the IV?" "Did they forget?" He lifted his hand. He turned his head: "Don't worry your mother." "He lost interest in everything worldly." He fell trying to go to the bathroom himself, fell, then cried, "I'm so ashamed." He slept. "He liked people in the room." "He turned his head." "He knew they were there." "Did he say anything about me?"

JB